Beautiful Nightmare

Beautiful Nightmare

Johnna B

www.urbanbooks.net

Urban Books, LLC
300 Farmingdale Road, NY-Route 109
Farmingdale, NY 11735

ISBN 13: 978-1-62286-515-4
ISBN 10: 1-62286-515-4

First Trade Paperback Printing July 2017
Printed in the United States of America

10 9 8 7 6 5 4 3 2 1

Distributed by Kensington Publishing Corp.
Submit Orders to:
Customer Service
400 Hahn Road
Westminster, MD 21157-4627
Phone: 1-800-733-3000
Fax: 1-800-659-2436

Dedication

In loving memory of one of the greatest men I have ever known, my grandfather, James Lett.

I love and miss you with all of my heart. You are my angel, and I know you will never stop watching over me. I wish you were here to see my dreams come to fruition.

Loving you always and forever!

Acknowledgments

First, I want to thank God for never giving up on me. I know my faith wavered for a little while, but he never let me go. Thank you, God, for such an imaginative mind. Through all my heartbreaks, he held my hand and walked with me. Now, here I am fulfilling my dream of becoming a published author.

To my mommy, you are the best. Dana Williams, you are not the most motivational speaker, but I know you always mean well. Lol. Our relationship hasn't always been the best, but I wouldn't have traded you for anything in the world. I am a better woman because of you. I have watched you my whole life make a dollar out of fifteen cents, and you always manage to bounce back. I love you, Mommy!

To my aunt Daphne Gillespie, I want to thank you for coming through for me, no questions asked. You managed to help me out almost over 500 miles away. That shows that nothing stops you from coming through for me. We've been thick as thieves since we were infants . . . me and you against the world. I love you, babe, and miss you so much. I'd kill and drown a drop of water for you, my favorite aunt. My aunt Shonettda Ball, you've been my rock for forever, and I love you dearly for always being there for me, no questions asked. Your support is immeasurable, and I don't know what I would do without it. I love you to pieces.

Acknowledgments

To K'wan Foye, I thank you so much for all of your help and one-of-a-kind wisdom. You gave me back that spark I thought I had lost, and I will forever be grateful to you for that. I thank you so much for answering all of my phone calls and answering all of my dumb-ass questions. Lol. Much love to you, hun.

Karoz Norman, you came in and helped me when I felt I had no one to turn to. I thank you so much for all your help. You are a true blessing, and you will forever be my friend. Thanks.

Chapter 1

Chance Meeting

Raven . . .

Standing a lean five feet eight with long, shapely legs, perfect D-cup breasts, a booty that would make Deelishis step up her game, and a tattoo right above the crack of her ass that read *slippery when wet*, Raven wasn't to be messed with. Beautiful, with skin that looked as if it had been kissed by the Egyptian gods, almond-shaped eyes the color of cherry oak wood, and long, flowing dark hair, Raven was everybody's fantasy, but, as the saying goes, everything that glitters ain't gold.

"You love this black pussy, don't you?" A pause filled the air. "Say it!"

"Yesss!" resonated between deep licks.

"How does it taste?" Raven asked, looking at the bobbing head in between her legs. Her body felt warm all over, but the heat she needed hadn't started yet.

"It . . . it tastes like . . . candy."

Raven thought for a moment, then spoke. "Naw, my shit tastes better than candy." She gyrated her hips. "It tastes like honey, doesn't it? Yeah, I like that better." She looked down at the head still bobbing and demanded, "Get the fuck up and lie on your back." She flipped her victim over like a rag doll. Raven wasn't a big woman, but when she was zoned out, she had the strength of ten men.

"Ooh, it's my turn! I hope I get my money's worth, you black whore."

"Oh, you will . . . trust and believe," Raven smirked, thinking of all the things she planned to do.

Raven stealthily walked over to her oversized bag and rummaged through her sex toys. She looked back at the freaky fifty-year-old white woman who lay eagerly awaiting what she had coming and pulled out a black, ten-inch dildo and a large paddle. As a dominatrix, Raven confidently strolled back over to the woman and stared down at her—her sex partner for the night, but mainly, she was just another victim. The woman was pretty well put together for her age. She was well kept. She had sandy-brown hair, which was slightly graying throughout, light brown eyes, a small keen nose, and thin lips. Her body was devoid of wrinkles or saggy titties. Actually, the woman had it going on. Raven was certain the woman had spent tons of money on plastic surgery, but what else was new? The woman eagerly grinned at Raven while awaiting what she had in store for her. Through a lidded gaze, Raven thought, *I'm going to enjoy this.*

Standing at the foot of the bed in a crotchless black leather jumper, Raven slowly crawled onto the bed with her head low and ass in the air. Once she got to the woman's foot, she picked it up and started sucking her toes one by one. Raven could see the muscles contracting in her victim's stomach as she took deep breaths. She placed soft, sensual kisses all the way up her toned thighs. Slowly, she spread her legs and looked at the pink pussy in front of her. It was void of any hair; her lips were so full and plump. She smiled at her swollen clit, which looked like a pinky finger. Instantly, she began to salivate at the sight before her like a rabid dog. She could see the juices running down and couldn't wait to taste them.

"You want me to fuck you?" Raven asked while rubbing her hand up and down the lady's pussy lips and occasionally slipping a finger into her wet slit. The woman's juices coated Raven's fingers as she watched the woman's skin tone turn five different shades of red.

"Yes, I want it hard," the lady said, barely able to breathe. Her stomach heaved in and out as she tried desperately to control her rapid panting.

Raven rose up and lay on top of the lady, taking her light pink nipple into her mouth. Now sticking her two middle fingers into her slit again, she fucked her with her hand as she made her way back down to get a taste. She took her fingers out and could see juices all over her hand. She placed her finger up to the lady's mouth, so she could taste her own sweet nectar while she sucked her jumping clit.

"Mmmm," the lady moaned at the feeling of Raven's tongue circling around her clit and dipping into her aching love box. She could feel her body tingling all over.

"Ahhh shhh ahhh." She couldn't form any words.

"You coming?" Raven asked while never taking her mouth off of her.

The vibrations from her mouth sent the lady over the mountaintop and into a new hemisphere. Raven watched her come as she finger fucked her. She loved to watch the fuck faces women made. She thought it was the sexiest thing in the world. She loved how it was usually a mixture between crying, anger, and passion, depending on how hard they were coming.

Raven looked at her toys laid out on the bed and opted to strap on the dildo and save the paddle for later. She stared menacingly at the woman and ordered, "Get on yo' knees and suck it." Raven could feel a tingling sensation starting at her toes.

The lady happily obliged and eagerly grabbed the strap-on with her small pink hand and began to lick and slurp the thick rubber dick as if it were the real thing.

Watching the woman's thin lips tease the tip of the dildo, Raven became angered as the tingling quickly turned into heat.

Slap!

Her hand slid across the woman's face as the sound resonated throughout the room.

"Bitch, is you playing with me?" she bellowed. "I said, 'Suck the muthafucka like yo' fuckin' life depended on it!'"

No more Miss Nice Lady. It was time to get this show on the road. Raven wasn't into being lovey-dovey, at least, not for too long and not too often. She had her fair share of lovers that she'd shared her tenderness with, but this wasn't one of the lucky few.

Without flinching, the woman became even more excited and reached down to play with her pussy. She moved her hips in rhythm with her fingers and moaned sensually. Raven heard how wet her pussy was and began to get even more irritated. Raven could feel this heat rising in the pit of her stomach and knew her orgasm was right around the corner.

"Oh, you wanna play, huh? Don't wanna suck my dick . . . Well, I got something for you!" Raven reached out and picked up the paddle off the bed. Forcefully, she ordered, "Bend the fuck over, and toot that old ass in the air!"

Ecstasy covered the woman's face as she seductively crawled onto the bed. While on her knees, she watched as Raven prepared herself. Clearly, she was used to the treatment she was about to receive. Raven licked her lips as she watched the lady flex her love muscles. Her ass was in the air while she played with and spread her lips apart so Raven could get a good view.

"I've been a very bad girl, and I need a spanking," she cooed over her shoulder.

"Shut the fuck up and do what I say." Raven's body was on fire as sweat dripped from her brow.

Again, Raven got no argument. In anticipation of the sexual punishment, the woman positioned herself on her elbows and knees. Her ass was as high in the air as she could get it. Sadly, the woman didn't realize that, not only was Raven a dominatrix, she was also a fucking lunatic . . . but she was about to find out.

Raven slapped the paddle against her hand, and then swung it across the woman's behind, twice.

Smack! Smack!

The woman screamed with delight as the large wooden paddle hit her on her creamy white ass with force. Raven spanked her with it two more times and then threw it on the bed. She positioned the dildo at the entrance of the woman's pussy. With one stroke, Raven roughly shoved the large toy inside of the woman. The sound that came from her mouth clearly indicated pain, but Raven didn't care. *Fuck this bitch*, she thought. Raven loved women, but she wasn't in the mood to be sensitive or affectionate. Tonight was all about her and her needs. As she pounded away at what was left of the old lady's walls, Raven snatched the woman by her hair and licked the side of her face.

"This how you like it?" Raven said through clenched teeth as she grinded her hips in slow motion, making the dildo go deeper.

There was so much anger in her that she could feel her heart about to beat out of her chest. She was so hot. It felt as if her body was literally on fire. This was the feeling she longed for. There was no detoxification for her cravings. She didn't know where this feeling came from. She'd discovered it one day while wreaking havoc on one of her victims. She didn't always get the urge, but when she did, there was no stopping her from fulfilling her needs.

Breathe, Raven, breathe, she thought. Her heartbeat had sped up times ten. This always happened. She had to pace her breathing before she had a heart attack. That was how powerful the feeling was. Every time, it seemed to take her breath away.

"Yes! Yes!" the woman cried out in ecstasy, throwing her ass back, taking in every inch of the dildo.

The woman was so into what she was doing that she never gave a second thought to anything else. When Raven had first approached her about a sexual adventure, she knew the lady would be game. Raven had watched the lady for a good twenty minutes before she approached her. She looked like she needed a little excitement in her life, and Raven was just the person to provide it. The lady was sitting at the bar of the Lumier Casino, waiting for her husband to finish a poker game. After a few drinks and a few affectionate touches here and there, Raven knew she had her.

But the woman was adamant about keeping it low key. She had said if she got caught, she would lose everything. Raven laughed to herself. She may not have gotten caught by her husband, but she was *definitely* caught. If the woman could see the sadistic shit Raven had going through her head, she would have been running for the hills.

One week later, here they were with Raven fulfilling the lady's every desire. She could have been a keeper, but tonight, Raven needed to feel that feeling that only a scene like this could bring.

"That li'l dick husband of yours don't do it like this, do he?"

"No," the woman huffed, making a circle motion with her hips. "Fuck me, you fuckin' nigger. Fuck me harder!"

Her eyes rolled to the back of her head. She and her husband hadn't had sex in almost a year. Between her going through the change and his flaccid penis, something had to give. She needed this in the worst way and would surely be coming back . . . or so she thought.

Raven looked at the woman through her squinted eyes. "You want it harder, huh?"

"Yes . . . harder!" the woman groaned lustfully.

Raven complied and pulled the dildo out of her pussy. After seeing how wet it was, she was shocked that a fifty-year-old pussy could generate that much wetness. Without warning, she grabbed the woman's ass, positioned it higher, and drove the dildo back inside of her.

The woman yelped like a wounded dog. "Okay! Wait a minute." She tried to move away, but Raven grabbed her hips and did not allow her to move.

"Stop! You're being too rough now."

The woman felt as though something was trying to rip right through her cervix. With each stroke, Raven could feel the back of the dildo press against her clit. The pressing on her clit brought on miniorgasms for Raven. They felt good, but they were nothing like the feeling she was searching for.

"Naw, bitch . . . It ain't no stop." Raven pushed deeper into the woman with a sinister grin on her face. It was showtime. "This is what the fuck you wanted, ain't it?" She plunged deeply again, and the woman tried to break free, but Raven stopped her, pushing her head into the pillow, making it hard for her to breathe. "Naw, don't run now," she ordered while pressing even harder on the woman's head. There was no fighting against Raven once she was in the zone.

The woman struggled against Raven's strong grip. Raven grabbed the paddle from the bed and began to swing precisely at the woman's head. The woman opened her mouth to scream, but nothing could come out. The repeated blows caused her to go unconscious, and she fell onto the bed in a heap. But Raven wasn't done yet. She hadn't got her shit off yet.

"Aaahhh, yeah! Come on! Yesss," she hissed at the feeling slowly taking over her body, the feeling her body longed for.

Raven looked at the woman with blood draining from the deep cuts on the side of her head and battered face, and grinned. She noticed that the woman was breathing shallowly.

The woman thought about her husband of thirty-one years and wondered if she would ever see him again. Would she ever see her children or grandkids again?

Repositioning her body, Raven hovered over the woman's ass, spread it apart, and rammed all ten inches of the thick rubber into her asshole, waking her up from an unconscious state instantly with a bloodcurdling scream.

The woman cried and frantically tried to get away, but Raven was relentless and fucked her ass with no mercy at all. Not only did each thrust bring pain to the woman and pleasure to Raven, but blood began to trickle down the back of the woman's thighs. The smell of sweat, pussy, and blood permeated the air, but Raven didn't care. Her continued thrusts put her where she needed to be. With her eyes rolling to the back of her head, Raven's pussy began to cream from the eruption it was having, feeling like her soul was shaking. The feeling was so powerful. Staying on the downstroke in the woman's ass, Raven had one of the biggest orgasms she had ever had.

She was now satisfied. Out of breath, Raven sat there a little longer to get the full effect of the orgasm. Her body was spasming out of control.

The woman's body fell onto the bed, forcing the fake dick out of her ass. She lay still, in a heap, with blood spewing from her orifices. Raven moved from her body without caring if the woman was dead or alive because she had to go. Calmly, she threw on her trench coat and put the dildo and paddle back inside of her bag. She pulled her cover from under the lady, making her fall to the floor and on her back. She would never lie her body on any surface in that motel. Smiling at a job well done, she looked around the decrepit room. Raven shook her head, and a sinister sneer crossed her face at the thought of the cleaning crew stumbling upon the gory scene in a few days.

"Maybe they'll just set the room on fire," she said to herself.

She took one last look at the lady and could see her stomach rising while she struggled to take her last breaths. *Maybe she'll still be alive when they come,* she thought as she walked out the door and straight to her car. She made sure to never go to a hotel where there could be witnesses. She always paid by the hour and made sure her car was very close. In St. Louis in the run-down hotels on Grand was where all the dopeheads and drug dealers did their dirt, so she knew there would be no surveillance cameras anywhere. The owners of the run-down hotels didn't give a shit who was in and out, as long as they got their money. So, as far as DNA or evidence, the rooms were so horribly dirty and cluttered with about twenty years' worth of semen, vomit, mildew, grime, and other parasites that she knew she would never get caught.

While making her way to her car, she exhaled in satisfaction. Raven chirped her alarm and hit the trunk button on her key ring, popping her trunk open automatically.

With renewed strength, she tossed her bag inside, and then closed the trunk. She walked toward the driver's side door and slid inside. Closing the door, she looked at herself in her rearview mirror, then smiled. The engine came to life as she turned the key to the ignition, and, as quietly as she came, she pulled away slowly and headed toward the highway en route home. It had been a long and fulfilling night, and now it was time for her to rest.

Chapter 2

Valencia

Valencia Ball sat at her cluttered desk, reviewing legal files. She had been a paralegal for three years and recently began working at Johnson and Associates. It was a larger law firm than she was accustomed to, but she hoped it would bring a little more excitement to her life.

Tired of looking at papers, she sat back in her high-backed brown leather executive chair and sighed. Her small office was quaint and unassuming. Nothing in her office identified her. There was nothing personal—no pictures, no plants, not even a sweater draped over her chair. Her eyes looked at the mirror that hung on the wall in front of her, and, when she caught a glimpse of herself, she shook her head sadly.

With black hair that cascaded down her back, deep brown skin, and slightly slanted, honey-colored eyes, Valencia captivated everyone around her. However, to herself, she was mediocre, to say the least. She didn't like her dark skin tone and felt she was too tall. Even though she didn't like her skin color, Valencia loved dark-skinned men. She just never thought that two dark-skinned people should connect, so she didn't date. Confined only to her 9 to 5, her life was boring. Outside of her best friend Sena, she rarely talked to anyone but clients. Some days, she found herself sitting and daydreaming about what her life would be like if she ever found love.

Would it be like the love she sang about in the music she listened to? Could someone ever really love her unconditionally? But she knew in the end, her life would never change, so there was no need in wishing upon a star. Besides, you can't miss what you never had is what she would always tell herself.

Chapter 3

Kidd

Kidd, his younger brother Moochie, and his homeboy Skillet were finishing up their breakfast at Goody Goody, which puts you in the mind of a bodega. It was small and family run. After a late night at the club and still slightly hungover, along with having the munchies, their table was full of empty plates that were once filled with chicken, waffles, eggs, turkey bacon, and hash browns. They also had watered down Pepsis and were awaiting refills. As regulars at the restaurant, most of the older patrons tried to ignore what they brought into the establishment—loud talk and raucous laughter, but, as usual, the females were trying to vie for attention.

"Hey, Kidd," a small, light-skinned honey purred as she passed by their table.

He looked up and gave her a head nod, then turned back to his boys. Kidd wasn't shocked by the attention he received. He was well known in the hood, and the ladies wanted him. Standing a full six feet even with brown skin, high cheekbones, shapely lips surrounded by a neatly trimmed goatee, dark eyes rimmed by long eyelashes, and a sexy swagger, he resembled a young Method Man.

"So, dig. I'm down on honey doing what I do best. This bitch screaming out my name and shit, talking 'bout 'stop for a minute please.'" Moochie became more animated as he continued his story. "I'm thinking I'm killing it and ole girl was loving it 'cause her face was all contorted and shit, so naturally I thought the bitch was 'bout to bust a fatty, but then this raunchy bitch fucked around and farted in my face." Everybody broke out into a fit of laughter. "Man, that shit ain't funny," he confirmed. "I punched that bitch in her pussy so hard she ain't gonna be able to fuck for a long time."

Moochie always had a good story to tell. He was exactly one year younger than Kidd was. They were born on the same day, only one year apart. He was Kidd's right-hand man and the only family he had left. You rarely saw one without the other. After their mother passed away, Kidd clung to his younger brother for sanity. Watching their mother struggle for life and wither away had done something to his mental. He latched on to Moochie hard and made him his only reason for living. He made sure he was taken care of. There was nothing he wouldn't do for his little brother. Moochie was the spitting image of his older brother with the exception of the shoulder-length dreads he sported.

"That's what the fuck you get," Kidd said sarcastically and slapped him in the back of the head. "You ain't supposed to do that shit to every chick you meet. I thought I taught you betta! You gonna fuck around and catch that nasty man's disease in yo' mouth." Sometimes, Kidd didn't understand the things that came out of Moochie's mouth.

"Right," Skillet cosigned, "and the catch of the day is only at Red Lobster."

Everybody erupted in laughter again.

The host, Gary, while making his rounds, returned to their table. "What story you telling now, Moochie? I know ain't nobody, but you got everybody over here laughing like this."

Gary was a tall, slim man who was three shades darker than a Hershey's Kiss. He had been watching the two brothers come in for years with their mother every Saturday. After she passed away, it took awhile, but eventually, they started coming back and kept up the tradition, and he always enjoyed them when they came.

"This nigga let someone fart in his face," Skillet blurted out in between laughs. Gary grinned at the admission and looked at Moochie. "So, how was it, man?" Skillet asked. "I know it couldn't have been that bad. She was a dime."

"Fuck that shit, man. Pardon my French, Mr. Gary," Moochie exclaimed. "But what look good on the outside definitely wasn't good on the inside. That shit smelled like a batch of greens that been sittin' out for ten days. You know how that shit sneak up on you? But that fart didn't. That shit hit instantly."

Laughter filled the air again at Moochie's expense. Gary joined in this time around, but he didn't stick around to hear any more. He was sure it would be too vulgar for his Christian ears.

"So we going out tonight?" Skillet asked looking between the brothers after the laughter subsided. He took a sip of his soda and chewed on the ice cube that he put inside of his mouth.

"I dunno," Kidd answered with a shrug, taking a long drink of his soda. "Where y'all tryin'a go?"

Moochie's mouth opened to answer, but Kidd cut him off. "I ain't going to that nasty-ass Pink Slip again. The last time I was there, this muthafucka here was getting his dome shined by some ho, and nigga was sitting right next to me." He nodded toward his brother with his lips turned up in disgust. "I ain't down with all that raunchy shit."

"Man, get out of here with that bullshit! Don't you two niggas still take baths together?" Skillet looked at the two brothers and started laughing, but he was the only one that found that joke funny.

"Fuck you, nigga." Moochie gave him the middle finger. "But, aye. Damn! You saw that shit? I told the bitch to be more discrete," Moochie laughed as he looked back at Kidd.

Once again, everyone laughed at Moochie's crazy ass.

Kidd reached inside of his pocket, pulled out four twenty-dollar bills, and laid them on the table.

"Where you headed?" Moochie inquired as he threw another piece of cold bacon in his mouth.

"To see Devin," he said, referring to his longtime friend whom he had helped to get his law firm off the ground.

Devin was actually a criminal lawyer, but he did everything for Kidd. When he decided to take extra classes to learn about investments and taxes, he'd contacted Kidd. He knew Kidd would be perfect for a good profit. If it wasn't for Kidd, he wouldn't have his own law firm that was currently one of the biggest in St. Louis. Devin knew all the ins and outs, courtesy of Kidd. Kidd saw potential in him and knew that, in his line of work, he would need him in the future. Kidd had a lot of illegal money to invest, but he chose to invest the money he got from his mother's insurance money and never touch it. The 200K had now grown to well over 5 million in seven years. He invested for Kidd; he was his tax lawyer, and he'd turned a lot of Kidd's money legal.

"Got some business to take care of. Y'all can follow me. Then, we can see what's up after that."

"Naw, man. I had a bad experience in one of them lawyers' offices," Moochie said with a stern look.

"Oh shit! I feel another story coming on," Skillet confirmed.

"I'm out, y'all." Kidd stood and gave everyone at the table some dap and strolled toward the door. As he was walking out, he could hear them laughing hard. He made a mental note to make sure his brother told him the story too.

After Kidd slid inside of his old-school Chevy Impala, the sounds of Lil' Wayne filled the air. Once he pulled off, he quickly changed his playlist from rap to R&B. He was particularly feeling the R. Kelly cut "You Bring Me Joy."

He cruised down Highway 170 toward his lawyer's office in Clayton, slumped in the seat coolly singing along with Kells. He thought back to when he was a child and his mother would always say, "Wanya, if you can't put a smile on a woman's face, then there is no sense in talking to her at all." Back when his mother kept a smile on her face, they were a happy family. He hadn't felt that kind of happiness since the day she took her last breath right in front of him and Moochie. Even with all of the women after him, Kidd always said he would never get married until a woman could make him feel the way that song portrayed love. Or until he met a woman that made him want to put a permanent smile on her face. He wasn't necessarily looking for love, but he also wasn't running away from it either. If Mrs. Right came along, he would gladly embrace her.

His boys always clowned him not only about living in the county, but also about being an R&B thug, but he didn't care, though. He knew the perception of county niggas—that they were weak, but he could come as hard—or harder—as any city nigga. Kidd didn't give a fuck who was from where. If he was disrespected, nobody was immune to retaliation. *Everybody bleeds when a full clip gets emptied in them,* he thought.

He admired the big buildings as he cruised the busy streets of Clayton. Lawyers' offices, courts, and expensive restaurants lined the streets, and the uppity rich folk walked hastily to their destinations. He had been driving this route for almost three years, and the hustle and bustle of this area still never ceased to amaze him. It was as though, once you entered the area, you were in a whole different world. These people seemed to have no problems and not a care in the world.

He had never struggled in his life, not even as a child. He was a hustler. He was the kid in school that came with a book bag full of snacks and goodies. Every day, he would come home with no less than a hundred dollars, hell-bent on saving every bit of it. His mother took good care of them, giving him no reason to spend his own money. Then, he moved up to selling weed, and, soon, he graduated into the real drug world. Soon after that, his boss offered him the deal of a lifetime, and there was no looking back after that.

Valencia looked at the clock on her desk and saw that she had ten minutes before her next appointment. Standing up from her chair, she stretched and ran her hands down her sleek frame, covered in a cream-colored Donna Karan suit. The matching Michael Kors pumps made her legs look even longer as she glided toward her door.

"Johnson and Associates, how can I help you? Please hold," the receptionist said three times before Valencia arrived at her desk.

"Hey, Sena, girl," she acknowledged her best friend who had gotten her the job at Johnson and Associates.

She held up her finger, signaling Valencia not to go anywhere as she answered two more calls.

"Girl, if I have to say that again, I swear my head is going to explode!" Sena's words were dripping with frustration.

"So, what you singing this morning?" Sena asked as she turned in her chair to face Valencia. She was referring to the game she and Vee played. The song would usually describe how they are feeling at that exact moment.

Valencia shook her head. "I can't even think of one right now. My mind is just blank. What about you?" Valencia really wanted to say "I Cry to Myself" by Chanté Moore, but thought better of it. She didn't want to dampen her friend's spirits.

"Shit! Sometimes, I feel I want to aann aann run away I want to aann aann get away." Both women broke into laughter.

"You better get them calls before Mr. Johnson jumps down your throat. Damn! Your switchboard is lit up like a Christmas tree," Vee pointed to the switchboard.

Sena shook her head and rolled her eyes as the switchboard continued to light up. "Where you goin'? To lunch?"

"Nah. Too late for lunch. Just to the bathroom before my two o'clock arrives."

The noise began to irritate Sena. "I'll talk to you later, V."

Moments later, Valencia passed Sena, who looked even more irritated. She laughed at her friend and then disappeared back into her office.

Sena rolled her eyes and continued to answer the ringing phones when the elevator chimed. A larger-than-life smile crossed her face when a tall man stepped out of the elevator. Walking toward her, she acknowledged him seductively. "Good afternoon, Mr. Brown. I'll let Mr. Johnson know you're here."

Her mouth began to water so much that when she licked her lips, it looked like she had put on a fresh coat of lip gloss. She had had so many nasty thoughts about this chocolate dream in front of her that, if people could read her mind, they would probably faint from all the freaky shit she wanted to do to him and wanted to let him do to her.

Sena eyed Kidd like a lion stalking her prey, but he was used to it. Like always, he turned and walked toward the waiting area, sat down, and began to flip through a *Forbes* magazine. Kidd moved off vibes and energy when or if he chose to approach a woman.

All the years he had been coming to the law office, Sena wanted him in the worst way and had explicit thoughts of him roughing her up, putting her in a full nelson while he hit it from the back. She got up from her desk and sashayed past Kidd, giving him the full view of her body. With her five feet four frame, she embraced her size twelve black girl ass and full set of perky double Ds. Although she was biracial, she denied her white heritage, but it was hard to ignore her big curly locks that hung down to the middle of her back and striking hazel eyes.

Without knocking, she walked into Valencia's office. "Girl, your two o'clock is here, and he is hot! I mean H-O-T kinda hot," she fanned herself.

"He? I don't have a man as my two o'clock appointment." Valencia frowned up her face.

"Oh, this is Devin's good friend. Everyone gets pushed around when he comes in. Devin can't see him now, so he has to see you, the next best thing!" Sena smiled big as she handed her the file with her next appointment's information in it. "Trust me, you will not be upset about this switch up."

"You're a mess," Valencia admitted truthfully, laughing at her friend. "But I'm not thinking about any man right now," she said with a wave of her hand.

"Song is 'Red Light Special.' You might not be, but I am, and he could get the muthafuckin' business right now." Both women giggled. "Don't say I didn't warn you, though, because, later on today, you'll be dreaming about him getting the kitty cat, and, when you come to your senses, it'll be too late because I will have already laid my vicious head game on him."

Valencia laughed. "You are stupid. Now, will you move so I can go talk to the man?"

"Whatever!"

Valencia walked toward the door and opened it. "See you later, and call in some takeout at Taylana's. I'm hungry now." Valencia walked out of her office with Sena on her heels.

"You tell me your song after you see him 'cause I got a few more that popped into my head like 'Sex You Up,' 'Half on a Baby,' and 'Bump N' Grind.' Girl, the list could go on forever," Sena yelled as Vee sped up her pace to get away from her crazy friend.

"Mr. Brown?" she spoke as she opened the door to the waiting room.

Kidd looked up and was instantly awestruck by the goddess who was walking toward him in what seemed to be slow motion, calling his name. She had him tongue-tied looking eloquent and statuesque in her suit and three-inch peep-toe pumps that adorned her small feet. He could tell her body was strapped from the front and wondered if she would need some help getting all of her hips and thighs out of her curve-hugging pantsuit. Her hair was pulled back into a bun, showing off her beautiful facial features. Her eyes were dark brown with hazel flecks dancing throughout them. Her eyes complemented her smooth complexion. She had just enough cleavage for it to look tasteful. He took a moment to admire everything about her. Her makeup was delicately applied with lips covered in a pale pink lip gloss that made him want to lick them. He had never seen anyone as beautiful as her in all his days. She was a far cry from the women he was used to on a regular basis. He had a few top-notch chicks in his stable, but she was in a league of her own.

"Hello, Mr. Brown," she extended her hand courteously without really looking at him. She wasn't paying attention, but he was. Her touch was soft and tender. He felt himself getting a little aroused. "I'm Valencia Ball. Mr. Johnson has appointed me to lead your investments. So, I will be meeting with you. I hope that won't be a problem."

Kidd didn't hear a word she said. He was captivated by her beauty. When Valencia turned to walk toward her office, he felt his heart take a double thump. He had to catch his breath. Her ass was magnificent.

"Oh my goddamn!" He bit into his bottom lip, imagining how her ass would feel slapping up against his stomach. *I have to call and thank my man Devin,* he thought.

"Excuse me?" She turned to look at him. "Did you say something?" *Ooooweeee!* she thought.

"Uh, naw. I'm just following you." Then he mumbled under his breath, "Anywhere you go."

When Valencia got a good look at him, she did a double take. He was fine, and lightning struck in her love tunnel, making her need to sit down ASAP. She smiled at him. "Has anyone ever told you that you look like Method Man?"

Damn! Sena gonna bug up when I tell her Silk's "Freak Me, Baby" popped into my head, she thought.

"Yes." He laughed. "I'm told that all the time."

Valencia's eyes spied Kidd's body. His facial hair was shaped to precision, connecting at his strong jawline and his goatee. His lips were thick and enticing. They just begged to be sucked while seemingly encouraging her to sit on his face. As sexy, bedroom eyes sucked her into his very essence, she caught her breath. Dressed down in a pair of Sean John jeans and a black V-neck, black Tims, and a red and black fitted Cardinals' hat, Kidd still held his own. He didn't wear too much bling, just a Bentley watch. Kidd felt that all the extras brought too much attention. Whether it was good or bad, he didn't want it.

Making her way into her office, Valencia said, "Come on in. Have a seat." She pointed to the chair directly across from her seat.

Kidd's eyes burned a hole through the seat of her pants, and he licked his lips hungrily as she walked to the other side of her small conference table and sat down.

"I've never seen you around here before," he told her, taking a seat across from her. "I've been coming here for about three years."

Although Valencia never let on, his gaze made her feel vulnerable. Being accustomed to being stared at by men and women was one thing, but there was something about him that deeply intrigued her. She tried her best to continue with the business at hand, but it was hard not to stare. His aura was emitting something into the air that demanded attention. And he had her full attention. No man had ever had that kind of effect on her, and he hadn't even done anything yet.

"I'm fairly new. I just started about three weeks ago." She tried her best to tear her eyes away from him, but she kept imagining how his strong arms would feel wrapped around her body.

"Well, welcome to the team." He extended his hand.

"Thank you." She graciously shook it.

At her touch, once again, he felt himself starting to rise to the occasion. Her delicate hand fit perfectly into his hands, and he almost didn't want to let it go. No woman ever had that effect on him, and he enjoyed it. She, on the other hand, began to get uncomfortable. His touch gave her feelings she never had before, and she quickly pulled her hand back. Noticing her uneasiness, he changed the subject.

"So let's get down to business. What's the word?" Kidd tried his best not to stare, but it was inevitable. She was breathtaking, and he wanted to get to know her a lot better. Her eyes were captivating. He loved how, when she turned her head, the hazel flecks made her whole eye look light brown.

Looking through the thick folder she had brought to her conference table, Valencia confirmed, "There's really nothing new from what I can see." Flipping through more pages, she continued, "As usual, your stock is still rising." Kidd's gaze was transfixed on her lips, and he hadn't heard anything she had said. "Mr. Brown? Did you hear me?"

"Huh? Yeah, I heard you. It's all good, right?"

She looked at a note affixed to the inside of the folder and read it. "Oh, also, Mr. Johnson said your name is still in the blue zone."

His smile instantly left his face. Not wanting her to know how he got his money, shame instantly shown in his eyes.

"That seems to be about all I have for you today. Either Mr. Johnson or I will contact you about any new investments in a couple of days." She extended her hand. "You have a good day, Mr. Brown."

"Wanya," he said as he took her hand in his, pulled it to his soft lips, and kissed it.

She was getting wetter by the minute. Her panties were so wet, she could probably wring them out. The man in front of her was working her over real good mentally. She stood to release the hold he had on her and backed up nervously toward the door as she watched him rise out of his chair. Instantly, a scene from a porno movie popped into her head. And just as quickly as the thought arose, she shook it off.

"Excuse me?" Valencia spoke with a perplexed look on her face. She wasn't able to fully comprehend him.

"My name is Wanya. Do you mind calling me by my first name? Makes me feel old when you call me Mr. Brown."

He began to walk in her direction. She watched every confident step he took toward her. She admired how the muscles in his arms moved with every swing of his arms. She almost reached out to touch him but quickly caught herself.

"I don't think that's appropriate. I'll just stick with Mr. Brown." She backed up a little more. *Damn! Please, God, get this man away from me.* She wanted to suck his bottom lip into her mouth.

"Just say it one time. I bet you'll want to say it again." He began to invade her personal space, looking at her with those sexy bedroom eyes that she was slowly starting to love looking into.

"Umm . . . You have a good day, Mr. Brown." She stepped around him to break the daze she was in from looking into his eyes.

"And you do the same, Ms. Valencia." He winked at her and walked out of the room.

At that moment, she needed to sit down. She didn't know how long she would be able to stand up on her wobbly legs. She found the end of the big cherry wood desk as Sena ran into the room.

"Girl, how was he?" Sena yelled, damn near making Valencia jump out of her skin.

"What the hell is wrong with you? You scared the hell out of me." Vee held her chest as she tried to catch her breath.

"Quit bitching! Give me tea. I want to know everything on that Methodical Man-looking muthafucka. Wait . . . no . . . Start with the song. I know something freaky popped into your head. What was it?" Sena smirked.

"Okay. Okay. 'Freak Me, Baby!'" she squealed.

"I told you. I *knew* it!" Sena practically squealed too.

"And there wasn't any tea. We simply discussed his investments, and he left. That's it." She was downplaying the electricity that was flying everywhere. She could still feel his presence in the room.

"You tripping. He fine as hell. That's one thang. Andddddd, second, you could use a little dick up in ya. Maybe your smile will brighten up around this joint, walking around all extraserious."

"Well, that was my last appointment for the day. I'm leaving early. I'll see you tomorrow."

"You want to go get some drinks at happy hour?"

"Naw, not today. I got a little running around to do," she lied through her teeth.

"Okay. I'll see you tomorrow."

Valencia rode down the highway, heading to her humble abode in South County. As she got closer to her home, she looked around at all the big houses that were scattered along the streets and the little kids and their parents out in their yards. It seemed like her well-to-do neighbors had everything figured out and had their fairy-tale ending already. Wives greeting their husbands at the door after a hard day at work. That kind of life seemed so far away, and there wasn't even a glimpse of a happy ending.

While listening to Chrisette Michele's "Is This the Way Love Feels?" she was in deep thought. She really wanted to know what love felt like. If it was anything like this song said it was, then she really wanted to feel that . . . the funny feeling in the pit of your stomach, a tingle, and everything else that came along with love, even the bad. She just wanted someone to love her unconditionally. To be hugged and kissed, for someone to look her in the eyes and say I love you and mean it from the bottom of his heart. She couldn't seem to shake Kidd out of her mind. Every time she closed her eyes, she saw some new part of his body. His eyes were so dreamy; she got lost in them every time she looked into them. She hoped he wouldn't contact her too soon. She needed to get him out of her system because there was no way in the world she could ever be with him. Life wouldn't allow it.

Every time she thought about her life, she wanted to cry. She asked God every day why her life was the way it was. She knew it was wrong to question God, but she really wanted to know. She was willing to give up everything she had—the money, cars, and her career—everything—just to feel love. Valencia wanted to find a love so hard that if they were homeless, they would still be happy and in love living in a cardboard box. As long as they were together, they would get through anything. But she knew she had to quit dreaming and deal with what she had.

Chapter 4

Excuse Me, Ms. Lady

Kidd and his crew were chilling in a booth at Club Home, and, from where they were sitting, they could see all the women walking by in too-short dresses, with their asses hanging out the bottom. Ass was in abundance, and his peoples was calling shotgun on damn near every ass that came bouncing by. Sitting in the back, trying to get Valencia out of his head unsuccessfully, he started thinking of ways to romance her. He had to have her, but she seemed to be a bit reserved for some reason. Is it because of the rule about "not mixing business with pleasure"? He hoped not because he really wanted to get to know her a little bit better, not even on a sexual note. He just liked being in her presence. She made him smile without even doing anything. In that short period of time, he wanted her to be his, and, if he had anything to do with it, she would be.

"So, like I was saying, I like for girls to make it clap, so this bitch bent over and started doing something with her ass. But I'm like, 'Yo, ma, fuck is you doing? Only one ass cheek is moving.' She turns around with an attitude and says, 'Nigga, you ain't paid me enough to make both ass cheeks move.' So I'm like, 'Bitch, I could buy ten of you and sell you back at half price.' She all like, 'Cash me out, then. Cash me out, then.' I looked at this chick like, 'Bitch, are you for real?' I had done already dropped like a hunnit ones on the floor, and she hadn't even earned that yet. So I picked up my muthafuckin' money back off the floor, leaving ten dollars down on that bitch, and walked away. She gon' yell, 'Cheap muthafucka!' and I yell back, 'Bitch, I'm going to find somebody that knows how to move both ass cheeks with yo' crippled ass.'"

Kidd glanced over at Moochie for a minute and chuckled a little at him. He was always so extra when he told his stories. But then something caught his attention at the front door. Valencia had just walked in the building, looking like a fucking superstar. She had on high-waist black jeans with some suspenders and a fitted white button-up shirt with a red tie on and some white Dsquared2 bone-heeled boots that went to the knees. Every curve on her body was there for all to see. The club wasn't that packed yet, so he could still kind of see the entrance to the right. Everybody noticed Kidd stand up and immediately followed suit, looking for trouble.

"Yo, Kidd. What we looking at?" Moochie asked, eyeing everybody in the club.

"My future wife!" He pointed toward the entrance.

"Daaaammmmmnn," they all said in unison, mocking the movie *Friday*.

"Damn! Mami is fire. You know her?" Skillet asked as he almost started drooling.

"Yeah, she works for Devin. Shit. She make a nigga want to commit some crimes just to be around her."

"You talking crazy, nigga. Ain't a bitch in the world look that good," Moochie said, scrunching up his face.

"Yo, man, why everybody got to be a bitch?" Kidd turned to Moochie.

"Shit, 'cause they rather be called a bitch than a ho, right?" Moochie was one of those "he treats you how you act" type of dudes and called it how he saw it.

"I don't know where you got that shit from." Kidd wanted to stay and chastise his little brother some more, but he had other things to tend to.

"Whatever, nigga, I got it from wherever you got it from. Now he want to act brand new. This guy is such a joker." Moochie put up the middle finger as Kidd walked away. He was used to Kidd's disapproving looks and comments.

"I'll be right back." Kidd walked in her direction, sizing her up from her head to the bottom of her feet. Indeed, he was smitten. She gave him butterflies and made him nervous. The anxiety of him not getting her to be his was making his stomach do somersaults.

"Excuse me, Miss Lady. I never thought I'd see you in a place like this." Kidd pulled her arm, so she was looking at him. His smile was bright enough to light the whole club.

"Excuse me. Do I know you?" Raven asked with an attitude, yanking her arm out of his grasp.

"So now you don't know me? And we had such a wonderful time together today." He just knew she had to be playing. With that one sentence, however, she knocked the wind out of him.

"I'm sorry, but you got me mixed up with someone else. I sleep during the day, sweetheart," Raven said, now backing up, getting a good look at him. Fine couldn't even begin to describe him. If she didn't know any better, she could have sworn she felt her clit jump. But that couldn't be. Wasn't a dick in the world look that good.

"So, yo' name ain't Valencia?" He had a look of pure confusion. He had been seeing her face all day in his head. He had memorized her smile, how her eyes squinted when she had an attitude, every dip, and curve in her body. This had to be her. But there was a hint of something different in her eyes.

"Nah, sweetheart, but, if that's who you want me to be, you can call me that bitch all night long if you want to." She was now all up in his personal space. But he was totally fucked up in the head at this point.

"Why you playing? If you didn't want to holla, that's all you had to say, ma. I ain't that hard up for no pussy." He was pissed that she would try to play him like that.

Raven's face shrunk to a small mask of anger, and her light brown eyes turned so dark that they almost looked black. "Look, I'm sorry if you have mistaken me for somebody else, but there's no need for the foul language. If you say the broad looks like me, then you better keep pursuing. There aren't too many women have that pleasure of saying such a thing. I would love to think I was a one and only, but, like I said before, if you can't find her, I'll be Valencia, Halle, Beyoncé . . . all them hoes, just for you."

He stood there, not believing her. That was her. It *had* to be her. He wasn't crazy. But the more he thought about it, she was a little lighter than Valencia, and her eyes looked sneaky. Valencia's eyes were the perfect blend of dark chocolate with a spoonful of milk, and eyes that made you feel as if you were looking into a kaleidoscope.

Skillet ran up to him laughing.

"Aye, man. She played you. Aye, this shit is hilarious. Billie D got kicked to curb. Yo! Go do it again so I can record it on my phone and put this shit on YouTube." Skillet loved this. Kidd never got turned down. Skillet wasn't a hater, but he damn sure was going to take the opportunity to get a "one-up" on Kidd.

"You ol' hating-ass nigga. She ain't turn me down. She wasn't who I thought she was," Kidd huffed.

"Yeah, a'ight. Let that be the reason," Skillet poked his lips out.

"Don't trip. She was with it too, so I'll take her if I can't get the one I want tonight." Kidd watched her watching him from the other side of the room. He knew exactly what that look meant. Shit! She was practically an exact replica of the woman he wanted. But her demeanor was on a whole 'nother level from Valencia. This lady in front of him exuded sexiness and lust while Valencia was more gentle, demure, and timid.

Raven was by herself. She always traveled alone while looking for her next high. She hadn't come out in a while, so it was time to get her groove on. She stood at the bar, eyeing this cute little honey standing next to her. She stood, leaning on her left leg with her hands on her hips, waiting for a waitress to come and take her drink order. Raven stared openly at the gap between her legs. The girl knew she had no business being out in public with her pussy print just there for the world to see, but Raven wasn't mad at her at all. It simply looked like a tight fist ready to throw punches at the first man's face who dared to challenge it. Raven could see herself getting all up in her hot box and couldn't wait to taste her. Raven could tell she wasn't gay per se, but she looked like she would experiment.

"Excuse me," Raven waved a hundred-dollar bill in the air, which got the waitress's full attention.

"Yes. What can I get you?"

"I want Pineapple Cîroc X-Rated." That was Raven's new drink of choice. It tasted like lemonade, but, ten minutes after finishing it, she knew she would be in the right place. Raven took her eyes off of the pretty waitress and looked up and down at the woman standing next to her. "And whatever this young lady is drinking." Raven smiled at her while licking her lips. The girl returned the smile. That was all Raven needed to know she was in. It wasn't just that she had smiled. It was the *way* she smiled and gave her the once-over.

"I'll have what she's having." She leaned up against the bar, very interested in what Raven had to offer. Hell! Her cheap-ass date didn't even have the decency to come buy her drink. She had never been with a woman before but was very curious, and what better way to break herself in than with the stallion standing before her?

"Thanks," Raven said as the waitress handed them their drinks. "So, what's your name?" Raven asked, giving the girl a "I want to fuck all night long" look.

"Toya. And yours?" she asked, returning the look.

Raven got a little closer, cutting to the chase, ignoring her question. She didn't know yet if she was going to keep her around. Raven didn't really care to get into conversations. A woman knows in the first five minutes if they are going to leave with you or not, and her five minutes were up. If she wasn't leaving with her tonight, then it was on to the next one.

"You look bored. Why don't we get out of here and have a little fun of our own?" Raven ran her index finger down the middle of her cleavage. She could see the reluctance in the young lady's face, but she also saw the goose bumps form on her arms too.

Toya looked around to see if her date was anywhere to be found. She had been gone for almost an hour, and he hadn't even bothered to come check on her. She couldn't believe that bastard still hadn't come looking for her. *He's probably got some bitch sitting on his face,* she thought to herself.

"I'm cool with that." She gave Raven a seductive smile. "Let me get my purse, and I'll meet you back here in ten minutes. Is that cool?" She reached out and ran her hand lightly up and down Raven's tie, pulling her in closer to her.

Raven bent down to her five feet four frame and licked the side of her neck and watched her ass as she walked away.

I might keep her around, Raven thought as she went to the dance floor till her victim/li'l tender came back. Her song, "Go Head" by Gucci Mane was vibrating through the whole club.

"Shawty got a ass on her, I'ma put my hands on her, I'ma spend a couple grand on her, I'ma pop a rubber band on her," she sang as she gyrated her hips, hypnotizing damn near half the club, including Kidd and his peoples.

"Aye, I know what them moves mean. She trying to get fucked tonight, and you better snatch her up before I step in, Kidd." Moochie was imagining her bent over, gripping her ankles, with her ass slapping up against his lower torso.

While watching a little longer, Moochie realized that there was something about her that he couldn't put his finger on. He didn't know if it was good or bad. He was a little too tipsy to get a good vibe off of her. But he knew it was something, and, if he ever saw her again, it would come to him.

"Don't move too quick. That's already got my name on it. Believe me." He strolled over to Raven on the dance floor, stood behind her, and slowly wrapped his arms around her waist.

Raven knew it was him before he got to her by the way his cologne invaded her personal space. The smell of his Dolce & Gabbana cologne mixed with his musk was an intoxicating chemistry, even for her.

"So what's your name, Miss Lady?" he whispered into her ear.

"Raven," she said with a swirl of her hips.

"Raven. I like that."

"So you got tired of looking for the knock-off version of me and decided on the real thing?"

She was now grinding her ass all over his crotch, liking what she felt. *If only I . . .* she thought. Liking what he was feeling, also, he held her a little tighter. She bent over and gave him a clear view of the *Slippery When Wet* sign on her lower back. Her pants were high waist in the front, but the back didn't have a prayer in the world.

"Is that right?"

"Is what right?"

"That sign on your back."

"Sure is . . ."

"Umm-hmmm!" he smirked.

"Well, I got to get going," she said, noticing her new friend waiting for her. "It was nice meeting you. I'm sorry, what did you say your name was again?" She turned around to get another look at him.

"Kidd. Where you going so soon? The night just started."

"I just came out to get a drink and to meet a friend. I have to go to work in the morning," she lied as she backed away.

"I thought you slept during the day." He crossed his arms over his chest.

"I do, but tomorrow I have some work to do. Besides, I'm a vegetarian. I don't do meat, but, if I did, I wouldn't hesitate to let you do whatever your little heart desired."

"Damn! It's like that, huh?" he said, rubbing his chin.

"In that order."

"Well, my bad, ma. I ain't mean to disturb you. It was a pleasure meeting you, though."

"Oh no. The pleasure was all mine." She walked away and waved her hand in the air, nodding her head toward the door, then a fine little honey walked up to her, and they walked out together.

"Twice in one night? We got to get this shit on tape," Skillet said, breaking Kidd from his concentration.

"Hush, my confused pupil. Even the best lose, at least, once," Kidd imitated Mr. Miyagi from *The Karate Kid.* "What a fuckin' waste." Kidd looked disappointed.

"Damn! She ain't shit 'cause she shitted on you? Don't tell me you one of those ole sucka-ass niggas that curse a broad out 'cause she ain't interested." Moochie had his lips poked out, waiting for the reason of his brother's sudden attitude change.

"Don't even play ya'self out like that, son. She a fuckin' lesbo."

"Damn! You right! What a fuckin' waste." Moochie had to agree with his brother. She was super-hot but wasn't giving a real man a chance to turn her shit inside out.

"Right. My sentiments exactly."

Raven lay on the bed, thinking about the fine, young tender that was trying to give her the business. She was trying to concentrate on what was taking place at the moment, but she couldn't shake Kidd for some reason. If she did do dick, he would definitely be a candidate. She would have experimented with him, but his mind was on someone else when he approached her, and, if he wanted to be with Raven, his mind had to be on her and her alone. She looked down at the PYT doing her thing down there on her clit, about to bring on an explosive orgasm. Just thinking about it alone, she started to convulse.

"Ooh shit! Do that shit, mami." Raven was feeling really good at the moment.

"You like that?" the girl said with a mouth full of pussy. She was trying her best to please Raven. She had never eaten pussy before, but she knew how she herself liked it.

"Yeahhhh." Raven felt as if she were riding on the stairway to heaven. "Come on up here. Let me taste it too."

The girl quickly obliged, putting her tongue into Raven's mouth to let her taste her own juices. They shared a long, passionate kiss that caused the heat to go up to what felt like 100 degrees. They slowly switched places. Raven was now on top and slowly working her way down Toya's body. She stopped at her caramel nipples and circled her tongue around one. Then, she rolled the other between her first finger and thumb. Raven's kisses made shock waves flow through Toya's entire body.

Raven moved down to her love tunnel, slowly spreading her legs, admiring the jumping clit in front of her. She was able to see the juices oozing out and couldn't wait to taste them. She stuck her tongue inside, and it instantly came in contact with Toya's fluids, creating a slimy string attached to her tongue. Raven smiled and placed a wet kiss on Toya's pussy lips, then devoured the kitty. Toya tried to run away, but Raven had a tight grip on her thighs, making it hard for her to move anywhere. She thought for sure she was going to have a heart attack if Raven didn't stop soon. She could feel her heart about to beat out of her chest and her muscles slowly getting stiff when, all of sudden, a feeling came over her that she had never felt before. She had come so hard that every muscle in her body went stiff as a board as shock waves went deep into her soul.

"Let's do something kinky," Raven said as she finally let go of her clit. Toya didn't think she was going to be able to take any more. She had never been to the heights that Raven was taking her to, and she could see herself cozying up real close to Raven. She had always had problems with the men in her life. Maybe she was supposed to be with women all along. Raven pulled out her sex kit. This one was a little different. It contained four pairs of furry handcuffs, two whips, some Ben Wa balls, a big black ten-inch strap-on dildo . . . and a noose.

Raven dove, face-first, in between her legs and sucked the girl's clit into her mouth, taking another taste.

"Ooooh shit!" Toya could barely contain herself, and Raven had barely even gotten started yet. Raven turned her on her stomach and cuffed her arms and legs to the bedpost.

"You're going to *love* this." She pulled at the girl's hips so that she was slightly on her knees and her ass was tooted up in the air. She stuck her face all the way in the immense ass before her and started eating her pussy from the back. Considering what she was about to do to the girl, she figured that she may as well send her off with a bang, but she was still undecided about what she was about to do.

"Ooh! That feels . . . sooooo . . . good. I'm about to come," Toya panted hard, anticipating the explosion that was sure to follow. She wasn't able to believe that this woman was taking her to heaven and back again. The tingling sensation flowing through her hot box was about to make her brain explode.

Raven made her tongue move even faster, knowing that she was on her way to an orgasm. Shaking and squirming all over the bed, Toya couldn't seem to control her body. Raven sat up, rubbing on Toya's ass, admiring it for the beautiful piece of art that it was. It looked like a perfect-shaped Georgia peach. Raven strapped on her dildo, softly rubbing it up and down her wet slit, coating the artificial dick with her love nectar. Then, she slowly inserted it into Toya, and she screamed with pure delight.

"Ooh yeah! Shit! That feels good," she said as she started working her hips, throwing that ass back at Raven.

"How do you want it?" Raven asked, gripping her ass firmly and spreading her cheeks apart.

"Hard, baby, hard." She was gripping the sheets and losing her mind, feeling another orgasm on the rise.

"*That's* what I'm talking about."

Raven pumped hard as she pulled out the noose, getting it prepared to do some work. Being that the girl was on her stomach, she couldn't see what Raven was doing. Hell, by now, Raven probably could hog-tie her, get up in her dookie shoot, and make her suck the dildo afterward if she wanted to. Raven was giving her the one-two punch, and she didn't want her to let up.

Raven's sex skills always got her what she wanted. That was her lure to get her victims comfortable and relaxed. She lay the noose back down, wanting to see the girl's face once more before she started squeezing the life out of her. So Raven removed the cuffs, turned her on her back, and put the cuffs back on her wrists, pulling her legs all the way back so that her ankles were cuffed to her wrists.

"Damn! Ain't nobody ever done me like this before," Toya exclaimed in pure bliss.

"Well, you know it's my duty to please that booty," Raven said, mocking Samuel L. Jackson in the movie *Shaft* as she went down on the girl once again. The need to taste her again took over her. The girl had some good pussy. It was such a shame that she'd met Toya on the night she needed a fix.

Now it was time to start the show. She eased the dildo back in and started to pump slowly, watching the girl's facial expressions. Raven was fighting everything in her not to do what she was about to do. But she needed a fix in the worst way. Still fighting within herself, she picked up the noose and put it back down, like four times, before deciding that it had to be done.

"Close your eyes."

Because she did as she was told, Toya didn't see the noose. But her eyes popped out of her head when she felt something slide around her neck. She started bucking and moving, trying to get away. This only turned Raven on more. She was fucking her like she could feel how tight the pussy really was when it constricted around the fake penis she wore. Raven, feeling a major orgasmic energy surging through her body, started pulling the noose tighter. The sight of the girl's contorted face brought on this blissful feeling that she had been longing for. She opened her eyes to see the girl with tears on her face. She had gotten so weak that she couldn't move anymore. Raven hurriedly removed the noose, and Toya took a long, deep breath. That was longest thirty seconds of her young life.

"I'm sorry. I just got carried away," Raven said, uncuffing her arms. Raven looked her in the eyes and could see the fear of God registered there. She didn't like to be looked at that way. That was why she was usually not around when they woke up, and, half the time, they didn't wake up. For some reason, though, she couldn't cause too much harm to this girl with the angelic face. She actually wanted to keep her around, but, by the way Toya was looking, she was going to run out of there as if her ass was on fire. Raven couldn't explain what she was feeling, but there was a sense of softness to it. Raven wasn't convinced that she'd liked it yet. At the end of the night, all she really wanted was mind-blowing sex and earth-shattering orgasms, which she had gotten.

"No, it's okay. I've never experienced anything like that before," she said, rubbing the burns that were forming on her neck. At that point, she would say anything to get out of there alive.

Raven had gone completely left field on her. It was confusing because she liked it rough, but that was a bit much, even for her.

"Okay." Raven rose up off the bed as Toya sat there, staring at her in awe. Raven didn't know why she was looking at her like that. She also didn't know why this girl was still breathing. Was she gaining control over her anger and addiction . . . or was something else interfering?

Chapter 5

Notebook

It had been two weeks, and Valencia still found herself thinking about Kidd constantly. His smile was like a warm breeze against her skin. His hands were so soft. She could imagine him running his hands all over her body. She wanted to take his lips home with her and put them on her pillow, they looked so supple and luscious. But she was well aware that they could never be together. She longed for love, to be loved, but even when she saw couples holding hands, walking down the street, or watched the movies where women got their men in the end, she knew that a fairy-tale ending was not her future. Then, there were the songs that portrayed love to be this wonderful thing that she knew nothing about, but so desperately wanted—no—needed—in her life. But her life's situation wouldn't let her. She belonged to someone else who had a death grip on her life. All she did was work. Occasionally, she allowed herself to get out and shop a little. Shit! Somebody had to make the money, and the lazy muthafucka she was tied to wasn't fit to do shit but spend money like it grew on trees. So she had to get her ass out of the house and get shit popping.

"What you thinking about over there? You looking quite pensive. What's the song?" Sena asked, sneaking up behind Valencia.

Valencia sighed. "Chrisette Michele's, 'Notebook.'"

This song fit her to a tee. She found herself scribbling Kidd's name all over paper with little hearts everywhere. She really wanted to be with Kidd, at least see him, if only for a moment, but knew it couldn't be.

"And inquiring minds would like to know where that song came from?" Sena asked, already knowing the answer. Valencia was looking all dreamy eyed.

"I don't know. It's just a song that popped in my head. Ain't that what the game is about?" she said while fidgeting with the pens on her desk. Valencia couldn't hide her feelings even if she wanted to. Kidd had really left an impression on her. The dreams she'd had were so X-rated and naughty that they turned her face red, just thinking about them. She tried to avoid eye contact because she knew if anybody could read her, it was Sena.

"Yeah, this is true," Sena chuckled. "It is about how you are feeling at the moment." Sena walked around to sit on Valencia's desk so she was face-to-face with her. "But it's cool that we got secrets now. At least, you think we do." Sena stared at her friend, waiting for a response. "You can keep quiet all you want, but remember, I know all, and I see all. You ready to do some mouth tricks for Mr. Brown Suga, ain't cha?" She couldn't help but laugh a little at her friend's innocence. "Don't answer. I told you I know already."

"Anyway, Miss Psychic Friends Network, what do you want?" Valencia was trying to change the subject to anything but the one at hand.

"Shit! Trying to get something to eat. What you eating for lunch?"

"I'm going down to Whole Foods," Valencia said as she watched about three deliverymen walk in with all sorts of flowers. Each had one vase in both hands. They stopped at the desk Sena was supposed to be at, and the person helping them pointed to her office.

"Oh yeah? Let me get some beef brisket. That stuff is the bomb." Sena licked her lips in anticipation.

"Huh?" Vee couldn't focus as she watched about three more men walk into the building with more flowers. She could see roses and lilies of all colors—red, white, yellow, purple, and some were blue. How the person got those colors, she'd never know. *This chick is lucky as hell whoever she is . . .* she thought.

"Girl, are you paying me the least little bit of attention?" Sena followed Vee's line of vision and could see Kidd walking through the door with more flowers in his hands, looking like something out of every girl's fantasy. There seemed to be a light around him. His smile was so bright, it melted her panties. His strides were strong, sexy, confident, and even.

Vee could have sworn she had stepped into R. Kelly's, *Half on a Baby* video, with his white linen outfit blowing in the wind while he was walking up the steps, leaving nothing to the imagination. She had imagined Kidd in that same scene, and she was the woman in the bed waiting. Kidd was the shit, and she wanted a piece of him in a bad way. She unconsciously crossed her legs so she could feel the muscles in her kitty thumping. She still couldn't get over how fine he was. She wanted to lick and bite all over him. The Egyptian gods had shown no mercy when they molded him. His golden bronze complexion shined brightly, and his body was a work of art that couldn't be described in words. From the looks of the bulge in the front of his pants, he was kind of right down there. She longed for the day they could be together, when he would hold her in his arms, and their souls would connect as one.

"Ummmm-hmmmm, and can you get me a side order of him with some gravy on top?" Sena asked, snapping Vee out of her daydream.

The deliverymen finally made it to her office, placing flowers all over the room, and, at the end of the line, Kidd was standing there with a look of sheer appreciation at the sight in front him. She was the most beautiful woman he had ever seen, and he wouldn't stop until he had wooed her heart right into his hands. He didn't just want her body—he wanted everything—her mind, body, and soul. He wanted to be the first thing she thought about in the morning and the last thing she thought about at night. He wanted to consume her every thought and invade her dreams.

"Hello, ladies. Miss Valencia, can I speak to you for a moment in private?" He licked his lips as he stared into Valencia's wanting eyes. "About my investments, of course." His smile brightened the room and made her feel warm inside. She looked around the room at all the flowers.

"I'll excuse myself," Sena said as she made her way to the door, but, before she left, she turned around and started humping in the air toward Kidd and rubbing all over her body, making Valencia laugh out loud. When Kidd turned around, Sena had jumped, stopped, and quickly closed the door.

"What is all this about, Mr. Brown?" Valencia questioned, still in awe of all the beautiful flowers.

"What . . . You don't like them?" Kidd hoped he wasn't being too pushy. He just wanted to show her he was very interested in her.

"No, I am not saying that. They are all beautiful. I just don't know what I did to deserve these." She smiled bashfully.

"You didn't do anything. These are just because I like the way you smile at me. Tomorrow, you may get some just because the sun is shining. And the next day because I had a dream about you." He looked her in the eyes.

"Hmm." She cleared her throat to give her time to think of something to say. She had absolutely no experience in this department. "Well, ummm, are those mine too?" She reached for the flowers in his hand, but he moved back.

"Naw. These are for somebody else. These are for this nice lady I want to take out to . . . if she'd allow me the honor."

"Oh, I see," she smiled. "Well, let me smell them. Those are my favorite flowers."

She admired all the pretty colors. To her, birds-of-paradise were, by far, the most beautiful flower God ever created. Most people wouldn't just pick that out of group of flowers, but he had, and that was very special to her.

"I guess." He handed her the flowers.

"Well, tell her she got ganked." Valencia snatched the flowers out of his hands and laughed.

"Okay. So I'm a punk now. You just gon' take something from me?" He laughed at her, loving the way her laugh soothed his heart. He loved her style. She was stunning today in a cream and chocolate-brown pin-striped pantsuit that looked as if it was made for her body only. The brown stripes going down her figure made her body look like a map with winding roads going up and down hills. The color bounced off her dark skin tone, perfectly illuminating the fresh coat of shimmering M.A.C. shadow she had applied that morning. Her chocolate-colored Mary Jane pumps made her legs look like they could reach the heavens.

"Taking sounds way better than stealing. Taking is gangsta and in your face, while stealing is sneaky and what punks do." She admired his chiseled jawline as he laughed. She could listen to his laugh all day long.

"So, I'm coming to the conclusion that you think I'm a punk." He looked at her all sexy eyed.

"We won't say that. Just that I'm gangsta. Yeah, we'll go with that." She laughed at him and pointed to the seat in front of her when she finally noticed they were still standing. She put a little wiggle in her walk when she went to the other side and slid her sexy frame into the oversized leather chair.

"Thank you for all the flowers. They are beautiful," she gushed, finally able to appreciate them as their fresh aroma invaded her senses.

"Well, you're welcome. Anytime." He couldn't help but stare at her. She was the personification of beauty.

"So, to what do I owe the pleasure of this impromptu meeting?" She couldn't give two shits about why he was there, just as long as he was in her sights.

"You said you would call me about the investments and never did." Kidd had racked his brain for a reason to come see her, and that was the best he could come up with, but it worked. The flowers were brought to put a smile on her face. Her eyes were beautiful, but he could see some sadness in them the last time he was there. If he had anything to do with it, she would never feel pain or heartache again if she only gave him the chance.

Valencia was trying her best to stay calm, but it wasn't working. Her heart rate had gone up drastically. She was getting hotter and hotter, and it was of no use in trying to hide her protruding nipples. This beautiful specimen of a man in front of her was turning her on. At first glance, she wanted to jump on top of him and ride him like a professional cowgirl.

"I'm trying to make things happen, and that can't happen with my money just hanging in the air. Scared money doesn't make money. Money makes money." He couldn't hide the lust in his eyes. He didn't really care about the money at that very moment. He knew Devin wouldn't let anything bad happen to his investments. Even if the stock market crashed right then and there, the money buried under his house would do him good for the rest of his life.

"I'm sorry if I have inconvenienced you in any way, sir, but I am a professional. And I'm damn good at what I do. But if you want me to just put the money anywhere until I find something suitable, that would be fine by me. I get paid regardless."

Attitude was written all over her face, and he loved it. Clasping her hands together on the desk, which pushed her breasts together, got his mouth to watering. His eyes were glued to them. Noticing his stare, she decided to play along.

"Can I help you with something down there? Did you lose something, sir?" she asked as she leaned forward to give him a better look.

He blushed like a shy, little boy. He hadn't known she was watching him or hadn't paid any attention. She'd bet on the latter.

"Naw, my bad. I ain't mean no harm, but you are beautiful, ma, and that attitude. I knew you had li'l hood in you somewhere," he laughed a little.

"Oh, am I beautiful?" She ignored the remark. "Or are my breasts?"

He leaned forward so he could get a closer look into her eyes. "Make no mistake about it. You are beautiful. I mean, I have never met a woman like you before. I like being around you. Let's be honest. I came here to see you. I usually call my man, he would fill me in, and that would be that. But you make me want to get to know the ins and outs of everything."

"While I am very flattered, that doesn't change the fact that I'm also in a very committed relationship. Plus, I never mix business with pleasure, Mr. Brown." She stood gracefully and took a deep breath to desperately attempt to lower her heart rate. There was an inferno in his eyes that was slowly melting the ice encasing her heart. He didn't even know it yet, but Kidd had her the moment he flashed those pearly whites at her. She'd follow him over a cliff if that was the direction he was going.

"I didn't ask if you had a man. I just said that you were beautiful and that I liked being around you. It flatters me that you feel you had to throw that out there. That means you were thinking about cheating," he laughed. "But, for real, for the time being, I'm not trying to wife you, just spend a little time. An occasional lunch date to discuss business, of course, and get to know you a li'l better."

That was a bold-faced lie. She knew what he wanted because she wanted it just as bad as he did.

"What do you want to know about me?" She sat back down.

"Everything." He leaned back in his chair.

"Liiiiiiike?" She threw her hands in the air.

"What's your favorite food, color, movie, flower, what makes you tick, what makes you smile, and, if there was any place on earth you could go, where would it be?"

"Birthday cake, sea blue, *The Five Heartbeats*, birds-of-paradise, liars, another smile, and Egypt."

"Now that wasn't so hard, was it? Egypt, huh? I never thought about going there. Now that I think about it, it does sound kind of cool. I'll put that on my things-to-do list. And birthday cake? That's not a food." He shook his finger in her face.

"Yes, it is. You could have a feast sitting in front of me, but, if I see the cake, it's most likely going to be the first thing I go for. It's the only kind of cake I eat. Maybe that's why I can't lose no weight." She laughed.

"Baby girl, you don't need to lose a pound."

"It's not what someone else thinks; it's about what I think."

"Okay, if you say so, but back to the subject at hand, no caramel cake, upside-down, 7-Up cakes, or any other kind?"

"Nope. Birthday cake with a lot of roses. I know. It's a shame." They both shared a laugh. "Ashanti," she said aloud by mistake. The song "Baby" was on repeat in her head.

"Ashanti?" he looked at her strangely.

"Oh, I'm sorry. That's something Sena and me do. Don't worry about it." She tried to play it off.

"What's this thing y'all do?"

"Nothing," she blushed.

"Why you blushing then, if it's nothing?" he questioned, giving her a knowing look.

"Okay, we like to say how we are feeling at a certain moment in time with the name of a song." She felt herself loosening up around him. He made her feel at ease.

"So, which one are you thinking of now?" he smiled. "Ashanti sings love songs. Hmm . . . Let me think." He looked at the ceiling like he was really thinking hard. "It can't be 'Foolish.' I would never break your heart. What about . . . 'Baby'?" She tried to hide the shock in her eyes. *I got this jones forming in my bones from a man who indeed took over my soul,"* he sang, teasing her, but she cut him off.

"Shut up. You will never know," she said with a slight chuckle.

"Yeah. A'ight. You'll tell me eventually."

"I don't see anything wrong with lunch." She was loosening up and had gotten totally comfortable by now. Valencia stood up to get some coffee. He walked into her personal space.

"Mr. Brown, this is totally inappropriate." She wanted to grab his face and stick her tongue so far down his throat that she would be able taste what he ate earlier, but opted to step back instead.

"Wanya." He looked into her eyes with an intense yearning.

"Excuse me?"

"My name."

"I know your name, Mr. Brown." She backed away.

"I know you know it. Just say it." Staring into her eyes intensely, he couldn't help but think, *Damn! No one has called me by my real name since my mother passed away eight years ago.* He would never allow it, but, for some reason, he wanted to hear it fall from her perfect lips.

"Wanya. Just say it." He was all the way in her face. Her panties were feeling really moist by now. Shit. At this point, she could call out his name from the mountaintops.

"Okay, Mr. Brown. Call me later on this week to schedule our lunch meeting." Taking a couple of steps back, only for him to take a couple of steps forward, he was seriously violating her personal space.

"Come on, ma. Don't be like that. Say it one time." Gazing into her eyes with those bedroom eyes, he broke down a few more barriers. He walked even farther into her personal space but never touched her. They were so close his breath tickled the skin on her face. His hands were clasped behind his back. He looked into her eyes hard and licked his lips like he had strawberry syrup on them, or, at least, that was what she had imagined. She couldn't understand, for the life of her, why he wanted her to say his name so badly. Or why he was having such an effect her. The damage was done, however. She reached for his face and stepped in closer to him.

"Vee, Mr. Johnson is looking for you." Sena burst through the doors, not knowing what was about to take place. "Oops! My bad," she giggled and tried to shut the door.

"Umm . . . Wait!" Valencia yelled nervously. "Keep Mr. Brown company for a moment." She rushed out of the room.

Sena turned to Kidd and smiled. Her smile quickly faded, however, and her face resembled that of a hungry wolf showing his fangs. She got right down to business.

"Look, I don't know what your intentions are for Valencia. She is the sweetest, nicest, most beautiful person you will ever meet." She was in *his* personal space now. "Now, that's my girl, and you better not ever hurt her." Sena paused to allow her words to sink in.

"What are talking about, man?" Kidd tried to get a few words in.

"Listen, she would give you the shirt off her back if you asked for it. People like her don't come around often, so don't go fucking with her emotions or her heart. She's been through enough, so, if this is a mission for a hit-and-quit, you walk out that door and don't come back unless you're looking for Mr. Johnson."

"So, I need your permission to continue to pursue her?" He stepped back out of her reach. For some reason she looked like was ready to swing on him. He wouldn't hit her, but he would definitely shake the shit out of her.

"Take it how you want to take it. She never has to know about this conversation. I'm just letting you know . . . that I have absolutely no problem with protecting my friend at *all* costs."

"Noted," He had to laugh in his head because she had no clue of who he really was. But he would let her have her moment.

She walked over to the door, but before she left, she left him with a few parting words. "They say there is nothing worse than a woman scorned. Well, they never ran into the best friend of a woman scorned. Because it would take you and your whole li'l crew to stop what you would have coming."

And, with that, she sauntered out of the room. Her point was very clear—come correct or don't come at all. Standing there, looking like a straight dickhead, he could not believe she had come at him like that. He just knew she was about to be on some *when-you-coming-over* type shit. But she was looking out for her girl. Seeing her in a totally different light now, he couldn't help but think, *She ain't a total slut bucket, after all.*

"*I'm a hustla, I'm a I'm a hustla homie nigga ask nigga nigga ask about me.*" Kidd's phone started rapping the Cassidy joint. Knowing it was somebody from the camp, he immediately flipped his phone open.

"What's the BI?"

"Get around the way. Skillet got shot!"

Moochie was damn near hysterical and was practically yelling in Kidd's ear. He and Skillet had been best friends since they were ten years old. In fact, Moochie was the one who named him Skillet because he said he was blacker than one of those big, old-school frying pans.

"I'm on my way." Kidd was out of that building and back on the highway in less than three minutes flat.

While riding, he was deep in thought, listening to Jaheim's "Just in Case," wondering if he could ever really have a chance to be with Valencia or someone like her. There was something about her that he couldn't seem to put his finger on. He figured a girl like her would never give the likes of him the time of day, so backing off was what he decided to do. She knew where to find him if she needed him. Soon, he would be out of the underworld and turning legit. He had invested enough money and also had quite a substantial amount of money under his three-car garage at his five-bedroom, four-bath, with a total of thirteen rooms minimansion in South County. He actually had enough money to quit now, but he had a lot of loose ends to tie up, and then he and his brother would be out. Switching into kill mode, he changed the song on his built-in iPod to Tupac's "Hail Mary" and put it on repeat and let it lead him the rest of the way mentally. This was the perfect song for today's situation because somebody sure as hell was going to die tonight.

After sitting in the bathroom and throwing water on her face, Valencia finally decided to go back out. She wanted to be with Kidd so badly that it hurt. Her heart felt like it was about to explode. But the fact still remained; she would never be able to live her life how she wished. She walked back into the conference room looking for Kidd, but he had got ghost. She tried to keep from getting upset and excited. For some reason, it brought on this horrible headache that made her feel like her skull was about to explode. And the rest of the night would be one long blur.

"Where did he go?" Valencia asked, asking no one in particular.

"Girl, that nigga ran out of here like his ass was on fire," Sena said, walking up on her. "What the hell did you do to him, Vee?"

"Probably ran him away for good." Feeling defeated, Valencia flopped down in one of the big leather seats that took up the most of the space in the room. She knew that she would never be able to have a fulfilling relationship if she didn't change some things in her life. She could feel herself getting upset. And Sena wasn't helping at all.

"And why the hell would you do some dumb shit like that?"

"Please, not now." Valencia's head was pounding.

"Do I need to run down his credentials to you? No kids, stupid hot . . . I mean, makes you wanna drink his bathwater. Again, no kids, and don't let me forget . . . rich!" Sena couldn't understand Vee sometimes. She knew women that would steal, kill, and destroy anything that got in their way over a man like that.

"No, you don't." She was angry and didn't know why.

"Like I was saying, the man is gorgeous and, most importantly, rich! You tell me where you can find another man with that many good qualities and I'll show you a red duck. Shit. Excuse my French, but they'd have to pry me off that dick with the Jaws of Life."

"Well, you fuck him then, and leave me the fuck alone about it!" She was massaging her temples while holding her head down.

"What the fuck is your problem?" Sena could see the sudden change in her friend. "Girl! Are you bipolar or some shit?"

Valencia smiled. "I'm sorry, girl," she said, trying to smooth things out. "I don't know what's wrong with me. If I didn't know you had a major buildup of coochie cobwebs, I would say you were a tremendous ho. Let's go eat, retard."

Chapter 6

The Reaper

"Okay, so run this shit down to me again, like I'm a slow third-grader." Kidd was not getting what happened, or, at least, it wasn't registering. He was talking to his crew, which consisted of Moochie and Li'l Tony, minus Skillet. Everyone was waiting on Li'l Tony to finish with the details so the plan could go into motion.

"Peep, he was over this skeeze's house he met. I guess he finished what was he was doing. When he opened the door, four dudes were standing there with pistols pointed at him. They robbed him. My source says he didn't put up a fight, and they had their faces covered, so they had no reason to shoot him. But my sixth sense is telling me that we need to go yoke this scandalous bitch up. I can feel the tingle of a setup."

Li'l Tony was their information guy. He knew everything and everybody. He knew shit before it hit Vine, Fox 2, NBC, and Channel 4. He kept his ear to streets at all times. Kidd paid him good money for the info he found out. Most of their jobs went smoothly because Li'l Tony was so precise, and, with Kidd and Moochie doing the dirty work, things usually went off without any kinks.

"You get the address?" Kidd questioned ready to get started.

"What's my name?" Li'l Tony boasted.

"I ain't ask yo' fucking name. I asked if you got the fucking address."

Everybody just sat looking, knowing how Kidd got when he was in kill mode, and everyone remained silent after that. He was calm and quiet, yet they could see that the caged beast within him was looking out at its prey as if he was remembering each of their faces, making sure to get every last one of them when he got loose.

"Yeah, man." He handed Kidd the paper, knowing he stuck his foot in his mouth. Kidd knew he had hurt the little pup's feelings and he'd apologize later. There was no room for remorse at that moment.

They loaded up in the hooptie, a broken-down 1994 Honda civic. There was no speaking because there was no need for words . . . only action. They were concentrating, and their minds were in the same place. They weren't going to fuck this up. They were going to find this bitch to get to the bottom of everything, and, if need be, dead the broad.

Kidd knew that once they got there, he was going to have to take total control of Moochie because the boy was a beast and very uncontrollable once he had his mind set on hurting somebody. Once he lost it, there was no turning back. Moochie was Kidd's right hand and usually made sure that Kidd didn't have to get his hands dirty. If there was a problem, Moochie never hesitated to make it go away, and he didn't discriminate when it came to his brother. Kidd hated the fact that it was a woman they were going to see, but shit stunk, and, as far as they were concerned, she was the reason for the foul stench in the air.

"This is her address right here," Li'l Tony said.

They pulled into a parking lot that had one way in and one way out. Everyone quickly searched for getaway routes, in case there was a need for a quick escape.

***

Shay-D was sitting in her living room thinking about how her life had made such a drastic change. She couldn't help but let a lone tear fall. She had moved to a new city to get away from her horrid past. After shaking that thought, she began to think about Kaylin. What was she going to do now? She prayed all day that he would make it. With him being her new lifeline, he had promised to help her physically and emotionally. He knew all about her. She had told him everything about herself one night after she awoke from a nightmare. A year ago, she would have never thought she could have fallen in love in such a short time or, better yet, even been able to give another man her heart. She knew she loved him the first time she saw him.

Knock! Knock! Knock!

"Who is it?"

"Aye. Somebody hit your car," she heard someone yell through the door.

"You have got to be fucking kidding. It's one thing after another." She swung the door open and stared down the barrels of about six different guns. Instantly, she had to shit after seeing Moochie with a menacing scowl on his face and a big sawed-off double barrel pointed right at her right eye. If she hadn't been raised in a brutal environment where guns were pulled and used as weapons on the regular, she probably would have lost all bowel control. "What's going on? I don't have any money."

"Look at this bitch. A pretty face will do it every time. Man's biggest downfall will always be pussy." The girl before them could put a few industry chicks to shame, but that alone wasn't helping her in any way, shape, or form. "Bitch, just back up, and you might make it through this," Moochie said while pushing her in the head with the gun.

"Wha . . . What is this all about?" Her ass seemed to be getting heavier and heavier, like she was going to lose complete control of her bowels.

"Fuck is you acting all scared for now? You wasn't scared when yo' scandalous ass was setting my boy up, now, was you?" Moochie could feel himself literally slobbering all over himself and spitting all in her face. As he pressed the gun to her head, he wanted to drive it through her skull like an electric screwdriver. His hand was itching, and his trigger finger was twitching to let loose.

"What boy? Who I set up? I ain't set nobody up. I don't even know nobody in St. Louis. I know one person. I've only been here about five months." She wasn't lying. She had come down from Detroit, looking for a fresh start. She had met Skillet on her third day in St. Louis. "Shit! I could have stayed in the D for this shit."

"So some niggas just *happened* to know where you live and when to get at my boy? So all this shit is a big-ass coincidence? Man, fuck this shit. Bitch, tell me who the niggas is before I blow your fucking noodles out." Moochie was now trying to choke the life out of her as he raised her body off the floor with one hand, without any resistance. His adrenaline was high, and he was ready to rip her fucking head off with his bare hands.

"Let her go, man. Dead people don't talk clearly," Kidd said as he placed a calming hand on Moochie's shoulder.

After seeing Kidd's point, he let go of her. Kidd hated that his boy got shot, but he also hated to see women get beat on. He knew that was going to happen, but he still had control over Moochie. Moochie backed up, still snarling at her menacingly.

"Talk, bitch," Moochie spat.

"Are you all here about Kaylin?" she asked, looking at all of them.

"Yeah," Kidd said while everyone was looking at each other.

"Listen. I met Kaylin like my third day here, at Sweetie Pies."

Everyone was still stuck on the fact that she was calling him by his real name. One, he hated his name. He thought it was a girl's name, and, two, governments were not given out 'cause they were into too much shit. This meant he really liked her, which was not making the situation any better for her.

"He's one of the nicest guys I've ever met in my life. Why would I set him up? I'd just told him I was pregnant, and he said that he would take care of us, that we would be all right and I had nothing to worry about." She started crying all over again, unable to hold back the tears that were choking her.

This hit them all like a thousand-pound boulder. Now, they were stuck. But she could still be lying, and Moochie didn't seem to want to let up just yet. Bitches were liars and very conniving by nature in his opinion.

"Okay, so what happened yesterday?" He folded his arms over his chest as he waited for her account of what happened.

She looked at all of them. She wasn't in the mood to go over what happened again, but by the looks on everyone's face, it was either speak or die. And she wasn't ready to go to the Upper Room just yet. She sighed heavily before speaking. "We talked about the baby and had our own little celebration. He said he was going to meet some guy named Moochie, his best friend, and that he couldn't wait to tell him he was going to be a godfather."

Tears instantly stung Moochie's eyes. The thought of losing his best friend made him want to vomit.

Shay-D kept going. "He said we were all going to celebrate and that we would be having the first baby out of everyone. He knew you all would be happy to be uncles. Well, I assume you all are the crew, with y'all comin' in here, pointing guns and shit. Anyway, he said that you would dig me as much as he did. Look. I would never do anything to hurt him. Do you know how hard it is to find a good man in this day and age?"

She looked all of them square the eyes. Even though she was only twenty-two, she knew a good man when she saw one. "Anyway, when he left, I heard something vibrate, and it was one of his many phones. I went to catch him before he left, but, when I got to the door, I heard a commotion and swung the door open. Then, this guy pointed a gun at my head, but Kaylin jumped in front of me and told me to go back in the house. I didn't want to, but then I ran and got the gun he gave me and called the police. By the time I got back, he was shot, and they wouldn't let me go with him because we aren't married, and I'm not a relative. And now he's on blackout, and I can't find out anything!" Shay-D, no longer able to control her breathing, started looking like she was hyperventilating.

"Did he say anything?"

"Yeah. Who is Moochie?" He looked up.

"Me."

"I figured as much. He said for you to be a good godfather to his seed."

Kidd sat behind an extralarge red oak desk in his office, staring at the contents of the package that was delivered to his P.O. Box earlier that day. In it was the info about what he would require for his next job. It was a picture of a man and the things he had done for the past three weeks. Some were of him leaving his home in the morning, kissing his wife good-bye. Others were of him playing in the yard with his young son and daughter. But most were of him having in-depth conversations with detectives. He had been receiving these kinds of packages for about five years. It used to get to him to know he was about to take another life, but now his heart had grown cold to the screams and pleas of his victims. It had pained his heart once upon a time to know he was taking someone's father, brother, or son away from them, but that was what his cards had dealt him in this game called life. He was a killer, a good killer at that, and had come to grips with that a long time ago. When his mother died, his heart went with her, and he replaced it with a piece of steel. At one point in his life, he had high aspirations of becoming an attorney, but, when his mother got sick, he took care of the home and Moochie. His plans to go away to college got swept away.

Kidd's mind switched gears, and thoughts of Valencia flooded his mental vision. He wanted her, and it was hard not calling or going to visit her because, indeed, he wanted to do everything in his power to get her be his rib. The possibility of what could be kept him hopeful, though.

His phone ringing snapped him out of his optimistic thoughts of Valencia. He looked at the black oak grandfather clock that sat in the corner. It read 12:45 a.m. Sleep didn't come naturally to him. The souls he had taken wouldn't allow his mind to rest in peace.

"What up with it?"

"It's ready," the caller said.

About thirty minutes later, Kidd sat in an abandoned building he owned, looking at four guys quaking in their seats. An feeling ominous was in the air, and death loomed in the atmosphere. It was damp and musky in the dark room. But the moonlight shined in just enough for everyone in attendance to see each other clearly. Kidd sat slumped in a metal chair with his head held slightly down with his hood pulled down over his head. They couldn't see him, but he could see them clearly. Moochie, who was never too far from him, stood adjacent to him in the corner awaiting instructions.

The special "guests" for the night had their mouths Gorilla glued shut, and their arms and legs were bound by thin razor wire. They had been badly beaten. He figured Moochie couldn't wait to give them some sort of punishment for their blatant violation. No words had been spoken in about ten minutes. He just sat there, watching them watch him. He observed as their facial expressions flip-flopped from fear to anger over and over again. Looking at them made his blood boil, and his rage had gone to a whole new level. He sat a little longer because he had to get his emotions in check. These dudes had violated in a major way, and he wanted to know why. If he acted now, he would have just put a hole the size of a grapefruit in their heads and would have never found out why they had targeted his peoples. No, he wouldn't be that easy on them.

He wanted them to feel his pain and wrath. No one fucked with his family, and Skillet was like a brother to him, so he would make them pay in blood. Skillet had survived the attack, but what if he hadn't? That thought alone made him jump into action, causing everyone else to become startled.

"I'm not gon' ask too many questions because I really don't give a fuck why you did it. All that matters really is that it was done." He looked into the eyes of the guys in front of him to see who was the most scared. He singled out the li'l bumpy-faced dude. His face looked horrible.

He pointed at him. "Rip Pizza face's lips apart," he told Moochie.

As Moochie went to do as he was told, he was thankful he had on gloves. He probably would have thrown up if he had to touch those puss-filled craters on the dude's face with his bare hands.

Kidd could see the hesitancy in Moochie and started laughing.

"You think this shit funny?" Moochie scrunched up his face. "This nigga got herpes to the tenth power on his face," he gritted, making Kidd laugh even harder. Even though there was laughter in the room, a dark feeling still loomed over them. "Nigga, you should have just killed yourself. How in the fuck you walking around looking like Freddy Krueger with acne?"

He pulled the guy's lips apart slowly, wanting him to feel every rip. That Gorilla glue was strong stuff. That was why they used it. They could hear his screams from his closed lips. The more they were slowly ripped opened, the louder the screams got. Blood was running down his face and neck. It felt like his lips were being ripped off. Technically, they actually were. While pressing down on his face, Moochie had to bust some bumps, so the dude also had puss running down his face—which only pissed Moochie off even more.

Vomit rushed to the back of Moochie's throat, and he had to breathe deeply to keep from spewing it out. "Man, if you wasn't about to die, I would've helped you kill yo' damn self."

Kidd chuckled a little more and then stopped. The dude thought the devil himself was standing in front of him. Moochie was usually the only one who got down and dirty, but today was special. This was personal, not business, so Kidd gladly jumped in on the action.

"What made y'all pick my peoples?" Kidd questioned, but the dude tried to act hard and sit with a stone face.

Kidd nodded his head and picked up his special bat. It was made from steel and had two three-inch spikes sticking out of it. It wasn't in his hands for too long before he came down hard on the guy's knee, crushing it and causing the spikes to come out the other side of his knee.

The sound of bones crushing was like a lullaby soothing Moochie's aching heart. Unrecognizable screams resonated throughout the abandoned building. The blaring screams didn't faze Moochie or Kidd, but it definitely got the other guys' attention. They were all mumbling something, but the glue on their lips stopped any words from coming out.

"Tape 'em up." Kidd was tired of hearing his screams. He was getting on his nerves. "Nigga, it don't hurt that bad. Man up, pussy," Kidd spat.

"Wait wait wait . . ." Pizza Face tried to talk, but Moochie put the tape over his mouth. He had blood, snot, and tears running down his face.

"You didn't want to talk then, so don't go ruining the fun now. Shit! I'm just getting started." He looked around. "Him!" Kidd pointed to the dude on the end.

The young man sat like a statue, praying he would die quickly. His eyes moved from the spot that they were stuck on just in time to see the bat shatter his partner in crime's knee wide open, and he never looked away again. His heart beat at rapid speeds. He'd done a lot of dirt in his life and never thought he would go out like this. During his life of robbery and vandalism, he figure he'd get gunned down, but this shit was like something out of a horror movie.

"Okay, I'm gonna start this one a li'l different. What's your name, dude? Pull 'em apart, Mooch," Kidd instructed.

The guy didn't scream like his friend had, but you could see the pain in his eyes. He took a few seconds to compose himself before answering Kidd's question. He was in shock, and it felt like someone had fire sitting on his lips. "What's ya name, dude?" Kidd questioned again.

"Kirvy," the dude said as blood ran down his face.

"What the fuck kind of name is 'Kirvy' for a nigga?" Moochie laughed.

"Yo' momma named me that when she saw my dick," he started to laugh.

Before anyone knew what happened, Kidd had slammed the spiked bat into the guy's mouth, making his head snap back. The other three looked on in horror as broken teeth fell from his mouth and blood spilled from the back of his head where the spike had made a hole.

"Now anybody else got any more muthafuckin' momma jokes? Come on. I'm all ears."

The fire behind his eyes made him look psycho, deranged even. Momma jokes were a big no-no. He didn't even play that shit with the crew. And they were tighter than fish pussy.

"I'm done playing with you muthafuckas. Now, the next one I ask a question betta come correct. Fuck with me if you want to, and, believe it or not, he went out the easy way. And I'm pissed about it," Kidd said.

Moochie quickly ripped the lips apart of the last two guys. More screams and moans escaped into the room.

"Shut the fuck up! You niggas like to rob and shoot muthafuckas and act gangsta, so don't bitch up now!"

Kidd had slowly morphed into a whole different person. Moochie loved to watch his brother work. The first time he had watched Kidd kill someone, it was like something out of a horror movie. Only he was watching his hero break a grown man down into little bitty pieces.

"What made you niggas target my peoples?"

He really wanted to know if they were aware of whom they had robbed. Their names weren't in the streets like that anymore. They were in a whole different league.

When Kidd quit hustling and moved on to bigger and better, that meant they all stopped hustling. Even though they hadn't tried to step on anybody's toes, a few niggas had to take a dirt nap because of them, but no one knew it was them that were behind any of those deaths. So what made them pick Skillet? Kidd and Moochie both tried to not have too many people in on the action. That way, if something ever happened, they knew they could trust each other. So, Skillet would, sometimes, come as backup.

"We had been watching him for some time. He came over to ole girl's crib a lot, and it was evident that he was holding a li'l paper. It was nothing personal," one of the dudes confessed. Kidd nodded his head, but, to him, it *was* personal.

"Which one of y'all pulled the trigger?"

"He did!" both the guys said in unison. If the other guy could have talked, he would have said the same thing, the way he was nodding his head in the direction of his fallen comrade.

"Damn! I wanted to cut some limbs off and make a muthafucka suffer, but . . . oh, well!"

And, in one swift motion, he pulled his .45 out of its holster and put a bullet in the middle of all of their heads.

"Clean this shit up," he mumbled as he walked out of the basement to leave Moochie to do what he did best—make shit disappear.

Chapter 7

I Want to Be Loved

As Valencia sat, she was astonished that it was about seven o'clock in the evening. Her good-for-nothing other half still hadn't shown up yet. Feeling ecstatic about it, thoughts of Kidd instantly flooded her mind. She really wanted to hear his voice, but she didn't know what to say after the way she had treated him the last time they were in each other's presence. While dialing his number, she quickly thought of a good reason for calling at the same time. She got butterflies just thinking about his voice and envisioning his sexy lips leaving soft, sweet kisses all over her body. She pulled a pillow between her legs to ease the tension building up.

"Pizza Hut," Moochie answered the phone, throwing her off her square and fucking up her quick fantasy.

"Excuse me?" she asked as a perplexed look took over her face.

"Pizza Hut, may I take your order? Would you like to try one of our specials?" She could hear laughter in the background.

"I'm sorry. I dialed the wrong number," but before she could hang up, she heard someone in the background calling someone an asshole and saying for him to give him his phone.

"Hello?" Kidd said after snatching his phone from Moochie.

"Yes, I was trying to reach Mr. Brown, please."

A broad smile spread across his face. "This is him, and how are you doing today, Miss Valencia?"

She blushed. "I'm doing just fine. I was just calling to confirm our lunch meeting for this Monday."

"I'll be there with jingle bells on. The Macaroni Grill, right?"

"Yes, sir." She bit her bottom lip to keep from overloading on excitement.

"So, how was your day today?" He wanted to keep her on the phone as long as possible.

"Excuse me?" She was in fantasyland and had completely zoned out.

"Your day. How was it?"

"Oh, it was all right, a long Friday, and yours?" She could feel her head starting to pound away. *I have got to get this shit under control,* she thought.

"It was hard, but it just got a lot better."

She blushed again. She didn't know whether she was coming or going being around him or just talking to him. He had that effect on her.

"You ain't nothing but a big flirt. See you on Monday, Mr. Brown."

"Indeed you will. Oh! And, Vee?"

"Yes, sir."

"I'm not a big flirt. I just know what I want."

"Bye, crazy." She hated rushing him off the phone, but because she knew what was to come soon, she didn't want him to witness any of it. So she decided to lie down and watch the news.

"This is Renée Williams, reporting live from the Congress Inn on Lindbergh Boulevard. There has been yet another brutal beating. The police confirmed the victim was found in the one of the hotel rooms. Reports say that the young lady was savagely beaten and sod-

omized. She was unconscious and has not awakened as of yet. Witnesses say she was seen with another young lady who looked to be in her mid-to-late twenties."

"Damn! That's messed up! What is that? Like number twenty or some shit? Makes me glad I'm not dating because people are crazy in the world," Vee said, shaking her head.

Valencia's head was pounding even harder, so she closed her eyes to see if that would help. She drifted off, no longer able to control her need to fall asleep.

"Look at this shit. It's on every channel. Serial rapist?" Raven laughed. "What a fucking joke! I ain't no fucking serial rapist. I just got a bad habit. Besides, these bitches be loving my shit. I do 'em real good before I do me."

Raven lay on the couch watching the aftermath of her latest work. The news had the pictures of thirteen women going across the screen. The authorities believed their assaults were committed by the same predator. The timeline spanned over a three-month period.

"If they had gone back a little further in time, they would have a thousand-person manhunt out for my ass," she smirked. "Naw, I think I'm gonna stay in tonight. I need the rest." Raven lay there, thinking about her first time out on the prowl.

She was at Club Bucca watching freaky white girls swing from the stripper pole. The girls were obviously too young to be in the club, but they were high on ecstasy. For some reason, it turned Raven on to see them grinding and rubbing on each other. When she decided to join in the fun, she walked up to one of the girls.

"Can I join?" Raven looked at the snow bunny lustfully from head to toe.

"Sure. What you on?"

Raven was confused but didn't show it. She kept her game face on. "I'm on whatever you're on."

The girl walked up to her and stuck her tongue in Raven's mouth, moved it round, and flipped two X pills into her mouth, and then backed up. Now Raven got it. But before she could react, the girl turned around with a shot glass in her mouth, flipped it upside down, and let the drink flow from her mouth to Raven's. The drink made Raven's body go real warm. Then, it turned really cold. It tasted like twenty pieces of Winter Fresh at one time.

"What was that?" Raven asked, trying to get used to the weird feeling.

"Rumple Minze. It's great, isn't it?" the white girl giggled.

Raven was intrigued at the way she moved her tongue. The high hit her quickly, causing her to feel loose and horny. Every time someone touched her, she felt it in every nerve ending in her body. The girl turned around and noticed Raven had stopped moving. Raven was holding her head like she had a bad migraine. She was just staring into space like she didn't know where she was.

"Are you all right?" The girl got scared. She thought she might have given Raven too much. Then, all of sudden, Raven started moving again and rubbing all over her again . . . and it was on again. They were vibing and practically fucking on the floor.

"I love your tattoo," the girl said, running her fingers across the tattoo on Raven's lower back as she bent over "So what's your name?" the girl asked as she pushed a clearly nervous Raven on the bed.

"Raven," she said, shaking her ass.

"Thanks."

Raven turned to look at her. "You know it's true?"

"What's true?" she questioned, never taking her hands off Raven's lower back, wanting badly to put her hands underneath her skirt.

"What the sign says," she replied, licking her lips.

"Hey, Reagan! Look at this tat. This shit is hot, right?" Kennedy asked her twin sister.

"Yes, I love it. Shit! She's hot, so that makes it even better," she flirted.

"I'm going to figure out something like that for my lower back. That shit is hot."

Raven wanted to tell them that it wasn't real, but why spoil their fun? She stuck it on whenever she knew she was going out. She really did want one, but just hadn't found the right one yet, but she'd get one before she took her last breath.

"You want to get out of here?" The girl flicked her tongue in and out of her mouth, flashing her glow-in-the-dark tongue ring, letting Raven know she was ready.

"I'm Kennedy. Is this your first time?" she asked, pulling at Raven's miniskirt. Raven raised her hips so she could get it off.

"Yeah." Raven didn't know what was going on.

"Don't be nervous. I'm gonna take real good care of you tonight." She stuck her tongue into Raven's mouth while squeezing on her breasts. Gently rubbing all over Raven's body created sparks that flew everywhere. She slowly kissed down Raven's neck, stopping at her chocolate dime-sized nipples. Kennedy made her way down her stomach, down to her aching clit. It began to feel like it was about to explode from throbbing so hard and jumping every second. Enjoying the feeling of Kennedy's tongue lighting small fires on her body had

Raven reeling in ecstasy. All she could do was clinch her teeth together to stop herself from crying out.

"Oh shit! What are you doing?" Raven had never felt such a feeling. In fact, no one had ever touched her private parts. At twenty-two, Raven had never let anyone get close to her. Bad memories and anger had never allowed her to. And the first sensual kiss she had ever received was given to her that night by the white girl. When she was younger, men would try to touch her, but she got that shit out of their minds real quick with a swift swing of the razor. Her mother had taught her how to keep it hidden under her tongue at the age of seven. Raven didn't just try to cut anywhere. No, she calculated and would go for either the wrist, the throat, or the face. She wanted everybody to see what she had done as a message.

"Just lie back. Let me take care of you," Kennedy said just before she worked her tongue double time. Raven's jaws locked. Her teeth clenched together tightly. She just knew she had chipped a few teeth. Her body froze as she felt the most wonderful tingling sensation she had ever felt in her entire life all over again in a matter of minutes.

Gripping the sheets, she panted. "What's that feeling?" Kennedy knew she was talking about coming. She could tell she was having an orgasm by the way her body had stiffened up, and she was a squirter, but Kennedy gladly lapped up every single drop.

"Let me show you how to make someone shiver like that." Kennedy got up, crawled on top of Raven, and they did another dance with their tongues. Raven took her ass in her hands and rubbed it as if it was softest thing on earth. They rolled over with Raven ending up on top. "Come on," Kennedy nodded toward her hot box, letting Raven know it was time.

"You mean put my mouth on you down there?" Raven pointed to Kennedy's pussy.

Kennedy found this hilarious; at first, she didn't believe Raven when she said it was her first time. She figured she was one of those that claimed she had never done it but was really a certified pro.

"Yeah, don't worry. It tastes very good."

Raven reluctantly put her mouth on Kennedy's wetness and slowly moved her tongue around. The taste was different, but she actually enjoyed it. She remembered what Kennedy had just done to her, so she had a pretty good idea of what to do.

"Yeah. You learn quickly. I like that."

Raven was handling her business, but a pounding headache was making it hard for her to concentrate. She stopped moving and grabbed her head, trying to shake the feeling.

"What the fuck?" Raven said with a confused look on her face. Her brain was pounding out of her head like a jackhammer. It felt like it would explode, it hurt so badly. Kennedy looked up to see what was wrong.

"What happened?"

Raven just stared at her, not knowing what to do. Then, it was like she blinked her eyes and went back to work. She kissed her way back up to Kennedy's mouth.

"Wait minute." Kennedy picked up her Marc Jacobs purse, which favored a duffle bag. At the bottom of the bag was skinny, long box. She retrieved a strap-on dildo from the box and started to strap it on, but Raven stopped her.

"Let me do you." Raven knew she would not be able to take that kind of pain on her first night out. Plus, she didn't want the first person to pop her cherry to be a girl with a big dildo. She, at least, wanted to try a little dick before totally knocking it out the box.

"Are you sure? Like, isn't this your first time?" She had a perplexed look on her face.

"Yeah, but that doesn't mean anything. I know how I want to be fucked." She pushed Kennedy back on the bed and climbed on top.

"Now, I like it rough." Raven looked confused, and Kennedy caught the look. "I mean, smack my ass, pull my hair, choke me, and bite me. You know, shit like that."

If she had noticed the look in Raven's eyes, she would have never suggested any of that. Matter of fact, she would have gotten her dumb ass out of that hotel room. Even as a child, Raven had liked to cause pain. It started with the men that used to visit her mother's house. Eventually, she would do little mean things to other people. Like, when walking in a crowd, she would stab somebody with a pin really hard just for fun.

"Oh, okay." She flipped Kennedy over on her stomach, pulled her ass up in the air, and rammed all nine inches into her soaking wet pussy. Kennedy screamed out, feeling nothing but ecstasy as Raven hit the bottom. Raven kept going harder and harder. The girl's cries only made her want to go harder and deeper.

"Wait a minute! You're going too hard now."

Raven had gone to a whole other zone by now. The cries coming from Kennedy's mouth seemed to please her and sent shock waves to every nerve in her body. The feeling that was slowly taking over her body was sensational. Never, in all her years, had she imagined a feeling like this was even achievable.

"No, I ain't. This is what you wanted, ain't it?" She smacked her hard across the ass. "Yeah, you like to be beat, huh?" She yanked damn near half of Kennedy's hair clean out of her scalp. "That's some straight stupid shit! You want somebody to beat on you while you fuck, right?" Kennedy tried to get up. "Naw, uh-uh. Don't leave so soon. I'm just getting the hang of this shit."

Raven had an evil tone in her voice. She could feel this heat rising in the pit of her stomach.

"Please stop! You're hurting me!"

I'm sorry, Reagan. *Kennedy thought about her twin sister who she had ditched to come have a little fun. Now, she would probably never see her again. Reagan wouldn't make it without her. Kennedy was older by five minutes and took her big sister role very seriously. She would have never let Reagan leave the club with somebody they didn't know. Now, here she was not practicing what she had preached and she was about to pay the ultimate price, and it hurt her to her soul.*

Raven's mind was in a far-off land as Kennedy's cries fell on deaf ears. Raven looked down and saw blood spilling out of her pussy, and it excited her even more. So she rammed harder, ignoring Kennedy's pleas for help. She held her down with all her weight and smashed her face into the pillow until she stopped moving. And, all of sudden, she felt that feeling in her pussy, and she started to quake. Her body froze, and her teeth clenched together. That magnificent itchy tingling feeling came to her pussy, and it felt like she was peeing on herself . . . So many juices flowed out of her that it seemed unreal. When her high came down, she realized what she had done. When she realized that Kennedy was still not moving, she was out of that room in two minutes flat, scared shitless.

After that night, it was a long time before she went back on the prowl. She didn't know how she was supposed to feel about the situation. She knew deep down she shouldn't have enjoyed what she'd done that much, but the feelings that took over her body that night left her with an intense yearning, like a heroin addict after his first high. Emotions were for the birds, so she never let anyone get that close to her. She kept a couple of her chicks around, but she called them. They were not allowed to call her. If they did, they got a number to her answering service, and, even then, they could only leave a message with an operator. She was like a man in many ways. She always wanted to be the one who did the fucking with no emotions. All that affection and shit was out the window. Let her taste it and bend over, get that ass in the air—plain and simple.

Chapter 8

Looking for Love

Valencia couldn't breathe, move, or think. The sight of Kidd sucking her toes was literally taking her breath away. His lips felt like velvet gliding up her skin as he made his way up her leg. Shivering uncontrollably, she closed her eyes because the sight alone was making a big puddle under her ass. Waiting with anticipation as he got closer and closer to her soaking wet pussy, she began to perspire. She could feel her heart beat in her pussy. Not being able to wait any longer, she began to pull his head to her wanting clit. It felt like it was literally jumping. He sucked her clit into his mouth as his fingers spread her lips apart, sending her into an orgasmic frenzy. He blew on her clit, and she watched him as he watched it jump. Slowly, he tongue kissed his way up her body, stopping at her chocolate mountains. He pushed her nipples together, hungrily sticking them both in his mouth at the same time.

"Are you ready?" he whispered in her ear.

"Yes," she replied softly.

Finally, her time had come. The man of her dreams was in her bed about to make love to her. Slowly sliding his dick up and down her pussy, teasing her clit a little bit, she squirmed, anticipating the pleasure to come. She could feel him at the opening, preparing to slide in. Then, the phone rang . . . bringing her out of her sweet dream.

"What do you want this damn early in the morning?" Valencia didn't even bother looking at the caller ID, figuring it could only be Sena calling this damn early in the morning.

"Girl, get the hell up. It's twelve o'clock on this beautiful Saturday afternoon." Sena was up and singing with the birds. She had wanted to call Valencia earlier but thought better of it. Valencia was not a morning person at all, especially on the weekends.

"What jitterbug jumped up your ass?" Vee asked, getting up to look out the window. She could see there was a beautiful day going on outside. Little kids rode their bikes down the street, and it looked as if the sun was shining a little brighter.

"Let's get out. I know there's some dudes in the malls."

Sometimes Valencia couldn't understand Sena's way of thinking. Like really, who even goes to the mall to hit on dudes anymore? That shit went out in the nineties.

"I don't feel like the mall today, and, like really, who does that anymore? Besides seventeen-year-olds, that is?"

"Quit acting brand new. Shit! You need some dick just as bad as I do. With yo' Virgin Mary ass, somebody need to gon' ahead and pop that cherry before that muthafucka turns into a rotten prune."

Point taken.

"Give me an hour." Valencia reluctantly got up, imagining the eventful day that Sena had planned for them.

"Now, aren't you glad you got out of the bed today? It's a beautiful day, ain't it?" Sena asked Valencia while walking through the Galleria Mall, looking for bebe, the clothing store.

"Yeah, yeah, whatever. I was looking forward to being lazy and getting fatter this weekend."

"Yeah, you keep thinking like that and you'll die a virgin," she scrunched up her nose.

"And what the hell is so wrong with being a virgin?"

"One, you twenty-five and don't know what it feels like to bust a nut. Two, you ain't never bust a muthafuckin' nut, and three, you ain't never bust a nut. When you get that first orgasm, that makes you feel as if your whole body is on fire and floating above the heavens, you'll see. You will know what you've been missing all these years." Just thinking about it, Sena felt her panties getting wet.

Shopping in bebe, Valencia got this eerie feeling, not like the one she always got, but a feeling like she was being watched. Looking up from the belt rack, the only people in the store were the young girls who seemed to not be paying her any attention.

"Aye! Isn't that ole girl from Society?" Moochie had been staring at Valencia for about five minutes now, trying to figure out where he knew her from. She couldn't have been one of his fly-by-night fucks 'cause clearly, he would have wifed her in a heartbeat. Kidd damn near snapped his neck, his head went up so fast. Kidd's heart started beating so fast it felt as if it would explode at any minute.

"Where?" he quizzed, looking around, zooming in on everybody.

"In bebe, and she with a nice-looking li'l honey."

Zooming in on them, Kidd could barely hide his excitement. It wasn't Raven but his actual future wife. A broad smile spread across his face. He and Moochie started heading toward the girls.

Kidd's smile seemed to get bigger and bigger as he watched Valencia talk and laugh with Sena. Every time he saw her, he found something else about her that was beautiful. Her beauty, to him, seemed so effortless.

Examining every curve on her immaculate body and imagining how good it would feel to hold her and sex her up real good had his joint jumping in his pants. She looked especially good in her skinny leg, high-waist jeans and tank top with flat knee-high Tims boots.

"Naw, that ain't ole girl from the club. Remember when I told you I got her mixed up with somebody else? *That's* her," Kidd said, pointing to Valencia. He knew it was Valencia because she was with Sena.

"Oh shit! They're practically identical," Moochie stated in astonishment. They headed in their direction.

Sena's antennas quickly went up from the smell of cologne, expensive cologne at that, lingering in the air. A good cologne mixed with the chemistry of a fine man just did something to a woman. Turning around a bit but not seeing anyone, she went back to her shopping. Now coming into her view, electric shocks shot all up in and through her pussy. Watching Kidd and Moochie walking up to them was something straight out of a movie. It was as if they were walking in slow motion, and she could hear the ocean crashing in the background. Kidd's butterscotch skin tone looked lickable in his all-black ensemble. His V-neck T-shirt fit him perfectly, and his jeans fit so good you'd have thought he and Sean John were good friends.

Moochie was always extra. He liked bright colors, so today, his outfit consisted of a multicolor button-up with a variety of greens, blues, and yellows, a pair of Sean John jeans, and the Tims boots to match his shirt.

Valencia was too busy studying the prices of the belts and wasn't paying Sena any attention as she was clearing her throat and hitting Valencia with the back of her hand. Sena, standing with this big-ass smile on her face, was trying her best to keep Valencia from saying anything incriminating.

"Girl, this is some straight bullshit." Everybody was looking at Valencia, but she still hadn't looked up yet. "Have you looked at the price of these belts? These people crazy. This damn belt is $265. This shit better get up and walk for me, make me tingle in all the right places when I walk, and take off about six inches from my waistline for this price." When she finally turned around to see everybody laughing at her, as dark as she was, you could clearly see her face turn red.

"You don't need any inches taken off. You are perfect to me as is." Kidd smiled at her.

"You didn't tell me you had company," Valencia said, clearly embarrassed.

"I tried to, but you were busy complaining about something you're still going to buy."

"I know, right? Anyway, you call *clearing your throat* telling me meat was approaching. Shit! I thought you had another hair ball," Valencia laughed.

"Are you going to keep bitching to me or pay attention to this double dose of mmm-mmm good?" Sena said, eyeing Moochie with what he took to be an *I want to fuck the shit out of you and drink all your babies* kind of look.

He was in total awe of Sena. She was definitely wifey material in the looks department, but he needed to see where her head was at first. She was beautiful and had a shape that could stop a heartbeat.

"How are you two ladies doing today?" Kidd asked as he eyed Valencia.

"Fine. Just out doing a li'l shopping. Well, attempting to do some shopping. Shit! If I get this damn belt, its gon' knock me down about two stores," she huffed.

"Well, you haven't put it down yet," Kidd pointed to the belt.

"I know. I'm gonna get it. It's a must-have," she said, admiring the leather stomach belt that was covered in studs.

"Why don't you let me take care of that for you? We wouldn't want you to have to cut your shopping spree short over a belt." She didn't realize he would have bought the whole store if that was what she wanted.

"Thank you, but I got it."

If Sena had been eating something, she probably would have choked. Truly not believing her dear friend, she tried to get her attention as she pinched the shit out of Vee's arm.

"Ahhh, bitch! What the hell you do that for?" Vee cursed while rubbing her arm.

"Girl, what the hell is your problem? I ain't did shit to you," Sena laughed.

"She pinched you because you're acting a little foolish. You shouldn't turn down a gift. It could hurt a person's feelings," Kidd said.

"Since you insist, here." She tried to hand him the belt, but he pushed her hand away and stepped back.

"Naw, I'll walk with you. I'm a gentleman, not Benson."

"Sooooo, you'd rather look like my suga daddy. I think I like that better than Benson anyway," she said while laughing and swishing a little harder for him as she walked to the cash register.

"I see you got jokes. You know that jiggle of yours could get this whole store bought for you." Kidd couldn't help but watch her ass shake hungrily.

"I'll keep that in mind when I get to Aldo."

"I'm Sena. I guess I'll introduce myself since everybody else is being rude," she said while holding her hand out and making that last comment loudly so the others could hear it.

"Ah, my bad, girl. You know I got sidetracked," Valencia said over her shoulder.

"I bet you did. Anyway, and you are?"

"Moochie, Kidd's little brother."

"I can see he's your brother. You two look like twins."

Younger brother? Maybe. Little brother? I think not, Sena thought as she couldn't help but stare at the print in Moochie's pants.

"Come on, skank," Valencia said as she walked up and wrapped her arm around Sena's.

"Aye, you know you look just like this chick we saw at the club last weekend? I mean almost identical, except she was a little lighter. Shit is ridiculous." Moochie couldn't get over how much they looked alike.

"Well, I know it wasn't me because I don't frequent clubs." Valencia kept walking.

"I know the hell it wasn't her. Shit! Do you know how long I've been trying to get her to go out with me after daybreak?"

"Anyway. What are you two gentlemen doing here today?"

Kidd, while looking right in Valencia's eyes, said, "Looking for love."

After hearing Kidd say that, Valencia's smile could have lit up the world if it was dark outside.

"Well, me myself, I came to cop them new Js that just hit the stores this morning." Sena, unable to get over how fine these two men were, seemed stuck in one spot.

"Sena, Sena!"

"Huh?"

"Girl, what the hell is wrong you?"

"Girl, ain't shit wrong with me. All is right in the world as far as I'm concerned. Shit! It's two of them, girl. The good Lord knew he was gon' be taken." She pointed to Kidd. "So he saw fit to place another one on earth. Shit. If it wasn't for you being stuck on this one. I'd be knee-deep in dick having my first ménage à trois." Everybody laughed but knew she was dead-ass serious.

"The one with the long hair is much cuter, though, don't you think?" Valencia joked with Sena.

"Aww! My feelings are hurt," Kidd pouted and stuck out his bottom lip.

Valencia could see herself grabbing his face and sucking his lip into her mouth.

"Don't hate, big brother. I told you that shit years ago. You just didn't want to believe it." Moochie patted Kidd on the shoulder.

"Raven, Raven! Bitch, where the fuck you been? I been calling you for weeks. This how you do me?"

Everybody turned around to find this superhot chick with her hands on her hips, staring at Valencia. They gave the hot number their full attention.

"Excuse me. Are you talking to me?" Valencia asked with a confused look on her face.

"Yeah, mami! Are you trying to act funny 'cause you got this new freak of the week?" She looked Sena up and down. "This bitch isn't even a mere fraction of me. She could never do what I could do."

Moochie's love stick jumped for joy, just thinking about the two in bed together. Imagining what ole girl could do made him have to slide his Foot Locker bags in front of himself.

Valencia stood frozen stiff. So, as usual, Sena stepped in to the rescue.

"First off, who the fuck is Raven? And, if you see a bitch, slap a bitch, you lose cock, ho." Sena was always ready to fuck anybody up. She didn't discriminate, but, before Sena said anything more, Valencia stepped in front of her after finding her words again.

"I'm sorry. My name is not Raven. You've me mistaken."

The girl, who was clearly confused, was looking at Valencia and trying to formulate her next words right because clearly, this bitch was trying to play her. She just *knew* this was Raven. She knew every nook and cranny on her.

"You know what, bitch? You could have been a woman about this shit. If you ain't want to talk to me no more, you could have just said it."

"Well, you would think the no answered calls for weeks would have sufficed," Sena said, still hot under the collar and still ready to work ole girl over real good.

The guys were just watching the exchange in amazement. It was like déjà vu for Kidd.

"So, if you say you ain't Raven, let me see your back!" she insisted.

"She ain't got to show yo' triflin ass shit!" She was working Sena's last nerve by now.

"Calm down, Sena," Valencia said as she dropped her bags. Then, she turned around and raised her shirt. Everyone looked to see if anything was there.

"I'm soooo sorry. Didn't mean to disturb your day! I could have sworn . . ." The girl walked away with a look of uncertainty plastered on her face.

As she walked away, Valencia bent over and picked her bags back up.

"You see. That's the same shit my boy went through, only he thought she was you."

"I don't know who this girl is, but maybe I need to see this chick too."

Everyone was clearly disturbed by the altercation. They were just standing in the middle of the mall, looking dumbfounded.

Kidd decided to break the silence. "Would you ladies like to have lunch?"

"Sure. Where?" Sena answered for them both.

"How about the Cheesecake Factory?"

"Damn right. They got my favoritest mash potatoes."

"Favoritest? Where in the hell you come up with that word?" Moochie asked, a little taken aback by her choice of words.

"I told her, 'Don't be using those words out in public,'" exclaimed Valencia.

"I'm going to come up with my own dictionary like that nigga E-40," Sena fired back.

Throughout the entire lunch, Valencia and Kidd found themselves getting to know each other a little better. Both were giggling like little schoolkids with crushes.

Now Sena was making it known that she wanted Moochie. He didn't mind because she was his type of woman—fine—and freaky to the core. During their conversation, she mentioned something that Moochie hadn't expected to hear. After throwing him for a loop with her statement, he couldn't help but look at her sideways.

"Get the fuck out of here," he said.

"I'm serious. Ask Vee."

"Whatever. Y'all gon' lie for each other."

"Just ask and see what she says. I'm dead-ass serious."

He looked at her for a minute before questioning Valencia. She's just a little too freaky not to have had sex in damn near two years. She has to be lying, he thought.

"Don't be putting me in the middle of nothing," Valencia said, putting her hand up.

"Naw, for real. When was the last time I had sex?"

"This morning, I bet, on the way to the mall," Kidd made a joke that only he and Moochie took a liking to. The girls gave them a look so fierce that their laughs stopped immediately.

"Anyway," Vee said with a roll of her neck and eyes. "You actually told him that? I'm embarrassed for you. It's been about two years," she said with a straight face.

"Get the fuck out of here!" Kidd quoted Moochie.

"My sentiments exactly." Moochie still didn't believe it.

"So, yo' first impression of us is we just some big hot cock hoes, huh?"

Sena and Valencia were looking them up and down, waiting on their answer. They were looking as if fire was going to start coming out of their ears at any moment.

"Naw, it ain't like that. It's just the way you came at a nigga makes it kind of hard to believe." Moochie wasn't quite sold. He just wanted to defuse the situation.

"Well, I hate to see what y'all think of my girl over *there*," Sena spoke without even thinking, and the look on Valencia's face told her she had just fucked up.

"Shut up, Sena! Do *not* put my business out there like that!" The last thing she wanted Kidd to know was that she is still a virgin. Not that it was a bad thing, but it was just a little weird, even for her.

"Girl, you should be proud of yourself."

"What she got to be proud of? She a virgin or something?"

Now, it was the guys' turn to wait for answers. They did not have to wait long because the looks on their faces said it all.

"Man, get the fuck out of here!" they both yelled.

Valencia could not have been more embarrassed than if she had just farted at the table. She wanted to run away and crawl under a rock, but she sat there stunned.

"They still make those?" Moochie couldn't help it.

Beyond pissed at Sena for that shit, Valencia couldn't even look up. She couldn't wait to tell her about it as soon as they were out of earshot from the guys.

"There's nothing wrong with being a virgin. Look at it like it's a good thing. That means your future husband will be a lucky a man," Kidd said, trying to make her feel a little better. That was the only thing he could come up with. Shit! He, himself, was a little shocked too.

Valencia fought within herself not to get too upset. Lord knows she didn't want that kind of lasting impression on their minds.

"Man, fuck that bullshit, so you've never busted a nut? I mean, a toe-curling, eyes-rolling-to-the-back-of-your-head nut? Damn, baby girl! I don't mean no disrespect, but what the fuck you been doing with yourself?" Moochie couldn't hide his stupidity even if he tried.

"You know you *are* a certified jerk." Sena got a little closer to his ear. "We gon' have to discuss those toe-curling orgams you talking about." Sena was clearly trying to defend her friend, but she got sidetracked somewhere in the conversation between "man, fuck that bullshit," and "toe-curling, eyes-rolling-to-the-back-of-your-head nut." Hell. She hadn't had a nut like that in all of her life, and she *needed* one. No doubt, he would get the business.

"What you looking for?"

Valencia was looking in her purse for something. Kidd hadn't said much since the revelation. Valencia reached in her purse and handed Kidd thirty dollars to pay for her food.

Looking at her like she had a real bad odor about herself, he asked, "What's this for?"

"My food. I have to be going." She began to get up to leave.

"Look, I understand you're a little embarrassed, but don't insult me like that. That's your prerogative on what you do with your body. I ain't trying to do nothing but be your friend."

"I have enough friends and don't need no more. Shit! The one I got can't seem to keep her fuckin' mouth shut. Petty, messy-ass li'l wanch." Instantly the cool breeze atmosphere had shifted into a burning inferno. If looks could kill, Sena would've dropped dead right there in that restaurant. "Are you coming? Better yet, y'all give her a ride home. I don't feel like this right now." Valencia could hardly get away quick enough. She didn't want to leave that way, but she knew that once she was upset and she started feeling that pounding in her head, it was a wrap, and there was nothing she could do to control her next actions.

"I'm sorry you had to see that side of her. Sometimes, I feel like I'm talking to a whole different person when we are talking." Sena got up to catch up with Valencia, knowing she wouldn't leave her. "Don't count this against her. This was a little touchy subject that I shouldn't have brought up. She is really crazy about you," she said as she ran after Valencia and prepared for the tongue-lashing she was about to get.

"It's good, ma. Just tell her to get at me when she's ready to talk."

"And you don't forget to call me. I'll be waiting," she winked at Moochie.

"I got you on speed dial. Don't even trip," Moochie said, holding his phone up in the air.

"Bitch, you know you got the biggest fucking mouth I have ever seen." Valencia didn't even wait for her to get in the seat good.

"I'm sorry! I didn't know the conversation was gon' take that kind of turn. Shit! We were talking about me and ended up talking 'bout you. The look on your face told the truth even if I ain't say much more, so don't be jumping down my throat. You my nigga if you don't get no bigger, but that disrespectful shit ain't for us." Sena loved Valencia to death, but being disrespected didn't sit right with her.

"I'm sorry, girl. You know I'm just totally embarrassed." Valencia put her head down on the steering wheel.

"It's all good. Shit! You know I got love for you to walk away from two of my favoritest things in the world."

"And what the hell is that?" Valencia asked, already knowing half of the answer.

"Dick and the Cheesecake Factory!"

"Girl, get the hell out of my car. I'll see you at work Monday."

Chapter 9

Am I Dreaming?

"Yeah, bitch. Just like that. Yeah. Suck it. Fuck is you doing? Stop playing with my fucking nut! I got something for people who play with me."

"I'm trying." The girl looked really scared. The sweet woman she had met at the store had flipped all the way out.

"Don't *try*, bitch. *Do it!*" She dug her nails into the top of the girl's head, smashing her face farther into her pussy. "You like it rough, don't you?" She yanked the girl by her hair and backhanded her across the face. The girl flew off the bed. When Raven got like this, she had superhuman strength. "You want a bitch that's gon' beat that ass?"

She literally jumped out of bed and on top of the girl in one stride. Her fist came down like a bolt of lightning across the girl's face over and over again until there was blood everywhere.

"What the fuck kinda shit was that?" Valencia said, waking up from yet another dream that she considered a nightmare. She lay in the bed staring at the ceiling as she tried to calm her nerves. Dripping from head to toe in sweat, she got up from the bed and headed to the bathroom. She pulled at the hairs that were sticking to her face as she stared at herself in the mirror. She had been having dreams about having sex with women, but she always ended up beating them really bad in the end.

Get control of yourself, Vee.

On shaky legs, she walked back to her bedroom and took the soaking wet red satin Ralph Lauren sheets off the bed and placed them in the hamper. Bits and pieces of the dream kept flashing through her head.

"Where is this shit coming from?" she asked herself.

She desperately tried to remember any portion of the dream that would answer her questions, but she came up with nothing sufficient.

She walked back to the bathroom and started a bath. She dropped some lavender bath beads into the warm water to sooth her senses. Because she always slept naked, she didn't have to undress, so, while waiting for the tub to fill up, thoughts of Kidd flooded her mind.

What could he be doing at this time? She was scared to call him after what had transpired yesterday. She really was sorry for the way she had left things. She looked at the clock. It read two-thirty in the morning. *Is he at home? Is he with a woman? He said he didn't have a woman, but that would be too good to be true.* She had studied his every move at lunch earlier and didn't see one flaw. His swagger was on point. He was sweet as could be. He looked "mmm-mmm good" like Campbell's soup, and he had two major attributes—no kids and he was rich. What were the chances of finding all that in one man? It was usually broken down and spread out sporadically, something good here and something worse there. Rich but looked like a fucking wildebeest. Fine but has four and a half kids. Sexy but straight lame. The kind of nigga that pulled his money out to get your attention 'cause he knew he wouldn't get it any other way.

"There has to be something. Shit! He's gotta have six toes or something. Some kind of turnoff." Valencia picked up the phone to call him again for the fiftieth time.

"Bitch, just call him. Either he can talk or he can't," she said to herself as she picked up the phone, took two deep breaths, and looked at the clock again. It read 2:33 a.m. Finally, she sat in the tub, waiting for him to answer. He didn't. That crushed her feelings.

"Figures. He must be somewhere laid up with his woman."

The phone began ringing before she could put it down. "Hello?"

"Yeah. Somebody just call Kidd?"

"I'm sorry. I must have dialed the wrong number. I was trying to reach Wanya."

"Vee?" Kidd asked, knowing it could only be her since he never told any women his real name.

"Yes, this is she," she smiled.

"What's good, ma? This me." He was glad she had called. He had been thinking about her a lot. He too hated the way things ended yesterday.

"Oh, were you busy?"

"Nah, my retarded-ass brother wouldn't give me the phone. Anyway, what's up? Why you up so late?" He could hear water splashing.

"Just woke up. Couldn't sleep. Thought about you and called."

He had this big stupid-ass smile on his face.

"I hear that. Good shit. If I could call you every time I thought about you, you would think I was a stalker or something. What are you doing? Washing dishes?"

"No, I'm in the tub."

"Now, I really feel special."

"Why is that?"

"'Cause first you called me when you couldn't sleep. Second, you called me when you are in the tub, and, third, you called me by my real name."

"What's up, sis?" she heard Moochie yell in the background.

"Tell Moochie I said hello, and how does he know I'm gon' be his sister?"

He could feel her smile through the phone.

"'Cause he says we're going to be married one day."

"And what do you say?" Her cheeks were on fire from sitting in their "big smile" position for so long.

"I say you never go against the grain, so I guess I have to agree with him."

"Umm-hmmm, I see." She was enjoying this conversation. His voice was sending vibrations through her body.

"What do you say?"

"I say nothing is written in stone. Destiny will lead the way, my young grasshopper."

"Okay. I see you got jokes." They shared a laugh.

"I called for a reason."

"And what's that?"

She paused for a moment because she knew her next move would be taking a chance, but her need for him to be by her side, if only for a little while, outweighed any repercussions. Moving fast and having so many emotions going on in her head had her feeling like she was on an emotional roller coaster. Being afraid, curious, nervous, sad, mad, just an emotional wreck, she threw caution to the wind.

"Umm . . . Do you mind coming over to keep me company for a little while? I had no one else to call so . . ."

He cut her off. "Not a problem. You want me to come now?"

Any chance he got to spend some time with her, he would jump on it. No matter the time or place, he would be there in a heartbeat. He wanted her to be his, and she would be very soon if it was left up to him.

"Yeah, could you?"

"Give me the directions."

When she was done giving him the directions, he was excited to get to be with her alone. Without any distractions, just her and him getting to know each other. She made him feel like a teenage boy with a crush.

"All right. Give me about twenty minutes. Stay right where you are."

"Boy, shut up. I'd be a prune by the time you got here. I'll leave the door unlocked for you."

"A'ight."

"What you looking at?" Moochie asked as he walked up behind him.

"Oh nothing, just thinking. She asked me to come over."

"Are you gonna go?"

"Yeah, I'ma go." Kidd felt his phone vibrate, and when he looked at the screen, it was picture of Valencia's legs covered in bubbles. He licked his lips. "Check these out." Kidd turned his phone toward Moochie.

"What the hell we looking at? Nice."

"That's enough, nigga. Stop drooling over my woman."

"Now, she's your woman? Whatever. You gon' fuck around and catch blue balls fucking with her. She ain't giving up the skins, and yo' nympho ass ain't gon' make it to the wedding date," Moochie said with a smirk.

"Have a little more faith in ya big brother. I ain't pressed for sex."

"Not yet. You always had an option. Once you get with her, you ain't gon' have no option but to wait till she ready."

"Why you say that? I got hoes throwing the pussy at me."

"True, but you ain't trying to catch it. You dropping and dodging that shit like it's the plague, and, once you get with her, you really gon' be in a game of dodgeball."

"Man, I ain't caught up like that. I mean, I dig her, but I ain't in love or nothing." Kidd was trying to convince himself more than Moochie. He knew she had stolen his heart the moment he laid eyes on her. Her smile was like his kryptonite.

"I know that, but I know you, and, once you see what I see, it's a wrap," Moochie said, remembering the promise they'd made to their mother.

"When was last time you called up a honey and did the do?" Moochie was waiting on the response because he knew the answer. Because the last time Kidd got some, it just so happened he had gotten some too. It was practically the last time they were separated. Lately, Kidd had been cock-blocking like a mutha. It was like he could feel when Moochie was about to get into something. He would call with something to do, when it was really nothing to do. But Moochie wasn't complaining because he loved his brother to death. It had always been him and Kidd against the world. Kidd practically raised him.

"Man, get the fuck out of here." Kidd was really trying to remember the last time he'd had sex. It wasn't as bad as Moochie made it seem . . . was it?

"You want me to tell you when it was?"

"Yeah, go right ahead."

"It was with that chick, Tiffany, the dark girl with the big titties," Moochie said with a knowing look.

"So what is really the point of this little intervention?"

"No shit, just opening your eyes to the situation. You dig ole girl. I can see it in your eyes. She would be good for you. She's a virgin, and that's a big deal, my dude. Either you gon' be her first and break her heart because you can't let go of your first love, or you gon' break it 'cause you couldn't wait to be her first." Kidd had to give it to his little brother because he had a valid point. Could he do it? She would be the last person he would want to hurt.

"Wait a minute. Who is my first love?"

"The call of the streets."

***

Kidd was sitting outside of Valencia's house really thinking. Should he take that step? He was halfway out of the streets for good, so that wouldn't be a problem. He wasn't worried about being faithful, so that wasn't a problem either. He had promised his mother that, if he ever found the right girl, he would love, cherish, and be faithful to her. She made both him and Moochie make that promise.

She didn't want her sons to exhibit the same behavior that their father had toward her. Loving a man that was unable to love her in return had done so much emotional and physical damage to her. So much so that she'd had three miscarriages, her hair had fallen out, and she had lost so much weight that she began to look skeletal. She made herself sick trying to do everything for him, but, in return, he left her with two young boys to raise on her own and cancer growing in her brain.

It crushed them to see their mother like that. Moochie ran from love. He didn't want to break the promise he'd made to his mother on her dying bed. While Kidd tried his best to embrace it, he wanted to prove to his mother that he could love a woman how she should have been loved.

"I can do it. I'm good. She gon' love me and give up the goods without a fight."

He got to the door and paused before knocking. He remembered she said she would leave the door open. He walked in, taking in the décor. The first thing he saw was a sign that said: PLEASE LEAVE SHOES AT THE DOOR with a stiletto in a circle and a red line going through it. After doing as the sign said, and, after further inspection of her humble abode, he couldn't help but notice that she had it decked out.

In the living room, there was a sofa made in the shape of a horseshoe that stretched across the whole room.

There was a big-ass marble colorful butterfly table in the middle. A baby grand piano sat in that corner, and there was a wall-size fish tank with what looked like a thousand piranhas in it. But what really got him going when he went deeper into the living room was that there was a sixty-four-inch flat screen with a Wii and a PlayStation 4 hooked up to it.

Then, there it sat in all its glory. A *Madden 2017* game. He knew right then—he was in love. He had to find out if it was hers or her little brother's. It had to have been someone else's. He had never met a woman that could understand the game.

He walked down the hall, opened a few doors, and walked up a small stairwell that ended at a door that he assumed to be her bedroom. The sign on the door said *"heaven this way"* with an arrow pointed up. *She really loves her signs, don't she?* he thought. But she wasn't done yet. There was another sign below that that read "No outside clothing on the premises" with a dress in a circle and red line going through it. *So am I supposed to get naked or something?* he wondered as he knocked on the door.

"It's open."

Pushing the door open, he asked, "This sign says no clothes, so what am I supposed to do?" He didn't know if he would be able to lie or sit next to her with no clothes on.

"Well, if you read the signs correctly, you should already have your shoes off. Now just take off your jeans and shirt."

Exhaling deeply again, he did as he was told. "A'ight. You love your signs, don't you?"

"People tend to do better with signs," she said while watching him remove his shirt and examining every curve and cut of muscle that was bursting out of his wife beater. He was a masterpiece that even Leonardo da Vinci wouldn't have been able to capture. She loved the way he always looked sleepy. His eyes seemed to be taunting her, beckoning her to come to bed with him. She could just imagine placing kisses all over his body because he looked so good. She wanted just to bite him. All the muscles in his legs were well defined. And his boxer briefs left nothing to the imagination. He caught her staring. Singing softly, all he could hear was "Half on a bayyyyybeeee . . ."

"Like what you see?" He turned around, modeling.

"Maybe," she smiled big time.

"Come. Sit down and talk to me." She patted the spot on the bed next to her.

He started to sit down, pulling the covers back, but he suddenly jumped out of the bed with the speed of light.

"What the fuck?" he questioned, looking at her like she was crazy.

"What happened?" she asked, jumping too 'cause he had scared the shit out of her.

"You . . . You're naked," he stammered, looking at her like she had three heads.

"Yes. Because I don't wear clothes in my bed," she said incredulously.

"What the hell you mean? Put some damn clothes on." He couldn't believe her. Surely, he would lose his mind if he had to sit next to her naked body, knowing the next step would not be sex.

"I told you. I don't wear clothes to bed." She looked at him like . . . *duh*.

"Well, you're going to have to do something. Shit! I'm being a man about the virgin thing. But I'm still a man. Come on, ma. You gotta let a nigga live." The damage was already done. He was doing just fine imagining. Now, he had the actual image stuck in his head. "You gon' fuck around and give a nigga blue balls and shit." She was now laughing at him hysterically, and he didn't find shit funny.

"I'm sorry," she said while still laughing. "I didn't know it was gon' be such a big deal," she said, looking down at the huge bulge building in his boxers. Having absolutely no experience with men, she honestly didn't know it would have that type of effect on him.

"Yeah, keep playing. You gon' get something way sooner than you had planned on." He was serious as a fucking heart attack.

"So, you're telling me you can't control yourself being around a naked woman?" she said, standing up to walk over to her dresser.

He closed his eyes. She was playing a little too much for him. He was not with the teasing. That shit was for the birds.

"Nah, I'm good on being around a naked lady. It's just, once she naked, there's usually something that follows or something that happened before it." He opened his eyes to see her in some boy shorts and a tank top. Her ass was hanging from the bottom, looking so good he wanted to kiss and bite it.

"That's a li'l better. You ain't got no sweatpants or nothing?" He sounded like a little boy whining.

"You're pushing it, buddy," she said as she got back in bed, mad as hell. *He ain't been around two minutes, and he already changing shit,* she thought.

"Can I ask you a question?"

"You just did," she said with a faux attitude.

"Naw, I'm for real. Why are you still a virgin? I mean, like are you waiting for Mr. Right or a wedding date?" He needed to know this, because he figured, nowadays when a woman doesn't have a man, she's usually a little crazy in the head. He wasn't trying to get caught up in a fatal attraction. Yeah, he dug her a lot, but he dug his life way more. He wasn't into putting his hands on a woman, but, if it came down to him or her, she would be dead wherever she stood.

"No, it just never happened. I've never had the chance, never really thought about it until lately," she said, looking out the window.

The stars were shining brightly. One caught her attention. It outshined all the rest, just like the man sitting next to her. She didn't know what she was doing; she just never wanted to be away from him. Valencia never knew it was possible to fall so hard for someone in such a short amount of time. But here she was, wishing for a shooting star to send true love and happiness her way.

"What you mean you 'never had the chance'? You are one of the most, if not *the* most, beautiful women I've ever met. I know niggas be trying to get at you on a regular. Plus, you told me you had a man."

"That stuff does nothing for me most of the time. They're just lusting over my body, and me saying I have a man just comes natural when I'm nervous." Being new to this, she didn't know what she was feeling, but she knew she was feeling something, and he was the sole cause of it.

"What are you nervous about?"

"This." She did a sweeping motion with her hands. "The last man to touch this bed is the one who set it up from the department store." She chuckled a little, never breaking her concentration on the shining star.

"Ain't no need to be nervous. I'm not going to rush you to do anything," he assured her.

"But what if I am in a rush?" The tears that just rushed the back of her throat were trying to choke her and make their way to the forefront.

"What's the rush for? You've waited your whole life for that special moment; don't throw it away just because.

If and when you give me your virginity, I would love to think I deserve it, and that it's not merely happening for convenience." He knew the value of a woman's virginity. His mother schooled him on everything a woman goes through and what goes on in her mind. He just didn't realize it was never her choice to still be a virgin.

"She's going to come back." She finally let a tear fall down her face.

"Who?" Kidd questioned as he looked around.

"Never mind. I really just want to be held. Can you do that for me?" She had such an innocence about herself. She was almost childlike. For the life of him, he couldn't figure out why he was so drawn to her.

Noticing that she was on the verge of a breakdown, he didn't push the subject, but he hoped that whoever she was talking about wouldn't come back anytime soon. He was making his way into her life and wanted nothing to stop him.

They lay there in bed together, but their minds wandered off in different directions. Lying as one, he held her tight. This feeling was too right to be wrong. This was the way her life was supposed to be. She was supposed to be in love with the man of her dreams with no threat of it being taken away in the blink of an eye.

In this short amount of time, Valencia had come to the conclusion that her life wouldn't be worth living if she didn't have Kidd in it. He put these feeling in her heart that she couldn't explain to save her life. All she knew was that to take him away now would be like taking her breath away.

Chapter 10

Love under New Management

Valencia rolled over and stared into Kidd's beautiful brown eyes. She wondered how long he'd been awake and staring into the dark. He held her tight in his comforting embrace. Apparently, Kidd couldn't sleep either. Neither one of them made a sound. The silence spoke volumes like a loud siren breaking the silence of the night. The way he looked at her made her feel as if her soul stood in front of him bare down to its core. If she could read his mind, she would want to know what he was thinking at the very moment. That moment in time was perfect, just their energies feeling the empty spaces where words should be filling in.

"Hey, beautiful," Kidd finally broke peaceful quietness.

"Hi" she spoke bashfully as she pulled the covers up over her face, not wanting to breathe her morning breath in his face.

"Don't be trying to cover up that dragon tryin'a break free." He laughed at her trying to cover her mouth.

"Shut up, fool!" She had to laugh herself. She knew she must have looked stupid talking with the covers over her mouth.

"Are you OK?" She made him want to make everything better for her. He'd happily take all of her hurt and sadness if she'd only give him the chance.

"Yes, I'm fine, and thank you for coming to keep me company on such short notice."

"No problem at all on my end. Whenever you need me, just call." He sat up on the bed and took in a deep breath. For sure she would be a major change in his life, and the words his brother spoke kept replaying over and over in his head. Was he really ready for everything that came along with being with Valencia? Clearly, she'd made a move on his heart, and he couldn't explain it to save his life. All he knew was he needed her like his heart needed its beat. "I'll let you get ready for work. I have to get going. It's going to take me three hours to get Moochie's ass out of bed." He laughed a little.

"Oh, OK." She tried to hide the disappointment in her voice. She wished they could have stayed in the bed all day together and blocked the world out. "Would you like some breakfast?" She would offer him the world to keep him close by.

Knock! Knock! Knock!

Instinctively, Kidd reached for his gun on the floor tucked under his pants.

"You expecting someone?"

"No, I'm not." Valencia was confused too. No one ever came to her house.

"You sure you don't have a crazy boyfriend that I'm gon' have to shoot?" Kidd asked as he got dressed.

"Really, sir, no, I don't have boyfriend. As a matter of fact, answer the door while I use the bathroom. Thank you." She got up and walked to the bathroom. He watched her ass as it jiggled with the intensity of a bowl of Jell-O. Once dressed, he head to the door.

"Who is it?" Kidd yelled through the door.

"It's me, nigga, open the door!" Moochie yelled back.

"Man, what the fuck you doing here?" Kidd asked as he swung the door open.

"You ain't bring yo' bald head home this morning, and I don't know this chick." Moochie made a mean mug at him, then walked past him into the house.

"My bad. Didn't know I needed to check in with my little brother," Kidd laughed.

"Don't get funny now, nigga!" Moochie looked around. "Aye, yo, this shit is nice. She got good taste. Can't speak for her choice in men, but her décor is sick!" Moochie was really impressed by the colorful marble table that sat in the middle of the living room.

"Thank you. Glad my taste in décor meets your approval." Valencia smiled as she walked in. Her smile immediately faded when she saw Moochie standing on her carpet with his shoes on.

"Oh, hey. Good morning."

"Can you please step back over to the door and take your shoes off!" she said with urgency.

"Is she serious, bruh?" Moochie looked over to Kidd and noticed he didn't have on any shoes either.

"Very."

"Hell, yeah, I'm serious! Now getcha footsie off my white carpet!"

"OK. Damn, calm down." Moochie walked back over to the door and took his shoes off. "This is some bullshit. I ain't never in my life heard of no shit like this."

"Yeah yeah yeah, li'l nigga whatever." She waved her hand at him and walked into the kitchen.

"Ha!" Kidd hollered out laughing.

"Oh, and good morning, Moochie," she yelled from the kitchen as she looked in the refrigerator to see what she had to cook. "Look at that. Here you are blaming *me* for the unexpected visit, and it's for you, sir." She added leggings to her attire so she could get some breakfast going. "To what do we owe this pop-up visit? You thought I killed him?" she asked as he walked back into the living room.

"Hey, I don't know you that well yet, and when a nigga start spending the night, I have to check things out."

"Well, are you staying for breakfast?" She hoped he said yeah, because she knew Kidd would have to stay a little longer.

"Wait, whose is this?" Moochie stared at the PS4 on the entertainment system.

"Well, it is my home." She looked at him like *duh*.

"This ain't your nephew's or little cousin's?"

"No, it's mine, and, yes, I know how to play it and all the games down there."

"Yeah, get them pancakes rolling, then, sis, we posted for a li'l bit."

"How you know she ain't got nothing to do?" Kidd asked, but he honestly wanted to stay.

"Oh, um, I'm good," Valencia answered with quickness. She'd already been plotting on how to get him to stay a little longer.

Moochie had already turned the game on and had his feet planted firmly in the carpet.

"Well, that settles it, then. I needs lots of meat, please, and thank you!" Moochie yelled over his shoulder.

Valencia busied herself in the kitchen with making breakfast. She could hear Moochie and Kidd in the living room yelling and laughing about the game. Apparently, Moochie was winning, and Kidd wasn't the least bit happy about it.

A few minutes, she felt a pair of hands sliding around her waist, and then a strong pair of arms squeezing her around the waist. She could have melted right there on the spot.

"You must have lost now you in here to mess with me," she laughed.

"Something like that." He turned her around so she was facing him.

"Can I keep you?" he asked as he put his forehead to hers and looked her in the eyes.

"I don't think I'm what you really want," she said sadly. She pulled her eyes from his gaze and looked at the floor.

"Let me make that decision."

"I'm serious, Kidd."

"I'm serious too. Can I keep you?" Silence. "Can I have you?" He pulled his forehead away from hers and began kissing her all over her face.

Goose bumps formed all over her body at the feel of his lips against her skin. A sudden heat took over her lower regions, and she felt her panties getting moist.

"Kidd, I—" she started to protest his advances.

"Stop calling me that. I told you my name." He pulled her face up so that she was looking up into his eyes again.

Valencia watched as his face got closer to hers. *Oh, bitch, he about to kiss you. Please don't mess this up. Please please please, kissing gods, be on my side right now,* she silently prayed as his lips touched hers.

Kidd noticed her reluctance and her inexperience. But that was all right with him. He had no problems with teaching her how to love him the right way. Her lips were soft and full, and thoughts of her kissing all over his chest and working her way down had his phallus superhard. He reached under her and picked her up and sat her on the counter without breaking their kiss.

Valencia's head was spinning. He kissed her so hard and passionately it felt like he was trying to breathe for her. And if she could give him her breath to breathe for her, she would. She wrapped her legs around his waist and pulled him closer. She knew she was doing horribly at kissing, but he never stopped, and that encouraged her to keep trying.

"Damn, you niggas don't smell that smoke or hear the fire alarm going off?" Moochie ran into the kitchen yelling.

"Oh shit." Valencia jumped down off the counter.

"Damn, man, y'all don' burnt all the fuckin' meat and shit!" Moochie was pissed. The aroma coming from the kitchen had his stomach growling.

"My bad," Valencia laughed as she ran to open the windows and doors to let some of the smoke out.

"You damn right, yo' bad. I'm hungry as hell. Y'all in here playing kissy face; meanwhile, the house 'bout to burn down," Moochie huffed as he looked at all the burnt meat.

"You seem a li'l upset. You need a hug or something?" Valencia asked.

Kidd spit out all his juice he just put into his mouth all over the wall. He fell out laughing because he would always ask Moochie why he was so mad all the time.

"Depends on who giving out the hugs. 'Cause I definitely don't want one from either of you two."

"Yeah, OK."

"And while you finding me a good hugger, make sure she can make that ass clap appropriately!" he yelled over his shoulder as he grabbed his jacket and put his shoes back on. He was preparing to leave and didn't see the panic set in Kidd's and Valencia's faces.

Valencia was panicking because she didn't want to be left alone with Kidd. She didn't have a clue about what she would do. She wanted him to go but stay at the same time. Would he want to finish what they started in the kitchen or would he leave too?

Kidd looked over and could see the worry on her face and decided it was time for him to leave as well. He mistook her want for him to stay as a panic for him to leave. He would never force anything on her. He knew she wasn't ready for anything past second base, and he was OK with that.

"Yeah, I gotta go back home and change. Can't be walking around smelling like burnt bacon." Moochie rolled his eyes. "Then again, it might work in my favor.

Cause bitches love bacon." He chuckled a little. "I'll catch you next time, sis." He walked over to Valencia gave her a hug, gave Kidd the middle finger, then walked out the door.

Valencia loved the way him calling her sis made her feel. She felt she really had family other than Sena now.

Kidd grabbed her by the hand breaking her train of thought. "I'm gonna get out of here."

"I figured you would leave like everybody else." She pulled her hand back with an evil-like glare in her eyes.

"Huh?" Kidd was baffled by what she'd just said. He didn't understand the sudden look of disdain in her eyes. The energy in the room had shifted quickly.

"Why are you looking at me like that?" Valencia asked. She could tell something was wrong with him. She prayed she didn't do anything to make him feel some kind of way.

"Why did you say that to me?" Kidd searched her face for answers. That remark came out of nowhere when he'd just asked her if he could have and keep her. Why would she think he was going to leave her?

"What did I say?" She had no clue about what he was talking about. What she'd said seemed to really upset him.

He stared at her a little longer before he spoke again. "Nothing, man, never mind. I'll call you later to check on you." He kissed her on the lips and left her standing in the middle of the floor feeling lost.

What had she done to make him run off? What had she said to him? Valencia finally had a small piece of light in her always dark and cloudy life. And now she may have ruined it before it even started.

Chapter 11

Love Me in a Special Way

Aphrodite must have been listening to Valencia's prayers that night. Almost three months had passed, and Valencia had never, in her life, been happier. Kidd was basically a permanent fixture in her home. She and Kidd were attached at the hip. They would sit and talk for hours about anything. He made it his business to keep a smile on her face. He brought so much happiness to her life, but she didn't know how long it would last. She just didn't foresee a happy ending. Happily ever after only happened in the movies. Everything was going too perfect for it to last. She couldn't remember a point in her life where she had been happy at all. Merely existing, not living was her life.

Valencia could remember, as a child, never being happy, and periods of her life would just disappear. The first time it happened was on her eighth birthday. Apparently, she'd slept the day away and didn't even know it. All she knew was that her mother's boyfriend had come into her room the day after and told her happy belated birthday and that he wished he could have been there the day before, so he could have helped bring in her birthday "the right way." She shuddered at the thought.

"Man, you cheating like a muthafucka!" Kidd yelled, bringing Valencia back to the present. Valencia was beating him *again* in *Madden*. "I can't play with these bullshit-ass controllers. The shit is bedazzled. Who bedazzles a fuckin' PlayStation 4 controller?" He huffed as he tossed the controller on the couch.

"Hey! You break, you buy! No dolla," she put on an Asian accent. "And don't be a sore loser, babe. I told you I could play. You doubted my skillablity. Ya girl comes through every time. And don't blame the bling. My shit is legit fire." She laughed at him as she got off the couch to get them something to drink. He admired her legs as she stood up in the little shorts she had cut from some sweatpants. She had no bra on, and her breasts sat perfectly in the air. He was totally in awe of her radiance. She was like the ninth wonder of the world to him. There was no explanation for this woman. He couldn't explain the hex she'd put on his heart, but she'd stolen it the first time he'd seen her. For all the bad shit he's done in his life, he couldn't figure out, for the life of him, how God could place something so beautiful and pure into his life. He thanked God every day for her and promised that, if he could keep her, he would change his life all the way around. And he meant that he would give up everything. All he needed was her.

"Whatever. If I hadn't taught you them new moves, you would be nothing!" he yelled over his shoulder.

"Yeah, all right. Let that be the reason," she said as she eased her arms around his neck. He took the drinks out of her hands. Then she climbed over the back of the couch to land on his lap facing him. She could feel his manhood as she straddled his lap. She put her arms around his neck. He put the drinks down on the table, put his arms around her waist, and rubbed her lower back. The look in both of their eyes said I love you.

"You know what?" Kidd said as held her a little tighter.

"What's that?" She kissed him on the lips.

"Do that again."

She obliged.

"One more time and make it good."

She leaned down to his mouth and placed a long, wet, passionate kiss on his lips that had sparks flying everywhere. Since being with Kidd, she had mastered the art of kissing. Because that's all they'd done so far. She was glad that she could add something even if it was just a kiss.

"Now, was that better?" She wiped the sides of his mouth like there was something there.

"Yes, ma'am." His eyes were still closed.

"Now, what was it you were going to say?"

"I love you." He looked her right in the eyes. She stopped breathing for a full thirty seconds before she could respond. He awaited her response patiently.

"Say that again." She could feel her heart flutter as the tears began falling down her face. She never thought those words would have hit her like they did. It felt like someone had punched her in the stomach and knocked all the wind out of her lungs. The words sounded so foreign that she didn't know how to respond. Completely lost in the words he'd just spoken, her mind went blank. She just stared at him, searching the inner being of her soul to say something—anything—that would make this moment make sense to both of them. Love was something she'd sung and read about, but something that wasn't supposed to be real.

"I love you, Valencia Ball." She had never heard that sentence from anyone besides Sena. Other than that, no one had ever told her that they loved her—not even her mother. She was completely stunned, and she didn't think he understood the magnitude of the words he'd just spoken to her. So many questions ran swiftly in her head. Did he really mean it? How was she supposed to be feeling? Was she feeling love at that very moment? What is she supposed to do next?

Finally finding her voice, she spoke softly. "No one has ever told me that before." She took a deep breath. "I'm sorry I can't say it back because I don't know what love feels like." She pulled her eyes away from his gaze, too embarrassed to look him in the eyes any longer. She didn't want to lie to him. She wanted the first time she said *I love you* to be real.

"I didn't say it for you to say it back. I said it 'cause that's the way I feel. You'll know it when it hits you. And I'll be right here waiting patiently for you say it on your own." He wiped the tears from her face and kissed the tears that replaced the ones he wiped away. He wondered what kind of life she had led to never have felt love before. She was the most amazing woman he had ever met. He wanted to announce to the world he loved her the first time he met her. So, he couldn't fathom the fact that no one had ever told her they loved her before. It didn't matter, though, because that just made another first for her that he would gladly participate in.

"If it means anything, you are all I think about. When I see you or even think about you, I get butterflies in my stomach. I smile just being around you. Your touch sends tingles all over my body. I don't know what I'm feeling, but I do know that you consume my every thought and my heart, Wanya Brown."

In his mind, she had just told him she loved him. Because that was what love felt like. That was the same way he felt about her. His name rolling off her tongue sounded like angels whispering in his ear. He pulled her face back to his and gripped her ass firmly as he stood with her holding on to him. She clasped her ankles together around his waist as he carried her to the bed. Slowly and gently, he laid her down.

"I love you," he said again as tears ran down the sides of her face.

He kissed her tears away and continued kissing down her face and neck. Kissing her passionately, he let his hands roam freely all over her body. The feeling inside of him was so intense that he had to take deep breaths to slow down. He'd never felt such excitement about being with anyone in his life. His dick was so hard it began to ache at the tip. He slid his hands under her back, unsnapped her bra, and allowed it to slowly fall. Gently, he took her breasts into his mouth and made circles with his tongue around her chocolate nipples. Hungrily, he took both nipples into his mouth, smashing them together. She rubbed the back of his head as her eyes rolled around in her head.

Valencia's moans gave him the cues that he was doing everything she liked. She had no idea there was such a feeling and couldn't describe it if her life depended on it. She couldn't believe this was finally happening.

Kidd made his way farther down and then sat up so he could get her panties off. As he pulled at her panties, she raised her hips to help him. He admired her body and rubbed his hands all over her one more time. Her body glistened under the moonlight, illuminating her curves. He felt like a boy doing it for the first time; his excitement was at an all-time high. He wanted to make sure that, after today, she would be his forever. Taking his time and giving every part of her body its own special attention was his plan for the night. He stood up and slid out of his pants and boxers. When he looked at her face, he had to hold back the laugh that was trying to break free. She looked at his dick like it was a machete. She had never seen anything like it in all her life.

"What a way to break me in." She nodded toward his thick and juicy pole hanging down his leg.

"Don't worry. We'll be gentle." He pulled her to the edge of the bed and got down on his knees. He rubbed his hands up and down her pussy, smearing the juices all over. He'd had dreams of this day for so long and couldn't actually believe it was happening. He was going to take his time and make this special for her. He licked her cat, slowly sucking it all the way in his mouth, kissing it as if it was her face.

She moaned and scratched the bed before grabbing the back of his head. She had never felt this good in all her life. He stuck one finger in her as he sucked. She flinched but relaxed.

"You want me to stop?" He looked up at her. *Shit, she can't even take a finger. How the fuck am I going to get my shit in her?* he thought to himself.

"No, I'm ready. I want to feel you inside of me," she panted as she looked down at him.

He rose up and crawled on top of her as she scooted back in the bed. He could see the fear in her eyes.

"You sure you ready?" he asked again to be certain.

"Yes, I know you'll take care of me." She pulled his face into hers. She could feel him rubbing the head of his dick up and down her opening. Slowly, he went in, inch by inch. She felt like she was being ripped apart. Her nails were planted firmly in his back.

"You all right?" He pulled his face away from hers to look at her. "Breathe," he coached, noticing she wasn't breathing.

"I can't!" She didn't want to move, it hurt so bad. He was too big to be her first.

"You want me to stop?" Hoping she'd say no, he didn't want to pull out. He could live in her pussy. It felt so good. She shook her head no.

"Take a breath, Vee. Relax, baby," he whispered to her.

"No." She shook her head left to right again like a little kid.

He laughed a little. "I need you to breathe, baby." Again, she shook her head no, but this time there were no words. He went in deeper until he filled her insides all the way up. He rested in that position until she got used to it. He could feel her walls pulsate around his dick. It felt like he had a warm, wet massager wrapped around him. Her legs loosened up, and he began moving in and out.

"Ummm . . . shhh." She couldn't get any words out. This moment was just too good to be true. He felt so good. She never wanted the moment to end. She felt him lifting her legs in the air and put them in crook of his arms as he started doing push-ups inside of her.

"Damn! You feel sooooo good, ma."

She was so tight. It was unbelievable. Every time he went out, it was like something was sucking him right back in. He let her legs go and stroked her slowly.

"I love you," he said as he looked into her tear-filled eyes. "Why are you crying?" he asked as he wiped the tears from her face.

"I'm so happy. It just doesn't feel real. I didn't think this would ever happen," she explained as she caressed the sides of his face.

"Well, it's happening, and I ain't going anywhere."

Valencia danced around her office while listening to 95.5. The radio station was jamming today. It seemed every song that came on was talking about her, and she found herself putting Kidd's name in all the songs. She had herself a man, she was laughing and smiling more, and the people around her took notice.

"If I didn't know any better, I would think that you got that cherry popped," Sena whispered in Valencia's ear as she walked up and sat on her desk. The smile on Valencia's face said it all.

"Noooo!" Sena jumped off the desk, excited.

"Yeeesssss!" Vee nodded.

"Umm-mm, gon', girl. That's what the fuck I'm talking 'bout."

"Oh my God, Sena! I never thought it would happen, but it did, and I'm so happy I did it. It was wonderful," Vee gushed.

"Well, I'll be damned. I'm happy for you! We got to get drunk and get into the details tonight, honey. I ain't had none in way too long. I'll live vicariously through you."

"You coming over tonight for game day? I got to get a rematch since you cheated me last time, but it's good 'cause I've been practicing, and I got a few tricks for that ass," Vee said, thinking about the moves Kidd had shown her.

"Whatever. I'll be there, and have my bed made 'cause I'm bringing the liquor and the SingStar. I just downloaded some more Beyoncé, and it's about to be on. Meee meee meee meee." Sena patted her throat as she practiced a little.

"Girl, whatever. You and Miss Bee ain't got nothin' on me and Miss Michele," she waved her friend off.

Chapter 12

Beautiful Nightmare

Kidd sat on the park bench watching some of the neighborhood kids play basketball. He was taking a break since they had run him ragged on the courts. He was daydreaming about his rendezvous with Valencia last night. He could still feel her love muscles clenching his joint. Her walls were so wet and tight. They felt like a sloppy, wet mouth. One of the little dudes slam-dunked on somebody, bringing him out of his daydream.

"Woo wee! He put some stank on that shit!" Kidd yelled out while laughing and cheering the young dude on.

"That's right! Make that nigga make the stink face," said the dude who had done the dunking. They laughed at the boy that had gotten the nuts in his face a little while longer. Kidd looked at his watch and shook his head. The sun was beaming down on him so hard that he just knew there was a heat advisory somewhere. He was waiting on Moochie and Li'l Tony to come so he could give them the rundown of what needed to be done for their next job. This would be his last job. He would soon be starting a new chapter in his life. He looked at his watch again for what felt like the hundredth time. Moochie would be late to his own funeral. He looked up to see them both approaching all cool like shit was sweet, and they weren't more than an hour late.

"I know. I know," Moochie said, raising his arms in submission as he got closer to Kidd.

"What you know?" Kidd asked, looking at his brother for an answer. Li'l Tony still hadn't approached. He was still trying to feel out the situation.

"What you mean?" Moochie looked at him with confusion in his eyes.

"Nigga, you said, 'I know. I know.' So, what the fuck do you know?"

"Man, get the fuck out of here with that bullshit," Moochie waved him off.

"T, what you know?" Kidd questioned but only got a shrug of his shoulders in response.

"I'm just saying, 'What you niggas know?' That I'm out this muthafucka losing weight by the second, that I'm trying to conduct business, and you niggas out here caking and shit, or that it's a thousand fucking degrees out this bitch? Let me know so I know *we* on the same page." Kidd was calm, but the threatening tone let them know he was upset. Moochie paid him no attention, though. Li'l Tony, on the other hand, was scared shitless. He had yelled at Moochie for about forty-five minutes, trying to get him to hurry up. Moochie wasn't tripping off what Kidd might do to him. He was his little brother, which meant Kidd wasn't going to do too much to him. But Li'l Tony wasn't blood, so that could mean open season on him. Noticing Li'l Tony's reluctance to come any closer, Kidd broke into a fit of laughter.

"Look at you, nigga, over there shaking and shit," Kidd laughed.

Moochie turned to see him standing about ten paces away. "The fuck you think he was gon' do? Shoot you or some shit for being late?" Moochie asked.

"Fuck that. The nigga crazy as fuck, and you ain't too far behind 'em," Li'l Tony stated as he walked up a little closer. He wasn't technically part of the crew, so he wasn't sure of his safety if things were to go wrong.

"Man, you good. I'm just fucking with you. I tell him a certain time and know it will be an hour later before he shows up. If money don't make the nigga jump, nothing will, and I have come to grips with that . . . from him." Kidd put emphasis on the "from him" part. "Let's get down to business."

Once again, Kidd found himself sitting in front of someone that was on their way to heaven or hell . . . whichever came first, and he would be the cause of it. Kidd had no idea what that man had done to deserve what he had coming, but it must have been something awful. It really didn't matter why this man was about to lose his life; he just knew it had to be done and quite harshly if he had to say so himself. The man that ordered the hit wanted him tortured in the worst kind of way. But Kidd wasn't into all that. Taking a man's life was enough, but taking his manhood was not an option. Kidd could still hear it clear as day: *I want this rat fuck fucked up the ass with a sick dick and no grease.* Kidd hoped he was just being sarcastic because there definitely would be no fucking of any kind going on.

The man lay on the cold, dirty basement floor, shivering, bleeding to death from all the cuts and whips on his body. Moochie had been whipping him for almost thirty minutes straight. There was so much blood everywhere that it could have been a scene from *The Passion of Christ.* Even though the man knew in the bottom of his heart that he shouldn't have been talking to the police, he did it anyway. It was either him or his partner. He was just grateful that the men had spared his wife and children. When he woke up to the screams of his wife and saw the men standing over his bed, he knew the Grim Reaper had come to collect the soul he had sold to the devil many years ago. He didn't put up too much of a fight, but he begged relentlessly for the masked men to spare his family's lives. However, he didn't have to waste his breath. Neither Kidd nor Moochie would ever kill a woman and her kids. The masked men had spared his family's lives, but he knew they would be forever haunted by the way he was snatched out of their home in the middle of the night. And that he would have to burn in hell.

The only thing that could be heard in the dark, musty room were the whimpers of the savagely beaten man. He hadn't even considered pleading for his life. He knew it would all be in vain. He had once stood in the same position as his capturers. He had shown no mercy to his victims; he'd even killed wives and children. He was so happy that his family didn't have to pay for his life choices.

"Let's get this shit done," Kidd spoke as he looked at the time on his watch. The only time they did a job without each other was when it was an easy hit, something like a bullet to the head. Neither one of them wanted to get a call saying something had happened to his brother. Neither would be able to forgive himself if he wasn't there to protect the other.

Kidd watched as Moochie poured gasoline all over the man's body. The victim tried to scoot away from Moochie. He was rolling all over the floor, trying to avoid the horrendous death that was coming. His eyes got big at the sight of Kidd walking toward him with a lit match. His screams were muffled by his glued lips. They watched as his body became engulfed in flames. The smell that took over the room was indescribable. Kidd was sick to his stomach. He had never set a man on fire and really didn't want to, but those were the orders. Moochie was used to the smell. This was how he got rid of the bodies nine times out of ten. His theory was, no body, no evidence, equaled no murder. Moochie had a funeral parlor that he paid quite a bit of money to in order to be able to use whenever needed.

As Kidd waited for Moochie to come out, thoughts of Valencia flooded his mind. He would never want to bring her into this kind of lifestyle, so he knew he had to get out very soon. He tried to shake the scent of burning flesh out of his memory. He didn't want her essence mixed in with this part of his life. She was the only good and pure thing in his life, and he wanted to keep her that way.

"Come on, man. What you doing? These muthafuckas over here kicking my ass, and you hiding behind a damn trash can!" Sena yelled at Valencia as they played *Resident Evil* on Wii. Sena was in her fighting stance, punching, while Vee was crouching down, shooting from a distance.

"Bitch, I'm helping. You just losing and can't take it."

They argued as if they couldn't stand each other when they played any game. It didn't matter what it was. They both went into the kill zone and acted as if they'd never been best friends.

Kidd and Moochie walked in and started laughing immediately. The scene was too funny. The girls were cursing at each other while Vee was under the table with a big gun shooting away at all the zombies while Sena was standing up boxing the air with some nunchakus in her hand, fighting for her life, but the zombies were getting in her ass. Her ass was jiggling all over the place with each punch, indicating she didn't have any underwear on.

The guys had brought liquor, but, from the looks of it, it seemed as though they didn't need to. There was already a bottle of Rémy Martin and Grey Goose on the table, and both were half-empty, so they already knew these two were really feeling themselves.

"I hope your thugalicious-ass man don't ever need you to help out in a gunfight 'cause the nigga is dead where he stand, 'cause yo' ass can't shoot worth shit. I done lost two lives fucking with you."

"Ah, bitch! Chuck it up. Shit! I go hard for mines. You better know it."

Kidd and Moochie, still standing at the door, started laughing again, knowing damn well Valencia wouldn't bust a grape in Welch's backyard.

Valencia and Sena were so into the game that they didn't even know the guys were there.

"Where he at anyway? I need a real shooter on my team. Bitch, you're fired," Sena said as she did the hand gesture mocking Donald Trump.

She turned around to pick her drink up and stopped when she saw the guys standing there. To say she was embarrassed would be an understatement. Valencia hadn't told her that they were coming over. This was supposed to be a girls-only night. But here they were, standing in front her, looking like a double dose of *Hot Damn* with a hint *Oh My God*. Had she known this, she would have chosen something way sexier. There she stood in her red Cardinals boy shorts with the big Cardinal sign going across the butt and a tank top that read "Bitch, I'm Me" across the front. Her hair was on point as always, but she was sweating from all the punching and jumping around. They went from playing *American Idol* to *Madden*, then doubles tennis, and now here they were shooting it out with the zombies.

She looked good as shit to Moochie. It had been awhile since he had seen her. He always asked Valencia how she was doing. But that was as far as he would go with the conversation. He couldn't help feeling some kind way about seeing her. He didn't want to have to explain why he'd never called. It wasn't on purpose. He had been busy with Skillet in the hospital and doing more since his brother had finally found love. He was happy for his brother, so he took up a lot of his slack.

They heard a loud thump coming from the floor. Everyone looked down and watched as Valencia tried to get up from under the table. She had already bumped her head a couple of times. She couldn't seem to find her way out.

"Ouch! Shit! Help me, bitch! You see me struggling!"

Valencia slurred her words while plopping back down on the floor, waiting for Sena to move the table. She could see the table being lifted into the air. Knowing her table weighed a good 150 pounds at least considering it was in the shape of five-foot butterfly and it was made out of bright colors of marble, she couldn't help but ask, "How in hell you lifting that damn table like that?"

She still hadn't looked up yet. Her head didn't seem to want to cooperate with what her brain was telling it to do. With her head feeling like she was in the ocean, she kept talking with her face in the carpet. "You got a lot of testosterone built up," she laughed. "That comes from not getting any ding ding. I'm gon' call Moochie and tell him to come get some of that good good. I'ma say, I'ma say, I'ma say, 'li'l bra, gon' 'head get cha some,' and I'm not gon' even charge him. It's gon' be on da house."

Sena stood there beet red she was so embarrassed. Thoughts of stepping on the back of Valencia's head crossed her mind. "Really, Vee?" Sena shook her head.

"OK, I'll charge him. We can't be giving it away for free. Shit, people paying for oxygen, so why can't they pay for a li'l cooter?"

"Vee, would you just shut the hell up and getcha drunk ass up!" Sena side kicked her in the leg.

Valencia's body finally cooperated as she was able to roll over.

"Oh, hey, honey! How ya doin'? Wait a min! Let me get hood, how you say it? What's the B. I.?" she said, deepening her voice. You could tell she wasn't a drinker. "Hey, Moo . . . chie." As she stood up to get her equilibrium together, she looked at both of them. "Oh, I get it. You came to redeem the Brown name in *Madden* 'cause you heard about them ass whippings I be putting down on ya big bra." She could barely stand, so she decided to sit on the edge of couch.

Kidd just laughed. She was not lying. She kicked his ass every time, especially after he'd taught her them tricks. She was looking so cute. She had her hair pulled into two pigtails hanging on each side of her head with a pink camisole that said, "I'm a Martian," and she had on the same shorts that Sena had on, only they were pink. You could tell that it was a real girl's night going on.

"Naw, my brother ain't told me nothing about getting his ass kicked by you in *Madden*. He knew he would have never been able to live that shit down, as much shit as he talks." He looked over at Sena. "How you doin', Miss Lady?"

"I'm doin' good, and you?" she said, trying to act like she wasn't hurt that he didn't call. She had got over it about a week after him not calling and hadn't thought much about him until now. Here he was standing in front of her, looking extrasexual.

"Okay. Now that the reunion is over, can we get this shit poppin'? Moochie's my partner. He looks a li'l more thuggish, like he got a good shot."

"A'ight, let me find out. It's all good. My girl over here seem like she got a good left hook, and, with my right hook, we good," Kidd stated confidently.

As Valencia went to pick up her gun, she got this feeling in her stomach, and her head felt like it was about to pound out of her skull. "Not now!" Everybody looked at her.

"Not now what? You don't want to play no more?" Sena was looking at her like she was crazy.

"Huh? Oh, don't pay me any attention. Caught a cramp. That's all." She rubbed her temples and shook her head, trying to shake the feeling that was coming over her. At any moment, she just knew her head was going to rupture. *Please, God, not right now. If you have any love for me at all left in you, please not right now.* She wanted to cry as she said her silent prayer.

"Don't punk out now. We going to war. We need your concentration, baby girl." Moochie patted her on her back.

"Don't even trip. I got you. What the hell?" She looked around at everybody.

"Girl, what the hell is wrong with you?" Sena asked, walking up to Valencia.

"Nothing. The liquor is getting to me. Let me go to the ladies' room. I'll be right back." She ran to the bathroom and locked the door.

Vee's migraine was getting worse by the second, and the feeling was no longer a battle. It had been won. She just wasn't as strong as the force she was fighting against. Valencia stared into the mirror . . . but Raven was staring back at her.

"Get rid of them!" Raven said through clenched teeth. Vee looked in the mirror, and the image before her was no longer her. Scared as hell, she knew her happiness had come to a complete halt. She knew it would be short lived, but this was too soon.

"Please! No! Don't do this," Vee tried to beg, but Raven cut her off.

"Fuck that begging shit, bitch. You said a little while, and I gave you that. I'm starting to get the feeling you trying to get rid of me."

"Well, you got the right feeling. Why can't I have my life? Leave me alone. Go find someone else to torture!" she screamed, punching the mirror, making the glass shatter everywhere.

"Ooooh, somebody's mad! Like I give a fuck. Bitch, I told you don't fuck with me. But you wouldn't listen, thought I was playin'," Raven taunted her.

"You expect me to let you live my life forever?"

Everybody ran to the door.

"Vee, you all right?" Sena yelled through the door as she shook the handle.

"I'm okay. I'll be right out."

"Open the door."

"No, I said I'll be out."

"Open this damn door before I kick it in." Sena was adamant.

"Would you just go the fuck away?" Raven hissed.

Sena's feelings were hurt.

"Why did you do that?" Vee couldn't believe this was happening in front everybody that meant the most to her. She knew if she didn't do something soon, Raven would hurt everybody in that house, and she would give her life before she allowed Raven to do that.

"Because I told the bitch to leave, but she wouldn't. I told you to get . . . rid . . . of . . . them before *I* do," Raven gritted. Everybody put their ears to the door.

"Who are you talking to?" Kidd asked.

"No one! Could you just leave, please? I'll call y'all tomorrow." Vee was trying to avoid a big commotion. Only the Lord knew what this crazy bitch would do if she walked out of the bathroom.

"Would you just come out, so we know you're all right?"

The door opened. Vee stood there with blood running out of her hand in puddles. She had this vacant look in her eyes like she was not looking at them but through them. Everyone looked behind her to see if there was anyone else in there because they knew they'd heard two voices.

"Oh my God, are you all right?" Sena tried to touch Vee's hand, only for her to snatch it back.

"Okay. I'm alive. Now could you just please leave?" Raven wasn't into trying to be nice to them at all. They weren't her friends.

"You want everybody to leave?" Kidd asked, just knowing she wasn't putting him out too.

"Yes, I'm sorry, but I have to take care of something." Vee could barely look him in the eyes. She could clearly see his feelings were hurt.

"Yo! What the fuck is going on? You were just drunk as shit, barely standing. Now, you're bleeding all over the place and putting us out. What the fuck type of time is you on?" Moochie said, scrunching up his face.

"Who the fuck is this nigga? You betta get this muthafucka out before I do."

It was like she just morphed right in front of their eyes. Vee was looking at Sena with tear-filled eyes. Now, everybody stood there, really confused. Vee and Moochie talked on the phone damn near every day, and he was always around when Kidd was over. The look in her eyes was deadly and sinister. This was not their sweet Valencia.

"Please leave . . ."

Tears were running down her face. She couldn't even look at them as she shut the door. Vee sat down on the toilet, crying harder than she ever cried in her life. She knew her life was over, and now all she could do was watch from the other side.

"It's my turn, bitch, and I'ma teach you a lesson about fucking with me," Raven said while trying to fix her makeup in the mirror. "Think you can get rid me. Give a bitch an inch, and she takes a foot. Look at this shit. Got my makeup running all over the damn place, crying and shit. Dumb ass, feelings is a fuckin' no-no. Weak-ass bitch, you want to know why I'm here? This why!" she yelled, circling her face with her index finger pointing at all the tears. "You too weak, just fuckin' pathetic! Why won't you just wither the fuck away and quit fighting the inevitable 'cause I'm here to stay, bitch, so get down or lie down."

"Why won't you just leave? Please leave. Let me have my life back. I need my life. I just want to be happy." Tears fell again.

"Didn't I tell you to stop with all that crying shit? That's all right. I'm gonna give you something to cry about. I'm gonna suck yo' little boyfriend's dick so good he gonna forget you ever existed."

"Don't you suck pussy?" Vee said, trying to have some sort of comeback. This can't be happening, not now, not ever. God can't be that cruel to finally give her happiness, only to snatch it away.

"Watch a real bitch work."

Chapter 13

1991

Valencia could hear the commotion going on in her house. There was a big fight going on downstairs between her mom Daphne and her boyfriend, Russell. Russell had been terrorizing Valencia's mom for years. He was a big fellow, considering her mom stood five feet eleven. Daphne would never consider a man under six feet tall. He wasn't handsome in the least bit, but he was six feet four and weighed every bit of 325 pounds. He also had a scar that went from his left temple to the corner of his mouth that resembled a railroad track.

Miss Daphne Ball had been one of the baddest chicks walking the streets of St. Louis before Russell got a hold to her. Valencia had never met her father. Daphne was so out of control as a teenager he could have been any one of the neighborhood players. She never approached any of them about being her child's father. She figured she didn't need them, and she was doing good physically. She kept Valencia clean and fed until she met Russell. But she herself had never been taught the motherly love part. She had become so materialistic that the only thing she knew for sure was that her daughter had to be clean as a whistle every day.

Russell considered himself a pimp. He had a few chicks scattered around, but he wanted Daphne to complete his stable. At age nineteen, Daphne was officially

Russell's bottom bitch, and she took much pride in it. She was an evil bitch. Every woman she came across she practically spit in their face.

Daphne had never emotionally attached herself to her daughter. She fed her and kept her in fine clothes. Then, in the blink of an eye, everything went from sugar to shit when she finally fell off. All the way off. Everyone had front-row seats to see Russell tear her down piece by piece. Russell had her on so many different drugs, she oftentimes didn't know what was getting her high. She just knew she got high whenever he was around. She had always been mean and cruel toward Vee. But she was all the child had. No matter how bad her mom treated her, Vee needed her mom. But when Russell got a hold of Daphne, it wasn't just her being hurtful toward Vee. It was him too. She would hide under her bed when he would come around because he would have this look of lust in his eyes when he would look at her. He would slap her on the ass when Daphne wasn't around. Valencia took after her mother in height, and, in looks, she was a beautiful little girl. She was tall for being nine years old, but her body had hardly even begun to sprout anything of substance. Yet and still, the men her mother brought around would look and make remarks about her looks. Valencia kept a razor under her tongue just as her mom had taught her to. It took a lot of bleeding from the mouth, but, at age seven, she had it down pat. She took her razor out of her mouth only to sleep, and, even then, she kept it under her pillow within arm's reach.

Valencia could hear every time Russel's fist connected with her mother's face and every time her mother hit the floor. She was scared for her young life standing at the top of the steps in her oversized nightgown rotating the blade she kept in her mouth. She did everything in her power not to look tempting to the men that ran rampant through their home. On many occasions, she would sleep on the back porch so she wouldn't be seen by the men who lusted after her body. On this particular night, she was done running away. This time, she decided to run to the fight. She didn't know what had come over her. It was as if someone was pushing her. She ran down the stairs with nothing but courage in her heart, rage in her eyes, and a razor under her tongue. Not knowing what to do, she lunged for the big, burly man who instinctively punched her so hard in the face that she flew across the room, landing on her head. He was charging toward her when she was finally able to open her eyes. As he got closer to her, he snatched her up off the floor. He held her by the neck in the air. Her little body hung in the air as he shook her as if she were a rag doll.

Slamming her into the wall, he snarled, "You want to be grown? I'ma turn ya young ass into a woman," Russell gritted his teeth, spitting in her face in the process. He held her by the neck in the air as he used his free hand to rub all over her body. He stuck his hand in her panties and started rubbing. Her head was hurting so bad she thought for sure it was busted wide open. Vee felt like she had to go to sleep and couldn't fight the feeling any longer. "You see yo' mama? I'm gonna turn you out like I did that bitch."

In that split second of him looking over his shoulder at her mother, lying there as if no life was left in her, Valencia had pulled the blade out of her mouth and sliced his throat in one quick motion. He didn't know what happened. He just felt her move and noticed that his green silk shirt was now turning bright crimson. Then, he finally acknowledged the look in her eyes. They held an almost demonic glare. He looked down to see where the blood was coming from. After dropping her, he realized it was coming from his own body and grabbed his throat. She got back up and watched him struggle to keep his blood from spilling out. The gurgling sounds that escaped his mouth as he struggled to breathe reverberated off the walls. But he couldn't do anything else as he fell to his knees looking the devil in the eyes as he died right there at Raven's feet. Raven didn't move until he was no longer breathing. She wanted to watch every ounce of blood drain from his body. If she could have, she would have sucked the life right out of him. His suffering made her feel good. Raven walked past Valencia's mother as if she wasn't lying there bleeding to death. She walked into the bathroom and looked in the mirror to see what damage had been done.

"Who are you?" Valencia asked as she looked at Raven through the mirror.

"Raven. And I'll be here to protect you forever, and no one will ever hurt you again," Raven said as she wiped the blood from her face.

"Oh, okay. I'm Valencia. Nice to meet you." Valencia finally had a friend and someone to protect her. She didn't care if she was talking to herself. It was as if she was standing right next to her. She never thought she would regret her decision to keep Raven around so many years later.

Chapter 14

Have You Seen Her?

"Vee!" Sena yelled as she walked into Valencia's vacant home. She looked around. It looked like no one had been there in weeks. "Valencia Ball!" she yelled out. *Where the fuck are you?* she thought to herself.

Room after room Sena searched for anything to be out of place. Confusion and heartache consumed her. Where had her dear friend gone? Why would she just up and leave without so much as a good-bye?

Bzzzzz Bzzzz Bzzz

Her phone vibrated at the bottom of her purse. Anxiety immediately set in. She prayed it was Valencia, and that she wouldn't miss her call. She looked at her phone screen and saw that it was only Kidd calling.

"Hey, Kidd," she answered solemnly.

"Still no word?" She could hear the worry in his voice.

"Nope, I'm here now, and nothing has changed. Still the same from when I cleaned it." She continued to look around to see if she had missed anything.

"Man, what the fuck is up with your friend? Has she ever done anything like this before?"

"Like I told you when she first left, no, she hasn't. At least not since I've known her."

"That's bullshit, Sena!"

"But wait, I ain't the one that left. The hell you yelling at me for?" Sena yelled back.

"I'm sorry." Kidd paused. "I'm just trying to get an understanding on what's going on, man." She could hear the defeat in his voice. She really felt sorry him. He'd given Valencia his heart, and she just ran off with it like a thief in the night.

"It's cool. I know we both are frustrated. We just gotta stay focused till we find out what really happened. I hope this shit don't turn out to be like one of those disappeared episodes like on the ID channel."

"I know, right?" Kidd paused again. "I'm gon' let you go. I'll check back with you again soon."

"OK, bye."

Sena took one more look around and fought the urge to cry. Memories of her and Vee playing the game or just sitting around laughing and drinking flooded her mind. She ran to the door. The walls seemed to be closing in on her, and she needed to get out of the house as soon as possible.

Sena sat at her desk answering the phones as usual. She couldn't concentrate on anything other than her missing friend. She'd gone by Valencia's house that morning again, with no success. She was lost in the world without her only friend. Every time the elevator chimed signaling someone had arrived on the floor, she would pray her friend would walk off smiling like she always did.

She looked down at her cell phone for the thousandth time checking to see if she missed any phone calls. Once again, she was disappointed. The tears that had welled up in her eyes fell like twin waterfalls. She got up and ran to the nearest bathroom. She hadn't had an anxiety attack in years. Her true strength was being tested, and she didn't know how long she would be able to hold it together.

How could you just leave me like this, Vee? Don't you know you're all I got? Sena wiped her face before leaving the bathroom. *I'm gone smack the fuck outta this wanch when she comes back,* Sena thought as she exited the bathroom.

Kidd sat at the table waiting for Moochie to show up. For once, he was appreciative of Moochie's tardiness. He needed to think. He had just left Valencia's house right before he called Sena. He had spent the night hoping she would come home for something. He needed to feel close to her. The moment he lay in her bed, the scent of her perfume consumed his senses, and he fought deep within not to cry. Things weren't the same without her there to make him smile. He needed her to make everything better again. He shook his head. This situation was definitely not in the plans.

Kidd and Sena had just missed each other by about five minutes. He'd searched high and low, scrounged through everything to see he could find anything that would lead him to her. His heart was hurting. He'd taken a leap of faith with her, and she took his heart and ran off with it. God had to be playing a dirty joke on him. This couldn't be real life. He knew deep down he didn't deserve a true blue love. He'd done too much dirt and ruined too many lives to expect to ever have his happily ever after.

"Aye, my man, you good?" Moochie asked as he slid in his chair across from Kidd. He could see the sadness in Kidd's eyes. He hadn't seen his brother like this since their mother passed away.

"I mean, I guess I don't have a choice but to be good." Kidd was all discombobulated and didn't know what to do with himself. His hurt was slowly turning into anger and resentment.

"So, Sena ain't heard nothing either?"

"Nah, man, she going crazy looking for her too. She even spent the week there hoping she'd come home for something." Sena cried on the phone to Kidd almost every day. Valencia was all she had in the world, and she just disappeared on her.

"Damn, that's fucked up. I hope ain't nothing wrong with her." Moochie had gotten close to Valencia, and even though she'd pulled a Houdini on everyone, he stilled loved her like the sister he'd never had.

"I put Li'l Tony on the case to see if he could come up with anything," Kidd stated as he ate more of his cold fries.

"Well, hopefully, he come up with something. I just hope nothing is really wrong with her."

"Shit, she better be kidnapped and being tortured for all this shit she putting us through."

"You got that right." Moochie chuckled a little, glad to see his brother still had a little sense of humor.

"But anyway, man, fuck her, dude. We out here tonight. I need to clear my mind."

"Damn right, my nigga, home too!"

Everyone was getting out tonight because Skillet was finally free from rehab. At one point, they didn't even know if he would pull through. And now to have him able to walk and talk and party, yes, there was definitely a need to celebrate.

"Bend over!" Raven instructed as she pushed her latest victim down so she was touching her toes. Standing behind the girl in a whole-body black leather jumpsuit, she admired the perfectly heart-shaped ass in front of her. The jumpsuit looked as if she would have to be peeled out of it. There were two holes where her breasts were sticking out, and it was crotchless in case she wanted to receive some oral pleasure herself. She couldn't wait to dig her face in between the girl's legs. Her mouth was watering at the thought.

"You are fucking disgusting!" Valencia spat.

She couldn't believe she was witnessing this happening. She was mortified. Raven just smirked. No one was going to ruin her fun tonight. She needed a fix in the worst way, and nothing was going to stop her high, not even Valencia.

"You ready?" Raven questioned as she pushed her fingers into the girl's dripping pussy. She pushed her finger in and out a couple of times, then pulled them out to get a taste. She licked every drop off her fingers and smiled.

"Tastes like honey," she said more to Valencia than the girl in front of her.

"Just trife, just fucking trifling." Valencia was beyond pissed. Why couldn't she turn her off? Why was she still here? They never coexisted before. What was happening now? Her thoughts were interrupted by Raven getting down on her knees.

"You have got to be fucking kidding me!" Valencia screeched. Raven ignored her and stuck her tongue deep into the girl's love tunnel.

"Umm . . . yeah. That feels so good." The girl worked her hips, trying to fuck Raven's tongue. She couldn't believe her luck. She had never been with a woman, although she and her friends had been talking about trying it. They wanted a girlfriend, but she just wanted to see what it was like. Now, here she was, with a beautiful woman making her feel like she had never felt before. She not only wanted to try Raven out, she now wanted to wife her. A man's tongue had never felt that good. She didn't know if it was the excitement of the experience or just pure lust that was pushing her over the edge. Raven's tongue seemed to be working overtime. The feeling of a huge dildo entering brought her out of her thoughts.

"How can you just fuck this girl like you're a man?" Vee wanted to know.

"'Cause this my pussy, ain't it?" Raven asked the girl but was really talking to Vee.

"Yes, this yo' pussy, baby, put cho name on it," the unknowing girl answered. Vee also had no idea of what was to come, but Raven was sure about to rock both their worlds tonight. Raven deep stroked her until she felt the girl trembling under her body. Raven had begun to literally hold the girl up because her legs had given out on her.

"Come on, ma. Pull it together. I ain't even gotten started yet," Raven said, frustrated with the girl's antics.

"I'm sorry. I'm trying to. I just ain't never felt like this before," the girl pleaded. Raven got an idea.

"Show me how sorry you are," Raven said as she slid the dildo out of her aching pussy.

"This is some sickening shit!" Vee yelled. She was beginning to fuck with Raven's moment, and Raven wasn't feeling that at all.

"Would you just shut the fuck up?" Raven yelled, startling the girl, who jumped, not expecting that reaction. Raven noticed the look in her eyes and got excited all over again.

"Now, come show me how sorry you are." Raven guided the girl's head toward her long dick. The young girl happily tried to swallow it. Raven got a better grip on the back of her head and slowly started fucking her face. The girl was going hard like a pro . . . until Raven's pace sped up, and she began to go too deep. She tried to push Raven off, but she couldn't. Raven's eyes were rolling around in her head. The dildo was pressing against her clit, and the thought of what was to come sent her over the rainbow.

The girl could barely breathe. She didn't know whether to push Raven off or grab her throat. It felt like her throat was being ripped apart. She had tears running down her face as she tried to fight off Raven. She was getting too weak to fight back. Raven had all her weight pressed down on the girl, as she clawed at Raven, but Raven was fully covered and could feel nothing but a rush.

"What are you doing? Let her up, you maniac!" Vee yelled, horrified by what she was witnessing. There was vomit everywhere, and blood had begun to spill from the girl mouth.

"Ahhh, yessss *sssss*," Raven could barely get her words together to respond to Vee. The feeling was too good to let go. Vee was not going to ruin her moment.

Vee felt horrible as she looked down into the eyes of the girl who was one breath short of death. She had created Raven and let her get away with what she was doing. She had no idea that this was what she had become. She wanted to cry, but Raven wouldn't allow it. The girl had stopped fighting awhile ago. Raven had reached the point of no return. She shook, shivered, and collapsed on top of the dead girl with her dildo still deep in her throat. After this night, Valencia would never be the same. This moment had shaken her to her core. Raven was a horrible person and was not fit to run the streets. Vee had no idea how she was going to get rid of her, but she was sure going to try.

For a month straight, Valencia watched from the side-lines as Raven got with different women. That first night out with Raven replayed in her head over and over again. Every time Raven would get with a girl, she would pray they made it out alive. She didn't think she could bear to see something so repulsive again. It was the grossest thing she had ever experienced. It used to be she wouldn't be awake to watch what was going on. Once Raven came in, she would usually fall asleep.

For some reason, they seemed to be coexisting now. The last time they had talked to each other was when Raven first appeared. Valencia couldn't seem to turn herself off. Raven hadn't been going to work, answering her phone; she hadn't even been back to the house. Every time the phone would ring, she could see it was Kidd or Sena's number flash across the screen. She knew they were going crazy with worry. Raven had changed all the locks on the house because she knew Sena and Kidd had keys. She only did that to be spiteful because after that, they basically moved into a hotel. She really missed her friend, and, most of all, she missed Kidd. She needed to feel his touch, see his smile, and hear his voice.

Raven had successfully sucked all of the happiness she had right out of her. Valencia's heart was crushed, and her spirit had gotten so low that she wanted to just let Raven have her life. But she couldn't seem to turn herself off. She still couldn't believe this was happening to her. She had seen the movie *Sybil* a thousand times and never once had she ever thought that could be her. Sybil was crazy in Valencia's eyes. Sybil had like ten different personalities while Vee only had Raven. But then again, Raven took the shit to a whole new level. Raven's personality was so big and strong, there wasn't any room for another one. Valencia wanted to take her secret to the grave with her. She knew in her heart of hearts that this was going to blow up really big. She only hoped it would be her standing at the end.

"You hanging in there, honey?" Raven asked Valencia sarcastically. Raven knew she was driving Valencia crazy. She hadn't even needed to get her fix because she so fixated on getting back at Valencia, that was a high in itself. She had so many girls' pussies in her mouth that it was a shame. But she loved every bit of it. Valencia was mortified by what she had seen.

"What do you want? Why won't you just leave me alone? You got what you wanted." Vee was defeated, heartbroken, and felt like committing suicide.

"Oh, buck up, buddy! The fun has just gotten started," Raven laughed.

"Where are you going tonight? To suck some more pussy?"

"I wish, but, no, if all goes well, I'll be sucking a li'l dick. Would that be all right with you?"

"Yeah, right." Vee would never believe that. Raven hated men, and wouldn't even fathom the thought of a man touching her body, let alone putting a dick in her mouth.

"Have a li'l more faith in me. As a matter of fact, I think you'll love to participate tonight. We are finally going to see what treasures your precious boyfriend has down in them jeans."

If Vee was standing on her own, her legs probably would have given out. But she had a comeback of her own.

"I don't know if you got the memo, bitch, but I already got the goods, and trust they are Grade A."

"What the fuck are talking about?" Raven was livid at the thought of Valencia making such a decision without her permission.

"Oooh, now look at this. Is Miss Raven mad because I did something without her permission? Well, so the fuck what! Bitch, it's a lot of things I had to get over."

Finally, Vee was able to get a little justice in all this madness. She knew Raven would hate it, and she was really happy she had done it.

Raven sat in the corner of Club Karma, scoping out the scene. She watched as Kidd and his entourage walked through the door and straight to VIP. It took everything

Raven had in her not to jump up and start throwing things all over the club. She wanted to walk up to Kidd and shoot him square in the middle of his forehead. How dare he take advantage of Valencia! He knew she was emotional, but he did it anyway.

Valencia, on the other hand, wanted to run to him and let him know she hadn't left him on purpose. But Raven was not having that.

"Hold ya horses, babe. I will be going to see my new friend in a minute. Let's drink a little, and, you know, mingle." Raven knew she was messing with Vee. She began to walk toward Kidd.

Chapter 15

Better Than Nothing

Kidd replayed the scene of Valencia putting them out over and over in his head. He still couldn't figure out what went wrong, what made her flip out like that. One minute, they were laughing and joking. Then, she flipped the script and was putting them out. No matter where he went, he couldn't shake her from his thoughts. He thought she was everything he could have ever prayed for in a woman.

It was as if she just disappeared off the face of the earth. He missed her like crazy and couldn't help but have some sort of resentment toward her. How could she just leave him with no explanation or good-bye? Even with all those feelings, he still needed her like he needed his next breath. He wanted—no—he *needed* to see her in the worst way. He really understood that Jordin Sparks and Chris Brown song "No Air" because he felt like his lungs would cave in at any moment. How could she say she loved him, then pull a Houdini? He would have never hurt her in any kind of way. To hurt her would be to hurt him.

Kidd wasn't perfect and had done a lot of dirty shit in his life, but he didn't think vengeance would come back in the form of heartbreak. Maybe a barrage of bullets or even a slow torture . . . but never this. The thought of never seeing Vee again almost stopped his heart every time.

"Fuck her!" he told himself, but he knew the words held no weight. If she were to knock on his door right at that moment, he would welcome her into his arms with no hesitation. Afterward, there would be a lot of cursing, but, for that moment, he would just relish in her beauty and warm embrace. But, for now, all he could do was visit her in his dreams.

Kidd was sitting in the back of Club Karma with his mind stuck on Valencia Ball. There was a party going on. Skillet had finally come home. The crew was celebrating, but he sat at the table keeping Shay-D company. She was not allowed to join the party, being that it looked like she was about pop at any moment, and she was only six months, but her stomach looked like she was nine. He laughed a little as he watched his crew walk it out and make it rain to their theme song, "Fuck You" by Yo Gotti. That was Moochie's shit. It was his ring tone on his voice mail, his get hype song, and you name it . . . He had an occasion to play the song for.

Kidd felt a light tap on his shoulder. When he turned around, his heart damn near leaped out of his chest. But his excitement soon faded when the realization sank in that it wasn't Valencia but Raven standing in front of him, looking gorgeous as usual. She was killing 'em in her knee-length white Donna Karan skirt with a red satin shirt that didn't leave much to the imagination, and her red Mary Jane Giuseppe pumps. Her hair was flowing freely straight down her back.

She noticed the change in his face.

"Now, is that any way to greet an old friend?" She smiled at him, and it made his heart melt. He missed that smile terribly, but why did she have the smile he longed for?

Valencia could see the hurt in his eyes. She saw it from across the room. She could feel his pain. She had the same hurt, but hers was multiplied by ten because she could see and hear him, but she couldn't touch him.

"Please let me touch him," Vee pleaded in Raven's ear, but Raven ignored her. "Please!" Vee became angry all over again. Raven could feel her head banging. But she ignored it because she knew she was much stronger than Vee.

"Oh, my bad, ma. How you doin'?" He stood up to give her a hug.

"How have you been?" She could see a million emotions flash on his face, but she was only able to decipher two: sadness and confusion. It was her mission to change that cute little frown into a smile. But with the combination of the music and Vee pushing hard to come through, it didn't look like it would be happening tonight, because Vee was on a mission to get to her man right then and there.

"I'm good, and you?" he said, not able to take his eyes off her. There was a sparkle in his eyes that hadn't been there in a long time. He sat back down and offered her a seat. She stood a little longer, shaking her head. Valencia was being very persistent. But it was of no match for Raven's revenge.

He introduced her to Shay-D.

"Aye, baby girl, this Raven." He pointed to Raven, then pointed to Shay-D and said, "Raven, this is Shay-D, my boy Skillet's woman."

Shay-D didn't pay her the least bit of attention. When Raven walked up, she brought a bad vibe around, and she didn't like it not one bit.

Raven couldn't help but notice the little attitude.

"Well, excuse the fuck outta me, bitch." She looked her up and down, then turned her attention back to Kidd, but not before Shay-D got her shit off too. Kidd just sat there. *Do they know each other from somewhere?* he wondered.

"How you can excuse yourself is you can walk yo' janky ass back to wherever the fuck you came from," Shay-D said, looking her square in her eyes. She and the crew had gotten extremely close, and she looked at them all as her brothers. She wouldn't allow anything to happen to any of them, and this bitch in front of her looked like she had come with a lot of shit. A bunch of bullshit with a capital B, and she would not hesitate to break this bitch's neck if need be.

"Do y'all know each other?" Kidd looked at both of them.

"Naw, I don't know her, but I do know this bitch is shiesty. You better watch yo'self." She was looking in Raven's eyes the whole time. She was pregnant, but that wouldn't stop her from sticking her six-inch heel in Raven's eye. Yeah, she refused to give up her Jimmy Choos. Pregnant or not, she must always look hot.

"You sure you ain't fuckin' her? She acts like she guarding the dick or something," Raven said with a slight chuckle. Any other day, Raven would have her face in the pretty bitch's pussy fucking shit up, and, after the girl got her rocks off, she would have watched the bitch bleed to death after slitting her throat.

Moochie stood watching the whole scene from across the dance floor, and he noticed the exchange between the two ladies. Shay-D didn't like Raven, and he was with her when she was right. He also thought there was something flaky about Raven. Her whole atmosphere, her aura, was dark. He lived, ate, and shit the streets and had danced with the dark side more often than not. He had also seen a lot of killers in his time, and, for some reason, she was giving off the same vibe as a nigga marking his next vic. Even though she looked just like Vee, there was a huge difference between the two. He felt as though he had to get this in his brother's head. He didn't know what it was about her, but he didn't want his brother having no parts of it whatsoever. He walked on up to them.

"Aye! Let me holla at you for a min," Moochie said, not even acknowledging Raven's presence.

"A'ight. Oh, this Raven—" Kidd started to point at Raven, but Moochie cut that shit short.

"Ain't no need for all that." He looked at her with disgust. He didn't want to get to know her at all. Now that he was up close and personal, he felt the vibe even more. Just on that observation alone, he wanted to blast her head off. He didn't discriminate when it came to his brother. Newborn on up was his motto.

Kidd noticed that look that took over Moochie's face. He too would get that same look when he was ready to kill.

"What's good, li'l bra? Why you look like you about to murk somethin'?"

Moochie just stood staring at Raven. Weirdest part about it was she was staring right back. "This bitch is bad news, bra. I don't like her." He knew Raven could hear him because he was purposely saying it loud enough.

"You ain't even meet the girl." Kidd couldn't understand what everybody was seeing that he wasn't.

"Has Shay ever met her 'cause, from what I saw, she ain't too fond of her either?" Moochie felt the need to talk some sense into his brother. Always following his gut feeling, he had to get his brother away from her. He got this feeling like he was walking into a bad drug deal.

Kidd looked back, still not understanding everyone's dislike for her.

"Y'all act like I'm 'bout to marry this chick. We just talking," Kidd rationalized.

"Shit! You *might* marry her," Moochie countered back.

"Why the hell would you say some dumb shit like that?" Kidd asked, already knowing the answer.

Moochie looked at him like, *"you can't be for real."*

"All I'm sayin' is don't let her looks fool you. There's something with this bitch. She will not replace Vee, so just fuck the bitch and be done with it." Moochie walked away to join the party. He missed Vee too. She was cool as shit. He always wanted a sister, and she fit the bill perfectly, but this Raven bitch had to go ASAP. He knew his brother was hurting, and he fully understood. Kidd was ready to be with Valencia and only her. He thought he had found his one and only.

Shay-D had gotten up to dance with the boys. She didn't care what they said. Shit! She was pregnant—not dead. Besides, she couldn't stand being around Raven for another second. Even though she had never seen Valencia, they had spoken often over the phone, and she could tell she was good peoples.

Raven sat there patiently. She didn't give a shit about what they were talking about. She had a mission to complete. Now that she sat there and thought about it, she wanted him gone. Erased from her and Vee's life . . . for good.

Valencia cheered from a distance. She had heard everything Moochie said. "That's right, li'l bra. This bitch ain't me."

"Bitch, please! You wish you had swag like me." Raven smiled and danced to the beat in her seat. If you didn't know any better, you would have just thought she was rapping the song instead of holding a conversation with herself.

"Yeah, well, we'll see, you dyke bitch. Why don't you go suck some pussy and stop sniffing around my dick?" Vee was getting hot under the collar.

"If that's your boyfriend, if that's your boyfriend, he won't be tonight," Raven sang an old Meshell Ndegeocello hit.

"You laugh now, but I bet I'll get the last laugh. You can best believe I'm coming for you," Valencia said, not sure of what her next move would be. Obviously, Raven was way stronger than she, but love was the greatest power, right?

She knew he would never love Raven. She wasn't lovable, but this was the only way she could get close to him until she came up with something else. She wanted to reach out and touch him. She missed him so much that it hurt. Sometimes, she wished she could turn back the hands of time and go back to the day she met him. She would have stayed at home and avoided the whole thing. Just knowing she would never be able spend time with him again, touch his face, laugh and joke with him, she wanted to end all her misery right there on the spot. Every time she thought about it, she cried, but Raven just laughed at her. Raven thought it was the funniest thing ever. Feelings had no place in Raven's world, and Valencia just had to get used to it because she would not have her precious Kidd ever again.

"I'm sorry about that, ma. That's my li'l brother. He a li'l overprotective of me. Don't pay them no attention."

"It's all good. Most people have to get to know me before they like me, so I'm used to it. So where you been? I haven't seen you out in a while."

"I got caught up in something." His eyes started to wander around the room, looking for something to focus on, trying desperately not to think of Vee, but that was a waste of time 'cause everything around him reminded him of her. Now he was sitting here looking into the eyes of a replica of her.

"Your woman put you on lockdown for a while, huh?" she asked, seeing if he would tell the truth.

"Something like that." He had a look of disappointment in his eyes.

"So you do have a woman?"

"Something like that," he repeated.

"What does that mean? Either you do or you don't." She was trying not to show her attitude.

"Ha! Bitch, back up, back up. Give him fifty feet," Valencia sang in her ear.

"I can't explain it. She kind of disappeared, so let's just talk about something else." He was getting uncomfortable.

"So are you waiting for her to come back?" she asked seductively.

"Something like that." He matched her look. Valencia wanted to break down and cry. Raven was really trying to seduce him. It was the right person, but he was hers and not Raven's.

"Well, I'm going to let you get to your party. I won't hold you up all night." Raven was getting bored and saw her next victim walking into the club. She was right on time, and Raven was ready to get her freak on. Tonight was a good night because she didn't need her fix. She wanted to get down with the get down.

"Wait! Please, just a little longer," Vee pleaded and begged. She needed to be around him like she needed air.

Ignoring Vee, she said, "Why don't you put your number in my phone? Maybe we can get together sometime." She already had plans for the night. She handed Kidd her phone.

He looked at it like it looked familiar. *But everybody has the same phone,* he thought. *Get your mind off that girl! She's gone. She left you without so much as a good-fucking-bye, not even a fuck you, a get a life, peace out—nothing, nada.*

He put his number in the phone. She kissed his cheek and got up to walk away.

Kidd watched her ass as it disappeared into the crowd. Why didn't his brother like her? What made Shay-D snap at her?

"Is it something I'm not seeing?" he asked himself. All he saw was Vee's face, her smile, her magnificent shape. He wanted to feel the warmth of her hands rubbing his waves. She had this goofy smile that he loved. She would show you all thirty-two teeth and brighten up the whole room. He wanted to feel her legs wrapped around him. He used to watch her sleep and wonder how he got so lucky.

How could God have known to place her with him? She could have landed anywhere in the world, but she ended up with him. Now she was gone, and she had taken his heart with her. He didn't even want it back; it would be of no use to him. He never wanted to feel that kind of pain again. He was a thoroughbred killer to the depths of his soul, but love had knocked him all the way off his square. Was he really going to try to replace Vee with a lookalike? No, there was no replacing Vee, but Raven would be better than nothing.

"Yo, Kidd! Come on, man. We finna take some pics!" Skillet yelled, bringing Kidd back to the here and now.

Kidd got up while walking to the picture booth. He could see Raven leaving the club with yet another beautiful woman. "Maybe, I can get in and make that trio one day," he said to himself as he reached his hand out to give a pound to the picture guy.

"What's the business, my dude?" he said, acknowledging the picture man.

"Not shit. You got it, big homie. How many y'all taking tonight?" the picture dude asked, knowing they always took at least ten pictures.

"I don't know. It's a celebration, so probably a lot." Kidd watched as Skillet and Shay-D argued about how to stand.

"Kaylin, how in the hell am I supposed to bend over in front of you?" She pointed to her stomach which was almost as big as her petite frame. She was five foot three, caramel colored, with big pretty brown eyes and was very beautiful. She refused to call him Skillet because she thought the name was ridiculous.

"Shit, you ain't have no problem this morning, did you?" he smirked.

"You know what? You sho' right. I didn't 'cause I'll get in any position as long as your face is in the right place." She put her hands on her hips waiting for his response while everybody laughed at him.

"You lucky you my main ho or yo' ass would be left right the fuck here," Skillet joked.

She turned beet red and put her finger in his forehead. "Nigga, you know damn well you ain't got no stable of hoes nowhere. I shut all that shit down. Yo' head be so far up my ass, nobody can tell where you start and stop. This discussion could go on for forever, and I'm still gon' be right, so let's go on and take this picture."

She stood in front of him. He wrapped his arms around her belly and kissed her neck. She pushed her ass into his crotch. She was his heart, and she was right too. She was the only woman that was able to talk to him like that. That shit made his dick hard as concrete.

"I feel that."

"You like it, though, don't you?" he said while rubbing his hardness across her butt.

"I love it." She smiled at the thought of what was to come when they got home.

This only made Kidd miss Vee even more. She was fun like that. When she left, she took his smile, his laughter, and his heart with her.

Chapter 16

Happily Never After

"You ready for this?" Raven asked her latest victim as she lay sprawled across the bed in nothing but a diamond-studded thong.

"Yeah, mami. You ready for me?" the girl asked as she made Raven a special drink, standing at the bar in some six-inch stilettos that wrapped all the way up her legs stopping midthigh. This was all Raven wanted her in. She had a fetish about sexing in heels.

"Come over here," Raven said to the girl.

She walked over and gave Raven a shot of 1800 Tequila. Raven threw it back. Ole girl lay there with a sneaky-looking smirk on her face. The girl climbed on top of Raven, waiting patiently. She didn't have to wait too long for the strong liquor and the number of pills she had put in the drink to begin to take effect almost immediately. Raven started getting a horrible headache as a look of pure confusion masked her face. Her head started to spin. She thought Vee was trying to come through and ruin her fun. But it was the liquor and the strong narcotics making her go away. Raven could no longer fight the feeling to fall asleep. The young girl had crushed the pills before putting them in a shot glass to make Raven feel it quicker, but she didn't expect it to be this quick.

"Wha . . . What's going on?" Vee shook her head, trying to get the feeling out of it.

The room started to spin, and her vision got blurrier and blurrier. She was trying to concentrate on the person in front of her, but blurry vision and her quaking skull wouldn't let her.

"Yeah, bitch, you thought you got away with what you did to my fuckin' sister!" she yelled as she jumped up and snatched Valencia off the bed, and she then kicked her in the throat and watched as she collapsed to the floor. Valencia couldn't breathe as she held on to her throat. She hurt so bad that she couldn't even cry. All the sound and feeling was knocked right out of her. The girl walked over to the door to let her sister in. Valencia could hear the two talking, but she was too scared to open her eyes. She feared she would see what was going to happen next. Even if she could see, she probably wouldn't be able to tell who it was. Raven had so many victims that it was ridiculous. Most of them never made it out of the room . . . except for one.

Raven was at Bottoms Up Strip Club, getting a VIP from this stallion of a woman named Portia. This chick fit the word *stallion* to a tee . . . long, dark chocolate legs with an ass so big it looked like another human was growing on the back of her. Raven was in heaven as this goddess gave her some mean head. She couldn't tell if the woman was trying to get a big tip or make her marry her. Just too bad she was tweakin' like a fiend that night. She let loose about six explosive orgasms before she stopped Portia. She had to taste it before she off'd her. It looked like it tasted too good to not, at least, test it out. Raven gave her a good tongue-lashing before she pulled out her goody bag. She always had it with her. The guard let her in with it because she promised to let him use her toys on her before she left, which was a lie because she wouldn't dare let a man touch her. She put on her strap-on dildo, bent Portia over, and went to work on the pussy like it was going to disappear if she didn't hit hard. Portia was screaming and loving how she felt. She was squeezing her eyes shut so tightly she didn't see the rope go around her neck. Then, her eyes popped open as she tried her best to fight Raven off her. But Raven had superhuman powers when she was in the zone. So the girl thought her best bet would be to fake dead. After another twenty seconds, she just dropped down. But she was scared as shit when Raven didn't stop pumping. "Please God, let me make it out of this mess, and I promise I will never do this again." And she meant that shit. Raven finally stopped pumping, got up, and put her clothes on. Lucky for her, there was a fight, and the guard had left the door open, so she was able to sneak out.

"You remember me, bitch? You left me for dead. But I'm back, bitch, and on some straight get back type of shit." She punched Vee in the face, and all the lights went out.

"Uh-uh, bitch, you gonna feel this ass kicking! Go get me some water and wake this ho up. Better yet, I got a better idea." She bent over and pulled her pants down and began to piss on Vee's face. This woke her up instantly. She didn't know what the hell was going on, but all she saw pussy and ass in her face. She tasted the tangy piss running into her mouth.

"What . . . are . . . you doing?"

She could barely get the sentence out. This had to have had something to do with Raven. *Just like that ole scandalous bitch to get me into some shit and run away like a fuckin' coward,* Valencia thought.

"Ahhh, please, stop!" she begged while trying to protect herself as they rained punch after punch at her.

They stomped every part of her body. Good thing she was drugged because she surely would have died on the spot if she felt that twelve-by-four-inch impersonation of a dildo go into her ass. While one sister fucked her in the ass, the other continued stomping her until blood was everywhere. When they were done, they just looked at her lying there, lifeless, and left her the same way Raven had left the other sister . . . *for dead.* Vee didn't stand a chance. She never even had a chance to defend herself. She figured Raven must have really fucked this bitch over for her to come back hard as she did.

Valencia finally woke up. Trying to move was like stabbing herself everywhere at the same time. It hurt like hell seeing her whole body covered in bruises, and big blood clots sticking to her skin made her want to vomit. Trying to crawl to the phone but unable to move, she just lay there crying her heart out. What could she have possibly done in her past life to deserve such treatment? Her whole life, people have been hurting her, and now it seemed as though she couldn't stop hurting herself. She wished they would have just ended her misery.

"Why would you do this me?" she cried, talking to Raven who, at the moment, seemed to have disappeared. Maybe she didn't want to feel the pain, so she let Vee take it all in. Vee lay there for close to three hours just crying and crying and crying. She had cried so much she started to dry heave, and that only added more pain to her head and damn near collapsed chest. Finally, she found enough strength to reach for the phone. She dialed Sena's number and got no answer. She figured as much because she didn't answer unknown numbers. She remembered telling Sena that she needed to stop that stupid shit. What if it was an emergency? She dialed the next person she figured she could count on.

"Hello."

Silence.

"Yo, who the fuck is this?" It was three-thirty in the morning. He was drunk as shit, irritable, and very horny.

"Moo . . . Moochie, I need help," she said barely above a whisper.

"Who is this?" he questioned, sitting up in bed. He swore it sounded like Vee.

"It's Vee. I need help."

"What's wrong?" He looked around the living room to see if Kidd was still there, but he was gone to his room. The last thing he remembered was he and Kidd walking through the door and his face landing on the big fluffy pillow on the couch.

"I need you to come get me and please don't tell Kidd. I don't want him to see me like this." She cried some more. "Please, I didn't have anybody else to call." She was in so much pain. Every move she made took her breath away.

"Where are you?" Sobriety quickly consumed him. His heart felt like it was about to beat out of his chest. He got up and walked out the door of Kidd's house before he could try to come along.

"I don't know . . ."

He stopped walking. "How am I supposed to find you if you don't know where you at?" He was getting worried because she didn't sound too good . . . sounded like she's holding on to her last breath.

If he only knew.

"I'm at a hotel. Wait a min—" She looked at the phone. It read Airport Holiday Inn.

"I'm at the Holiday Inn by the airport." She was out of breath and ready to pass out again.

"What room you in?"

"I don't know, I don't know, I don't know." She started crying, about to lose her mind as she looked around at the blood that was caked all over her body. "I can't walk to the door." Moochie's attempt at staying calm was fruitless, since patience wasn't his strong suit.

"Fuuuuck!" he screamed while banging his fists against the steering wheel. He took a deep breath. "I need a room number, baby girl. I need you to try to get to the door. I'm about ten minutes away. Do you think you can crawl to the door?"

"Hold on."

Placing the phone's receiver down, willing herself to get up. She reached the door handle and turned it, but let it go when she heard people walking past. She wouldn't dare let anybody see her like that. Opening the door, she looked up at the sign that said 166. Slowly, she made her way back to the phone.

"Room 166. I'll leave it open so I won't have to get back up." She couldn't bear the thought of moving again.

"Okay. I'm on my way now. I'll be there in two minutes." He heard something hit the floor before he got a response. "Hello! Vee! Hello!"

She had passed out again. The pain was much too unbearable.

He couldn't wrap his head around the situation. Why hadn't she called Sena or even Kidd? Where had she disappeared to?

Moochie approached the door cautiously, not sure of what he was walking into. His heart was beating in overdrive. He wasn't sure what a heart attack felt like, but he thought he was close to it. Vomit instantly rushed to the back of his throat from the fumes coming from the room. The stench of feces, urine, vomit, and blood mixed is a smell he couldn't even begin to describe. He looked around with his gun drawn in case some more shit popped off, but he didn't see Valencia. All he saw was blood all over the floor. He thought his heart was about to burst through his chest.

"Vee!" He called her name but didn't get an answer. Sliding his body against the wall like a soldier at war, he was preparing himself for anything . . . except for what lay on the other side of the bed. He dropped to his knees and crawled over to where Vee was lying. Gingerly, he turned her over to assess the damage. He felt as if his heart was about to beat its way through his chest cavity. Her left eye was swollen shut, and her jaw looked like it was totally disconnected from the rest of her face. Softly, he shook her to see if she was still conscious, causing her to wince in pain.

"I'm sorry. I didn't mean to hurt you. I was just making sure you were still alive. What happened?"

She opened her one good eye and started crying all over again. "Help me, please . . ." She barely got those words out before her lungs felt like they were on fire. It broke his heart to see her this way. This was way worse than he had imagined. Whoever did this had to have hated her because he himself would have just shot a nigga and been done with it, unless his hand called for drastic measures.

"Can you call Sena again? I need somebody to help me into the tub," she said, wrapping her arms around his waist. He was kneeling to pull her up to his chest.

"Yeah. What's the number?" With a million things flowing through his head, he really hoped she answered the phone. He didn't know if he would be able to handle this alone. He picked up the hotel phone, but she pushed it away.

"She won't answer a number she doesn't know."

"She doesn't know mine either." She gave him a look as if to say, *yeah, right.*

He dialed her number.

"She didn't answer. You don't have anybody else?" He sounded exhausted.

"I thought I called him." She started crying again.

"Yeah, you right, you did. I'll help you. First, let's get to another room. I'll see if the room next door is available." He knew that he wouldn't be able to take that smell too much longer.

He lay her on the bed before he left the room. He had managed to wrap a sheet around her. When they got to the next room, he knew he would have to be the one to help her get all that blood and shit off her. He had to. He knew his brother would have wanted someone to help her even if that person had to look at her naked. But he was going to try his best to block that part out of his mind.

Going back into the room, he picked her up off the bed and carried her into the bathroom and gently lay her down in the tub. As he unwrapped the sheet, fury and rage rushed through his body. He tensed up, and his muscles flexed on every part of his body. He couldn't believe somebody had violated her this way. He had done some shit to a few niggas in his day, but damn! Somebody really worked her over. There was a bruise going down her back, and, even with her dark skin, you could still see the bruise clear as day. He couldn't pull his eyes away from all the bruises. He could feel her body shaking. He looked up to see her staring at him and crying. She knew she looked bad but didn't know it was *that* bad. The way he was looking at her made her feel like the Grim Reaper was speeding her way.

"It's all right," he said, trying to comfort her and himself.

"No, it's not. I don't know what I did to deserve this." She continued crying.

"Can you tell me what happened?"

"I don't know . . . can't remember. I woke up, and there were two women in here punching and kicking me. I didn't even know who they were."

"How did you get here?"

"I don't know," she lied, knowing it had something to do with Raven.

He reached and grabbed the towel and soap off the sink and started to scrub the blood off her gently. All she could do was lie there and watch as the blood ran down the drain. She couldn't even find the words to say to him. Looking in his eyes, she could see that he was angry, disgusted, and scared as hell. She hurt so badly all over, she could barely lift any limbs.

He would wait till she was ready to talk. She could feel him lifting her arms and washing her. She lay there, just watching as he gently rubbed the towel all over her body, cleaning like a scared parent would. Silently, tears fell from her eyes. She couldn't believe Raven did this to her. She swore on her life she'd die before she let that bitch out to play with her life again. She didn't even notice he was cleaning down below her waist. Her whole body was so numb. She wondered what he was thinking. Did he still look at her the same? Was he going to run and tell Kidd? Where the fuck was Sena? Everything was going a mile a minute in her head. Then, the thought of the beating flashed through her head. It was like watching a scary movie over and over again.

"I need you stand up," he said, snapping her out of her thoughts. She reached her hands out for him to help her stand up. Looking at her body again, he couldn't think sexual thoughts even if he wanted to. It looked like some shit off a horror movie. If it wasn't for him seeing her before all this and the little spots that weren't bruised, he would have never known what color she was. Looking at her face was very hard for him. The beauty it once held was now replaced with purple and black bruises and a lot of swelling. He began to wash her back. He couldn't help but feel sorry for her *and* the muthafuckas who did it, because this was not going down without revenge. That's if she even *knew* who did the shit.

"Are you going to go the hospital?"

"I think that I need to. It feels like I have couple of broken ribs and they also did a number on my ass. I'm sure you can see and smell it," she said with a slight chuckle of sarcasm, but he didn't find shit funny. He sure as hell did smell it, and it smelled to high hell, but he would never tell her that.

"As soon as we get you cleaned up."

"I don't have any clothes. They took my clothes." The tears just kept flowing.

Who the fuck is they? he thought.

"I'll go run and grab you something to wear. You think you can finish cleaning yourself?" He asked with a worried look on his face. He didn't really want to leave her alone again.

"Yeah, I'll just stand here and let the water run on me until you come back. But you're covered in blood. I don't suggest you go out like that." Taking heed, he looked down but didn't care.

"Man, I'll be right back." He ran to the Walmart about ten minutes away and grabbed her and him a pair of sweatpants, a pack of tank tops, her some ugly-ass granny panties, and some flip-flops. He had flipped his clothes inside out as if that even helped any. He still looked like he worked in a slaughterhouse. He was gone twenty minutes flat. He got back thinking she would be ready to push out, but she was still standing in the same spot in a daze. Looking but not really looking, thinking but not really thinking. Just there. It seemed as if her body was there, but her mind was somewhere else. She hadn't heard him come in.

"Why would you do this to me? What did I ever do to deserve this? First, you practically take my life. Then, you take the one man I love, and now this. Why didn't you just kill me?" She was talking to herself, and Moochie could hear it all.

"Who you talking to?" He looked around, but there was nobody there. He was hoping she didn't start that crazy shit again.

"God," she said point-blank.

He helped her slowly get out of the tub. Walking over to the bed, she looked at the clothes.

"I just grabbed the first things I saw. I thought you might want to be more comfortable than fashionable."

"It's okay. Thank you. You don't know how much I thank you for all this. You didn't have to answer the phone, but you did. You didn't have to come, but you did. You didn't even have to help clean me, but you did. Why would you do all this for me when I left your brother without so much as a good-bye?" She turned to him. He was sitting in a chair across the room with his head bowed.

"This had nothing to do with my brother. My *sister* needed my help, and I'm here, plain and simple." He looked at her. She just stood there looking at him looking at her. He wasn't lusting over her body like she was used to men doing. He was doing everything in his power to hold back the horror in his eyes. He walked over to her and began helping her put on her clothes. He had misjudged on the panties measurement. They were a bit snug, but they would have to do.

When they got to the hospital, as usual, a million questions were being asked, and no medical care was being administered. Moochie had to step out of the room while they examined her, like he hadn't seen it all already. By this time, it was about nine o' clock in the morning, so he decided to try Sena again, and he needed to tell his brother about this. He knew his brother would want to be there with her.

"Hello!" she answered very irritated

"Uh, Sena. This Moochie."

"I know who it is. What do you want?" He had to look at the phone, but he checked himself because he was getting ready let her ass have it, but there were bigger problems.

"I'm at the hospital with Vee. Can you come down here with her? I have to get going."

"Vee? Hospital? What happened? How did you end up with her? What hospital you at? Can I speak to her?" Her body was moving without her knowledge. She was going through a full Code Blue while she put on her clothes, and didn't she even know the half of it. Grabbing her keys, she was out the door before he could finish the sentence.

"St. Johns."

"I should have known that. That girl would rather go to her grave than go to any other hospital."

"Can you come?" He was almost pleading.

"Yeah, I'm in my car." She threw on a Juicy Couture sweat suit and was on the road in two minutes.

"A'ight. She in room 929."

"Wait a minute! Isn't that like ICU?"

"Yeah. We been calling you since four this morning. It's bad. Man, just come on." He hung the phone up not feeling her attitude. She had the right to be mad at him, but today wasn't the day for that shit.

"Sir?"

Moochie turned around to find a fine little nurse was calling him.

"Is everything all right?"

She couldn't help looking him up and down. "Your sister is looking for you. You may go in now."

"Thank you." He walked past her not giving her a second look. His mind was on Vee and helping her get through this.

"Hey! How you feeling?" He stood above her. He could tell her spirit had been broken, but was it before all this happened? He still had tons of questions running through his mind.

"I've been better," she answered still not able to look him in the eyes.

"I finally got in touch with Sena. She's on her way."

"That's good. You can go if you're in a rush. I understand. I've taken up a lot your time." She was feeling very weak and honestly didn't know how much longer she could fake being all right. Her head was spinning, and she was beginning to feel disoriented and nauseated. The morphine had taken a lot of the pain away, but not all of it.

"It's not a problem at all. I'll wait till she gets here. I don't want to leave you alone in this cold-ass hospital. I know I wouldn't want to be alone in a situation like this," he said, looking around. "My mother was in the hospital off and on for years, dying of cancer, and we stayed with her. Every day, either me or Kidd was with her. She once told me being in the hospital alone breaks your spirit. With no one around to tell you everything will be all right, you start thinking all kinds of crazy stuff. Listening to doctors twenty-four hours a day telling you what's wrong with you, and no one there to counter with what's right with you, all you think is negative. I think that's part of the reason she died."

"I thought you said you all were there every day?" Vee said just above a whisper.

"Yeah, my brother and I were, but my father never came, not once, not even to say good-bye." He got a little choked up at the memory of his mom in the hospital bed helpless.

"I'm sorry to hear that."

"Don't be. At first, I was a little mad at her 'cause I thought she gave up."

"You don't still believe that, do you?"

"No. I believe she died of a broken heart. No matter what the doctors told her. She would always say, 'When your father comes, everything will be all right.' That's all she wanted was for the family to be together. I don't know, maybe that would have made her feel better; maybe it wouldn't have. But I do know she didn't get sick until my father left and the doctors started treating her."

"What kind of person was she?"

"She was June Cleaver to the tenth power," he laughed. "She cooked, cleaned, read to us, taught us how to play sports, taught us about women. She was Superwoman. I say love was her kryptonite."

"No, it wasn't. It was her love for you two that kept her going as long as she did."

"I guess," he mumbled, looking down at the floor.

"Look at Mr. Moochie! He does have a softer side." They both shared a laugh.

"Aye, can I just ask you a question? Why didn't you call Kidd?"

She knew the questions were going to start soon. "I didn't know how he would react to me calling."

"Shit! He would have been happy as hell to hear from you . . . to, at least, know you was still alive." Rubbing his hands down his face, every time he closed his eyes, he saw her bruised body and all the blood.

"I know. I've missed him like crazy. I just couldn't bring myself to call him after the way she—I mean—I did him."

"How did you get to the hotel?" Moochie just looked at her.

"I was at home asleep and the next thing I know, I'm getting my ass kicked in a hotel room."

"Sooo, you have some kind amnesia or something?"

"I don't know. Maybe," she said, hunching her shoulders. "I don't feel so well . . ." Her words faded as her head fell back and her eyes rolled around in the back of her head. She had lost a lot of blood.

"Nurse!" Moochie screamed as he ran to the door.

It seemed like every nurse and doctor in the hospital came running once they heard *Code Blue in 929 STAT.* He didn't know what that meant but knew it had to be serious. They started pushing Moochie out of the room.

"Sir, we need a moment," the nurse said before shutting the door in his face. About ten minutes later, they were all walking out, but one of the doctors stopped to talk to Moochie.

"What's your name, sir?" The doctor stuck his hand out for a shake.

"Deshawn Brown, sir." He reached out to shake it.

"And you are Miss Ball's brother, correct?"

"Yes, sir. Please, what's wrong?" He had panic written all over his face.

"She has lost a lot of blood and is bleeding internally. We need to operate to find the source of the bleeding. She is a very strong young lady. Someone slipped her a date rape drug and somehow tripled its potency. To be honest, she should have thanked them for that."

"What?" Moochie couldn't believe this muthafucka said some dumb-ass shit like that.

"Don't misunderstand me, sir. Without that drug, I'm sure she would have died hours ago given the kind of pain she is in. She would have more than likely had a heart attack or went into shock. Without the drug, she would have felt everything done to her. We've managed to stabilize her for the moment. You can go in until we get an operating room prepared. She is currently in a medically induced coma until we get an operating room available." He patted Moochie on the shoulder as he walked away. Moochie just stood there, not believing everything that was going on.

Chapter 17

Broken Wings

Sena walked off the elevator, looking and smelling good. She looked him dead in the eyes and turned to head toward Vee's room. Moochie ran up behind her trying to catch her before she saw Vee, but he was a moment too late. When she saw how Vee looked, her knees buckled and it felt like all the blood had rushed to her head. Luckily, she wasn't that far away from Moochie because surely she would have hit the floor. She was hysterical, feeling like she was hyperventilating and needed a seat. There was her best friend, lying up in a hospital bed, bandaged from head to toe, and most of the bandages were soaked with blood. She had tubes and machines attached to damn near every hole in her body. It was unbearable to look at. Sena's chest heaved as if she were pushing the weight of the world up and down. She was trying to stand, but Moochie was still literally holding her up. Her legs wouldn't move. They just wobbled under her. The sight before her was horrible, and Sena was mortified. No matter how many tears clouded her eyes, they could never take away what she was looking at.

"What happened to her? Oh my God!"

She was barely breathing as she walked over to the bed. He pulled a chair up for her. She looked at her dear friend as the tears ran down her face. The only family she had was lying up in a hospital bed in God knew how much pain. When they were only about fourteen, Vee came to live with her family because her own mother was too far gone on drugs. Then, when they were eighteen, Sena's mother passed away from breast cancer, leaving just the two of them to take care of each other.

"Where did you go? What happened to you? Why would somebody do this to you? I don't understand," she said, crying as she held and kissed Vee's bruised hands. "Why didn't you call me? How did you get here?" she quizzed Moochie.

"She called me when she couldn't reach you," he said, looking at her, hoping his answer didn't make feel her worse that she wasn't there for her girl. Vee had never asked her for anything but friendship, and she couldn't even come through for her the one time she needed her.

"Oh. Why didn't she call Kidd?" She wiped her face with the sleeve of her jacket.

The doctor and about three nurses came rushing into the room.

"Okay, you two have to wait here. We'll update you in a little bit," the doctor said while pushing Valencia out the door to the operating room.

"Where are they taking her?" Sena asked as tears started to flow freely down her face once again.

"To the operating room. They say she lost a lot of blood, and she's hemorrhaging internally."

"What happened?"

After he gave her the rundown on what happened, Code Blue would be an understatement on how she was feeling. All the color drained instantly from her face.

"You want me to stay with you?" he asked, already knowing she wouldn't want to be alone.

"Would you?"

"Yeah, let me go make a phone call, and I'll be right back."

Sena put her hand to her face to wipe away the tears that seemed to have no end.

Moochie walked out of the room, dreading the phone call he was about to make. He didn't know how his brother was gon' take the news. He pressed the number one and send on his phone and waited for Kidd to answer.

"What's the business? Where you run off to this morning, nigga—"

Moochie cut him off. "I'm at the hospital."

"What happened? Are you all right? Which one? I'm on my way." Kidd rattled off question after question without letting Moochie answer any of them. Going into full panic mode, there's three things Kidd does not play about: his brother, his crew, and his money, in that order.

"Naw, I'm good, kinda, in a way. It's Vee, man."

Kidd just knew he heard his younger brother wrong. "Vee?" He scrunched up his face.

"Yeah, man. She in St. John's Hospital, and it's bad."

"Why *you* there?" Kidd was feeling some kind of way about that.

"She called me about three-thirty this morning to come help her, and when I got there, she was lying in a big-ass pool of blood."

Kidd could hear his brother's voice crack slightly. His heart went out to her, but this had nothing to do with him. At least, that was what he was trying to convince himself of.

"So what you telling me for?" Kidd was done with her.

"What the fuck you mean what I'm telling you for? Because you need to bring yo' stupid ass up here and be with her!" Moochie yelled heatedly.

"Naw, I'm good. Tell her to call whoever she disappeared with to come up there, or, better yet, you stay. Apparently, you who she wanted around." He was a little jealous that she had called his brother and not him. His emotions were in a whirlwind. He didn't know if he was angry at her or scared for her.

"She called me because she was afraid of the way you would react, and I don't blame her. She's in the fucking hospital on her deathbed, and all you can think about is who she called first. I thought you would want to run to her like I did and help her get through this, but I see you still on that li'l kid shit. So, if you looking for me, this where I'll be. You can handle things without me, right?"

Click

Moochie hung up. He couldn't wrap his head around how his brother responded. He didn't even ask if she was all right or nothing. Kidd claimed he loved her and she was the one. How could you turn your back on someone you love? He couldn't even fathom it. Because if you had a place in Moochie's heart, hell, even if you were in his life, that meant he had love for you, and he wouldn't hesitate to help you through anything. He knew his brother was hurt from the way she disappeared, but you don't just turn love on and off like a light switch. Shit. Apparently, she had been in some kind of trouble. If he loved her the way he said he did, he would have been on his way to hospital before Moochie was able to finish his sentence.

Moochie took a deep breath as he walked back into the room to keep Sena company. Sena was sitting in the windowsill, rocking side to side, hugging herself, crying, and praying all at the same time. He walked over to her, then picked her up and walked over to the bed to lay her down. He lay down behind her and held her tightly as she cried silent tears for her friend. He could feel her body vibrate as she cried. Not able to imagine life without Vee, it felt as if the air was being sucked right out of her lungs. This is exactly what Moochie was trying to avoid. He knew, from the first time he met Sena, that she was a winner, freakiness and all. They clicked well together,

and the chemistry was there. That was why he had never
called. He wasn't ready for love yet. He didn't think he
was ready for an emotional attachment. But no matter
where you run, love will find you in the strangest places.

Kidd was driving down the highway feeling like he
couldn't breathe. Tears were burning the rims of his eyes.
What his brother had said kept replaying in his head,
*"She on her deathbed, and all you can think about is who
she called first."*

Deathbed?

Knowing he was wrong for what he said, he quickly
made a U-turn when Moochie had called. And honestly,
he didn't mean it. He was already on the way while his
little brother gave him the business.

Actually, he wasn't that far away. He was at his boss's
house out in a small community called Town and Country,
buying his freedom. He was officially out of the game and
a legal man. He had made it out unscathed. Not many
men could say the same. Although, technically, he wasn't
in the game. But still, he participated in some dangerous
affairs. He was young and a millionaire. Now, all he
needed was his queen, but it looked like she might not
make it to see his dreams come true. He still wanted to
share his dreams with her. She said she wanted a house
full of kids, ten to be exact, and he was cool with that.
They wouldn't have to struggle to care for them. So he
could see a house full of kids that looked just like her. He
wanted that life with her. Kidd started laughing at how
his brother put his check game down. For one, he would
get his ass kicked, and two, he loved and respected his
brother too much. "She can't die. God can't be that cruel
to bring her back to me just to snatch her away . . . again."
He was driving in silence as he let his favorite song "I
Can't" by Lyfe Jennings, lead the way to the hospital.

He hesitated before walking into the hospital. He honestly didn't know if he could take her being taken away again. He stopped at the nurses' station and got her room number. As he got closer to the room, his legs felt like they weighed a ton. He stopped short of her room. He paced back and forth outside the door, not knowing what to say or do. He knew his brother hadn't told her what he said. That was a given. He just didn't know what to expect. What the hell does knocking at death's door look like? As he walked in, he only saw one bed, but it contained Moochie and a crying Sena. Moochie was holding her and rocking her back and forth. He instantly felt bad. Sena was crying like Vee was already dead. He took a seat on the other side of the room and looked around, hoping they had taken Vee somewhere as he prayed it wasn't the morgue. He didn't want to disturb them with questions right then. He just sat there, watching them, as the tears started to run freely down his face. Shaking his head, he whispered, "Not the morgue. Please, God." No, it couldn't be that bad . . . could it? He thought again as he watched Sena start to get up.

"I need to get some air," she said, feeling like the walls were closing in on her.

"You want me to come with you?"

"No, somebody should be here when she comes out of recovery. I don't want her to be alone."

"I'll be here."

They both were surprised to see Kidd sitting there in the window seat with a tear-streaked face.

"How long you been here?" Sena asked as she got up to walk over to him. She stood to give him a hug. Moochie just sat there, not really saying anything. He was happy that his brother got his head out of his ass, put his pride aside, and came to the hospital.

"Not long, maybe about ten minutes."

"You been sitting here that long and didn't say any-thing?" questioned Sena.

"I didn't want to interrupt. You looked like you had a lot on your mind."

"Right. Did you hear anything?" she asked, hoping he had good news.

"Nah, they just told me the room number."

"What's up, man?" Kidd looked at Moochie.

"Not shit. What's good?" he said a little too dry, Sena noticed.

"Okay, I'm gonna say this shit right now because I don't know what's going on between you two, but you niggas better get it together. My best friend will be back from surgery any time now, and she doesn't need you two adding to her pain so get that shit out now!" She looked at both of them, neither one said anything. She just had a way of speaking her mind and making you listen.

"We good, ma. Don't trip. You ready to go outside?" Moochie stood up and walked out the door before Sena got a chance to say anything else. He was feeling some kind of way about the whole situation. He and his brother watched every day as their mother cried and prayed night after night that their father would walk through those hospital doors and tell her everything was going to be okay. Moochie didn't think it was the cancer that killed her so quickly. It was a broken heart in his opinion. Because, not once did she ever ask if she was getting better, if there was any change. No, all she wanted to know was if her husband had shown up. Maybe he was a little angrier because he saw Vee when it first happened. And he couldn't erase that horrible sight for nothing in the world.

"Moochie, man, let me holla at you," Kidd yelled.

"I'll be in the hall," Sena told Moochie as he walked back in the room. Kidd knew when his little brother was uptight about something, and it didn't sit well with him that he was the reason of him feeling this way.

"What's up?" Moochie asked nonchalantly.

"Look. My bad about earlier. I was still mad at her for not calling me and leaving me the way she did. You know I would never shit on her like that. You know me better than anyone. My pride just got in the way of my feelings. I knew I was coming, though. It just felt a little good to act like I didn't care," he said, hunching his shoulders and sitting back down.

"It's cool, man. It's not you. It's just, when I found her in that room, it was like Momma all over again. But this was way worse. Somebody did her dirty, dude, and I mean straight fucked her up really bad. Every time I close my eyes, I see her lying on the floor caked up in blood. Then, when I put her in the shower to get some of the blood off, my blood got to boiling. There is not a spot on her body that is not bruised."

Shower? Kidd thought. He knew his brother would never do him dirty, so he just listened to the rest of the story.

"So that's why you left in a hurry this morning? When I came out of the bathroom, you was gone."

"Yeah, she had called and told me not to tell you because she didn't want you to see her like that. I don't think you would have been able to take it. You got more invested in her than I do. I was looking from a brother's point of view, but you would have been looking from a lover's point. And if I know you like I think I know you, you probably would have hit the roof. You know I was gonna tell you. I just had to get the whole story first."

"So did she tell you why she disappeared?"

"Naw. Didn't get a chance. Hell! She couldn't tell me what happened. She said one minute she was 'asleep,' and the next she woke up in a hotel room getting her ass kicked by two chicks."

"So she wasn't raped or nothing, was she?"

Moochie looked away not able to look his brother in the eyes.

"Come on, man. Don't hold out on me." Kidd's whole body went completely numb at the thought. He couldn't imagine another man being inside of her. He was her first. Her one and only, and he wanted it to stay that way. He knew he was thinking selfishly, but he didn't care. The thought alone made his heart hurt even worse than it already did. He was hurting all the way to his soul. Someone was going to feel his wrath tenfold.

"Well, sorta, kinda." Moochie couldn't seem to find the words.

"Fuck you mean 'kind of'? Either she was or she wasn't." Every muscle in Kidd's body felt like it was on fire. He felt it in the pit of his stomach. He was about to send someone to their Maker.

"Well, from what I saw, they did a number on her ass."

The room was spinning and seemed as though the walls were closing in on him fast. He had to grab hold of the walls to keep from falling. He couldn't explain the feeling that was flowing through him. He felt hot and numb at the same time.

Punching a hole in the wall, he yelled, "Fuuuuuuuccck!" causing Sena to run back in the room, followed by two nurses.

"Is everything all right?" the women asked in unison.

"Yeah, we cool. My brother just a little upset about his girl. That's all."

In walked a doctor. "Deshawn Brown?" The doctor looked back and forth between the two men. He wasn't the same doctor that had spoken with Moochie prior to Valencia being rushed to surgery.

"Yeah, what's going on?" Moochie turned around to face the doctor. Sena sat on the bed to brace herself.

Then, she stood up, and then she sat back down. By then, the men were looking at her. She stood back up, then sat back down. She didn't know what to do with herself.

Moochie's heart went out to her because he couldn't fathom the thought of his brother being taken away. He walked over to her and put his arms around her to help hold her up. Kidd walked on the other side of her.

"We were able to find the bleeding and stop it. Her colon was also badly ripped. We were able to repair most of the damage. However, we were unable to wake her up from the anesthesia."

Moochie tightened his grip, and Sena's body shook so bad it looked like she was having a seizure. Kidd had to find a seat quickly, his legs felt so wobbly, and his heart felt like it was about explode.

"Don't go planning any funeral arrangements. It may just be an allergic reaction to the anesthesia. We'll know for sure in a couple of hours. At the moment, she's in recovery now, and only one visitor at a time is allowed."

"We can see her?" Kidd asked, looking up.

"Yes, one at a time and only for a few minutes."

Sena's hyperventilating slowly turned into normal breaths as she thought about seeing her friend again. She started toward the recovery area feeling like she was walking *The Green Mile*. Just when she had her hand on the handle, a slew of nurses burst past her into the room and told them to stay out.

"What's happening now?" Kidd looked like he was about to throw up. He was just walking up to Sena and Moochie when he saw all the nurses and doctors fly into the recovery room. He had stayed a little longer in the room to prepare himself for his encounter with her. He missed her so much it scared him. His anxiety was at an all-time high. He didn't know if he wanted to hug and kiss her or yell at her from the top of his lungs.

Chapter 18

Secrets

On the other side of the door, Valencia had awakened. She was looking around and watching out of one eye as the nurses checked her vital signs and made sure she was cognitive, taking in her surroundings. The nurses were in their fresh uniforms, the tubes, the IVs, the smell of antibiotics, that awful hospital smell, the cold feeling, and the pain, she experienced them all. All she could do was let the one functioning eye cry. She cried for herself, for the pain, and for Raven. What could a person have done to deserve such a beating? She was thinking about the conversation she had just had with Raven. *"What did you do for them to beat me like that?"*

"I ain't do shit to that bitch. She was just jealous!"

"Don't forget, I've seen your work."

"Whatever," Raven dismissed her.

"You can't be that dumb. You can't be that damn stupid to think that this was done just out of jealousy. What made you this way? Why are you so fuckin' evil?"

"Bitch, you made me this way. You made me mean and evil, and a pussy licker, as you call it, with all that whining and crying. Why won't they stop teasing me? Can somebody please help me get away from this man? Why won't my momma help? You needed help, and there I was to take all your pain away. To make sure no one else was able to hurt you. Hurt us! I took in all

the abuse, the stankin'-ass kids teasing you 'cause you had piss stains on your clothes. The Uncle Bos, who would rather stick their dick in a child's mouth than the pussy of a grown-ass woman. That was me, bitch! Me! So you can judge me all you want. Fuck you. No, fuck that! Yeah, I like women because men disgust me. When I see men, all I see is the nasty old men who touched and fondled me as a child—not you, but me!"

Raven was now crying, but she went on. "But you know what's so crazy? I don't like for nobody to touch me. Hell! I beat women until they don't move no more. Now where that came from, I don't know. That's all your anger and rage, not mine. Then, you had the nerve to try to get rid of me. Why? When I did all that for you? When I went through all that shit for you because I knew you wouldn't make it without me?"

"How do you know I wouldn't have been able to get through any of that when you didn't give me a chance?"

"Who are you kidding? I mean, like, for real, in real life, for real, for real? You're too weak. I did all that for you. Don't I deserve to have a life, to live a little?"

"Look. I appreciate all that you have done, but, in the end, it's still my life. Besides, I never knew all of that was going on. You never said anything!"

"You damn right you didn't know because I protected you. I did, not your funky crackhead of a mother, not your dear friend Sena, not even that boy you like. But I'm the one you want to get rid of. What the fuck is wrong with that picture? Here I am, protecting you all your life, all your pathetic life, and now, you want to get rid of me. They don't even know you because, if they did, they would know that half the time they think they're talking to you, they're talking to me. You lived with Sena for years? Hmm . . . How do they love you so much but don't even know you're a fucking lunatic? Riddle me that," Raven said with an evil chuckle.

"You don't understand. If you get to live, when will I?"

"Baby, can you tell me your name and birthday?" a friendly looking older lady asked, breaking her out of her thoughts.

"Valencia Renée Ball. July13, 1982."

"Good. Who is the president of the United States?"

"My president is black," she sang hoarsely.

The nurse couldn't help but laugh. She felt as long as her patient was still able to make a joke and smile through all the tears, then they would be all right. Laughter was good for the soul.

"Okay. Good. We want you to rest before we allow your visitors to enter."

"Visitors? I have visitors with an 's'?"

"Yes, a young lady and a couple of fine young men. Girl, I don't even want to know how you picked one 'cause I would have taken them both. Honey chile, back in my day, one would have been my husband, and the other would have been what you youngins call my plan B."

Valencia wanted to laugh so bad but thought better of it. Even the slightest movement felt like a thousand knives digging into her. She knew it could only be Kidd and Moochie that would make her say such a thing. They were a fine duo.

"I'll come back in another hour to check on you." She started for the door.

"Wait! Can you please let me see Deshawn Brown first, please? If only for a few minutes, I need to talk to him first."

The nurse walked out of the room to find three anxious faces waiting for answers. Time seemed to stand still as the nurse walked up to them. With everyone holding their breath, it was like everyone exhaled at the same time when they saw her smile appear.

"She's awake. We don't want her to have any visitors for a while, but she really wants to talk to . . ." she paused as she looked at her clipboard. Sena just knew it was her, and Kidd wasn't so sure. "Deshawn Brown." Moochie looked surprised. He just knew she would want to have Kidd or Sena with her.

"Did she know I was out here?" Sena asked, full of attitude.

"Yes, she did, but she requested to see Mr. Brown," the nurse said, giving back the same attitude. "Now, back to you. You're only allowed about five minutes, and I'm counting, so make it quick. Everyone can visit in a few hours."

"What's up, ma?" he said, walking up to her bed and felt slight pain in his chest. It hurt him to see her this way.

"I just wanted thank you for everything," she said, trying to keep her composure. She was going through an emotional whirlwind.

"It was nothing. I would—" he started to say.

Valencia cut him off midsentence.

"I know. I know. You're Mr. Save-a-Ho. I just wanted to say thank you. I don't know how I could ever repay you." Now she was crying.

"I do. You could make my brother happy for the rest of his life." He tried to look her in her eyes. But one was still closed shut from the swelling, and the other was a blink away from being closed shut itself.

"I don't know that I can do that."

"Why not?" Moochie asked.

"I can't explain it right now."

"Well, when, then? Because I think I deserve a little explanation for all this," Moochie said, doing a sweeping motion with his arms.

"I know, and I will explain, but I don't think I can ever be with your brother." She was crying even harder at the thought of never being with Kidd again. The pain that filled her heart was a million times worse than what her body was feeling.

"Yo! You still haven't told me why the fuck not!" Moochie really didn't want to get mad, but she wasn't making it easy. Shit! This was his brother, and apparently she was playing with his feelings.

"Because . . . she . . . won't . . . fucking let meeeee!" she yelled out.

"Okay! This visit is over! You are not supposed to be upsetting her." The nurse burst through the doors.

"I'm sorry. I'm leaving." He gave one last look at Valencia and walked out of the room. He could hear her calling his name, but he just kept walking.

"Are you okay?" the nurse looked at her with concern.

"Yeah, I'm all right. I just need some rest. I don't want to see anyone for the rest of the day, please," she said, turning over on her side. The tears were flowing and seemed to not have an ending in sight.

"Okay, Ms. Ball has asked me to tell you all that she doesn't want any more visitors. She's a little upset." The nurse shot Moochie a dirty look, and everyone else did too.

"What y'all looking at me for? I ain't even do nothing." He rolled his eyes at them. Shit, screw them. All he was trying to do was help, he thought.

"Well, what were you two arguing about?" Sena needed to know.

"I asked her a question, and she couldn't answer, or rather, she wouldn't answer. I told her she had a lot of explaining to do, and she went all Sybil on me. She just needs time to rest and think." He didn't know what was going on with Vee, but she had better get her story straight real quick.

Sena sat down in the nearest chair. She didn't know what the hell was going on. First, Vee disappeared, and then, she showed up half-dead, Moochie ended up with her, and now no one could talk to her 'cause she was upset about something. She needed to talk to her like yesterday. But it would have to wait.

"Man, what happened in there?" Kidd wanted to know too, because he, also, wanted to see her.

"I told you. I asked her a question, and she flipped out talking 'bout *she* wouldn't let her be with you."

"*She?* Who the fuck is *she?*" Kidd asked with an almost worried look on his face.

"Fuck if I know, man. Just try to visit tomorrow," Moochie said, hunching his shoulders up.

"Wait a minute. She said that she wouldn't let her be with me?"

"Yeah."

"Remember that night she called I left to go to her house about three in the morning?"

"Yeah."

"She told me that night that she was going to come back. I asked her who was she, and she got real quiet and switched the subject."

"You think that's what happened to her?" Moochie looked at him like he was crazy.

"I don't know, man. I just know that she has mentioned this to me before. I got some thinking to do, so I'll see y'all tomorrow." He gave Sena a hug and kiss on the cheek and dapped Moochie.

Moochie took a squat down in front of Sena and pulled her chin up. He could see that she had been crying again, and her beautiful eyes were red and swollen.

"Are you gonna be all right?"

"I think so. I'll just sit here for a while to clear my head." She was so distraught she didn't know what to do with herself.

"You don't need to stay here by yourself. You should go home and get some rest." He hated seeing her this way.

"Naw, I think I'd rather be here than home alone. I'll be all right. You go on ahead and handle your business. Are you coming back up here tomorrow?"

She finally looked him in the eyes, and he could actually feel his heart start skipping beats. She was beautiful, even with puffy, red eyes. He wanted to hold her and tell her everything would be okay. He wanted to kiss her tears away and bring back that smile he hadn't seen in a while.

"Yeah, it may be in the evening."

"Okay. Thank you for everything, and thank you so much for being there for her. I'll never forgive myself for not being there for her. I let my ego get the best of me when you called. I'm sorry for having an attitude with you. I had no right to be that way," she said, defeated.

"It's good. Don't sweat the small stuff. I understand. Do you need anything before I leave?"

"Yeah."

"What's that?"

"For you not to leave me."

He knew and hoped this was coming; he was already prepared to stay with her. He knew she wouldn't want to be alone. He could honestly say he was glad she wanted him to be there with her.

"You want to follow me to my house or go to yours?" She smiled for the first time that day, and Moochie could feel her chipping away at that wall he had built many years ago.

Chapter 19

Where Do We Go from Here?

"You want something to drink?" Sena asked as they walked through her front door. She was so nervous she could feel her palms starting to sweat and her heart rate had gone into overdrive.

"Yeah, what you got?"

"Lemonade, Kool-Aid, Vitamin Water, and orange juice."

"Man, you gonna name everything in your refrigerator?" He was watching her as he stood in the doorway to the kitchen. She was moving a mile a minute, like she was supernervous. He admired her body and beauty from afar. He was willing himself not to sleep with her, but she wasn't making it easy on him. The way she moved around, her ass and titties were bouncing all over the place like they had a mind of their own.

"You asked me what I had. I keep a variety of drinks around, just in case I get a little thirsty," she said, turning around to find him leaning in the doorway looking superdelectable and sexy. She wanted him in the worst way, but she had to put her feelings in check because it was obvious he didn't feel the same way. After all, if he did, he would have called.

He also stood there, taking her all in. She was beyond sexy to him, even with puffy eyes and a sweat suit on.

"Well, I'll take some Kool-Aid. It don't taste syrupy, does it? You ain't one of them people who keeps pouring until sugar has filled half the pitcher, are you?" he laughed.

"Noooo, I measure, thank you very much." She handed him a cup.

Taking a sip, he said, "This is good. You don't find too many people who know how to make Kool-Aid that well."

"Well, if you had given me chance, you would have seen that I'm multitalented." It got real quiet. "I'm sorry. I shouldn't have said that. Make yourself at home while I shower. I smell like the hospital," she said while practically running past him.

He could tell that she was really nervous about him being so close. It was like all her sass ran away, and now she was like this shy little girl with a crush.

He walked around, taking in the décor. She had a nice little three-bedroom apartment. He looked in each room finding a computer room and a workout room. The last room was the bedroom, and it had sexiness all over the room, with a king-size canopy bed with black satin sheets and sheer black curtains that hung down the poles. It looked like there were a hundred candles all over the room, although none seemed to ever have been lit. They had the room smelling real good. He got comfortable on the bed and started flicking the channels on the forty-two-inch plasma screen that was mounted on the wall. He could hear the shower turn off just before she walked into the room soaking wet with nothing on. His dick damn near jumped out of his pants. He wanted to lick every drop of water off her body.

"Oh shit! I thought you were in the living room," she said as she ran back into the bathroom. She had no idea he had come into her bedroom or else she would have had a better entrance planned for him. He shocked her, so she did the first thing that came to mind—run.

"You ain't gotta run now. I done already seen it." He laughed so hard he had to sit up because lying down with a hard-on had started to hurt. It was hard as steel.

"Oh, shut up, you jerk! You weren't supposed to see anything in the first place," she yelled out the door, and then she walked out in a floor-length silk black robe and put on a little show with her hips for him with the fabric sticking to her body. He could see every curve.

Watching the show, he couldn't take his eyes off her.

"You know it's rude to stare." She walked around the room gathering the things she needed.

She laid her underwear and lotion on the bed, then lifted her leg to place her foot on the bed before she started to rub her Very Sexy Skin Body Butter by Victoria's Secret all over her body.

"I wasn't staring. I was just observing. There's a difference," he said. Then, he picked up the remote and started channel surfing again, crushing her little feelings.

I really do nothing for him, she thought.

"You know I could do that for you." He didn't even have to look her way to see the big-ass smile that spread across her face. He not looking gave her time to compose herself. "So is that a no?" he asked, turning his head to find a naked Sena sprawled across the bed much to his surprise. "So that's a yes, I take it?" he smiled at her.

"What do you think?" She handed him the lotion really wanting this rubdown. It had been way too long since a man had touched her body. She was done fantasizing. It was time for the real deal. Juices were already soaking her thighs from the thought. He got up off the bed to walk around to the other side where her legs were. She watched him take off his shirt, then drop his pants but kept his boxer briefs on. She could still see that wonderful-looking bulge and was ready to say, "Fuck the rubdown. Let's get this shit popping."

He picked up one of her legs and put it on his shoulder. He started to rub up and down her leg. He looked down at her pussy and could literally see the juices flowing from her love tunnel. He never knew his dick could get so hard. The head was starting to hurt. He put her leg down and picked up the other one and started rubbing that one. In heaven at this point, Sena's mind had gone into a different orbit. The feeling was so good she knew for sure she would come even before it started. She could feel him put her leg down. Then, his lips were on her stomach. Electricity shot up and through her body. He was now up to her breasts and was sucking away like a true professional. If they paid titty suckers, he could get top dollar.

"I've been wanting to do this ever since the first time I saw you in the mall," he told her in between kisses and licks to her neck.

"Well, what took . . . so . . . umm . . . long?" she managed to get out in between moans.

"I wasn't ready for this," Moochie explained. He was finally letting go, and he wanted to make love tonight. To see what the big deal was all about.

"What is this?"

"Love." He started kissing his way down her body, heading to her aching pussy. She could feel her heartbeat in her clit. Sopping up every juice that her body produced, he worked his tongue in and out all around, just driving her crazy until she came so hard it felt like her chest would explode. He slowly sat up and pulled down his boxers to unleash the beast. She had imagined what his dick would look like, but her imagination did him no justice. He had the most beautiful dick she had ever seen in her life. As he slid in, she came on contact. Feeling like he was literally ripping her apart, she didn't know whether to moan or cry out. Whatever the case, it was a welcomed confusion.

"Umm, shit, you feel so good, ma," Moochie said, trying his best not to nut too early. Her pussy had his dick in a choke hold. It felt like there was a suction cup at the end of her love tunnel. He had no choice but to hit bottom with every stroke.

"Ohh, yesssss. Right theeerrreee," she moaned with her eyes rolling around in the back of her head.

"Right there?" he asked, poking her spot, making her teeth clench.

"Yes, don't move. Stop moooo . . . vving." She half-pushed, half-pulled at him.

"What you mean stop moving? You want me to stop?" He stopped moving, teasing her clit with just the head of his dick.

"Don't stop. Keep moving. Stop playing." She dug her nails in his back.

"Umm-hmm . . . I thought so." He went to banging her spot and sucking both her titties at the same time.

"Oh my Ggggg oooo dddd!" she managed to say before her whole body locked, and she wasn't able to move her mouth to form another word. Once he felt her muscles come back to life, he went back into motion.

Making love until the wee hours of the morning after multiple orgasms for her and a few for him, she fell asleep sore and very satisfied, with him snoring very loud sounding like a bear. Before she fell asleep, she lay there and thought for a little while. Did he really mean it when he said he was feeling love for her? Where would they go from here? Should she expect something more from him after tonight? She didn't want to make it seem like since she gave up the goodies, he had to be with her. That wasn't the case. He satisfied her and was there for her when she needed him. She didn't want to trap him into a relationship. Hell, a rubdown every now and then would be cool with her. Even though she would love to have him in her life permanently, she didn't want him to feel forced. God knows she wanted him to stay. She wanted to offer him the world to stay, but she didn't want to come across as desperate. In her mind, she didn't deserve such a man. He was too good for her. She couldn't wait to tell Vee. She missed her girl like crazy. She needed her wisdom. Vee would talk to her and let her know that everything would be all right.

Moochie finally woke up in the middle of a bed that wasn't his. Now, he knew it wasn't a dream. He really had had sex with Sena. He stared at the ceiling, thinking about what this would mean. What would she be like now? Would she be cool just being friends? Does she want a relationship? He had been digging her since day one. *Fuck it. Just go with flow,* he thought as he got out of bed and headed for the shower. He looked down at his flaccid genitals that were glued to his thigh with sex juice. When he got to the bathroom, she had it prepared with towels and an extra toothbrush waiting for him. He smiled. She could hear the shower going, and she too couldn't help the cheese-eating grin from creeping across her face. She loved the thought of him waking up in her bed and showering in her home, and soon, he would be eating breakfast in her kitchen. About ten minutes later, he came downstairs to find her in the kitchen eating an extralarge omelet with salsa on top and Chrisette Michele's "Mr. Radio" playing low in the background.

"Yours is in the oven, if you're hungry." Sena almost choked on her food when she looked up at the sight of him standing there in his boxers. His body looked as if it was chiseled right out of chocolate.

"Cool," he said, walking over to the oven. "Good looking out."

"Not a problem at all." She couldn't help but think about getting round six in. Maybe it would be a round seven or eight, whichever one. She wanted it right then and there. She hadn't got a chance to taste him last night. Now she was ready to bite into that caramel candy bar.

Now finished with her food and waiting on him to finish before she pounced on him, she sat there playing with her orange juice. She didn't have to wait long. The way he ate that omelet, it was gone within three bites. He must have really worked up an appetite.

Standing up and switching the song on the radio to "If I Had My Way," and putting it on repeat just in case this went a little longer than planned, she sauntered toward him and let her robe fall to the floor, showing her glowing naked body. Finishing up his OJ, he could see her through the glass. He now knew what time it was. He pushed his chair back to see what she was getting ready to do. Not expecting her to drop to her knees right there in the kitchen, he couldn't hide his shock as she slid his dick through the slit of his boxers. He could feel tingles up his spine as she wrapped her lips around the head and slowly made her way three-fourths of the way down. He wasn't expecting her to be able go that far down, but she was taking it in like a champ. With his toes curling and eyes rolling in the back of his head, he had to stop her before he came too early.

"Wait a minute." He pulled her up and spread her legs so he could slide in between them. Pulling her down on his joint felt like it was being wrapped in wet silk. With all the blood rushing to tip of his dick, he sucked on her neck to keep from screaming out.

"Umm *ssss*," she moaned as he hit bottom. Pulling her hair so that her neck was bent all the way back he started to place sloppy wet kisses all over her neck and breasts. Not one to be outdone, Sena started rolling her hips as if she had an imaginary hula hoop around her waist. She was riding the dick like a true professional cowgirl.

"Yeah, yeah, ma. That's right. Fuck me back," he coached her in between moans.

He could feel his nut building again. He damn near sucked her breasts down his throat. Bouncing up and down, Sena could feel something incredible building in her body. She was on fire. Sweat dripped off both of them like they were running a marathon.

"Come with me, baby," she moaned. She didn't think she could take any more. She wanted to wave the white flag and give in, but the feeling was too good. She couldn't let it go just yet.

"Huh?" His head was in the clouds. He couldn't hear shit but the music, and the moans coming from her mouth. It was the sweetest sound ever.

"Come with me, baby," she moaned.

"You want me to come?" He grinded into her going deeper as his adrenaline was so high he couldn't even feel her rip the flesh on his back with her nails. The feeling that was going through his body was unheard of.

"Yeah, come with me." It felt like he was trying to come through her throat. She never knew pain could feel so good.

"Umm, a'ight." He slid to the edge of the chair and pulled her hair again all the way down so it looked like she was lying in his lap, locking her legs in the crook of his arms and holding her back. He stood up and walked over to the kitchen counter never letting his dick slide out. He lay her down on the counter; then he dropped to his knees.

"I ain't ready to come yet, so don't be rushing me. I ain't no quickie-type nigga," he said before he sucked her pussy into his mouth.

"Umm, wait . . . please . . . I only want one . . . don't do this to meeeeeee," she pleaded through her moans. She could feel her body tingling all over.

"You coming?" Silence. "Are you coming?" Still silence. She couldn't speak even if she wanted to. Her jaws wouldn't move. She was stiff as a board. Now standing, he slid back in. He decided to go easy on her as he deep stroked her into oblivion. Now, he was ready to release himself.

"*Urrggg!*" He growled as the orgasm that seemed to come from his soul came bursting through his dick, making his knees buckle. He fell on top of her, breathing hard as he placed small little kisses all over her stomach. Sena had passed out right before he came.

Sena woke up in her bed again not remembering how she got back there. The last thing she remembered was them having sex in the kitchen. Looking to her left, he was still there, lying right next to her.

She watched him sleeping so peacefully, and he had a little smile on his face. She hoped he was dreaming of her. She still couldn't believe the events that had taken place in the last twenty-four hours of her life. First, Valencia had come back half dead, but it reunited her with Moochie, and they shared an explosive night of lovemaking. Not even in her wildest dreams could she have imagined the lovemaking would be that good.

Sena was in kitchen again when Moochie came walking in with his muscles glistening from the shower he had just taken. She had to stay focused because he almost got her again. But, this time, she was fully dressed and about to walk out the door.

"You going somewhere?" He looked surprised.

"Yeah, I want to get to the hospital as soon as possible. I took family medical leave for the next four weeks so I can help Vee get better. You don't have to leave yet. I know you must be tired since you were up all day yesterday. And I know you must have exhausted yourself last night and this morning." She smiled.

"Naw, I'm good. I could have kept going. You looked like you were about to pass out, so I took it easy on you. Then, when I had to carry you to the bed this morning 'cause you actually did pass out, I knew you couldn't hang." He laughed at her.

"Hold on, cat daddy. Don't get it twisted. I can hang, homeboy. It's just been a long time." She wasn't lying. Sena could outfreak the freakiest of freaks hands down.

"Oh yeah! You can hang? So you ready for another round?" He was now in her face with a firm grip on her ass as he licked her neck, causing her to get goose bumps everywhere.

"Bbbooy, you better get back. I got to go." She pushed him back softly, not really wanting to push him but, instead, pull him into her arms and sex him down one more time. If she could live in this moment forever, she would.

"Um-hmm. I bet. I better get going myself. I got to meet up with Kidd today." He had to make up something. He really didn't have any plans till later on. He really just wanted to spend the day with her. But he understood her need to get to her friend and never would he want to stand in the way of that. "Then, we'll be out to the hospital later."

"Anyway . . . How's he doing?"

"What you mean?"

"I mean with Vee being back and all, then the way she came back?"

"He all right. He just wants to know what's going on with her."

"You know we been best friends damn near half our lives, and I still don't know a lot about her. She came to live with me when we were younger. She was kinda of strange then too. She never speaks of her past, and, in the last few years, we only really hung out at lunches and work, and shopping, of course, and we catch breakfast here and there. I would ask if she wanted to do something, but she would always say she had to be home at a certain time. I just let it go. I think that's got something to do with her disappearance."

"Who is she?" he asked, hoping Sena knew what the deal was.

"She who?"

"I don't know. Vee just kept saying *she* wouldn't let her be with Kidd, and why would she do this to me. She just kept saying she this and that. I thought maybe you would know who *she* was."

"Never heard of her, but I'll be sure to ask when I get there. But I got to get going. I'll see you later." She stood to leave and tried to walk past him, but he grabbed her arm.

"Are you all right?" She seemed a little distant like she was trying to get away from him. Moochie could read people like a book. It was a gift and a curse. And he didn't want her feeling uncomfortable around him because of what happened between them.

"Yeah, I'm good. Look, what happened last night and this morning was great, but don't think I'm gonna turn all psycho obsessive on you. I thank you for being there for me in my time of need, and, if the need comes again, I hope I can call on you. I don't want to make you love me or be with me. I want you to want to be with me. So you can go on with your day maybe even your life as if this never happened, if you want."

She walked out leaving him sitting at her kitchen table staring at the door.

He didn't know what to say. Hell, she didn't even give him a chance to say anything. If she would have stayed she would have known that he wanted to be with her and that she didn't have to run away. He already had it in his head they would spend the day together to get to know each other a little better. He liked being around her. She didn't bug him or get on his nerves. Most of the time, he could only stay around a woman for a little while because they would start to act and talk stupid, thinking they were being cute and not total idiots. She was freaky, and her head game was vicious. Not to mention, she was drop-dead gorgeous, an all-around winner, which she was.

Chapter 20

Why Would You Stay?

When Valencia woke up, she found Sena sitting in the windowsill reading a book. Sena had been sitting next to Vee for hours, watching and studying her while she slept. Her once beautiful best friend was covered from head to toe in bruises. She couldn't understand why this had happened to her. Valencia was the nicest person Sena had ever met. She couldn't take looking at the bruises, so she pulled out a book she had in her purse.

"Hey, chick-a-dee." Valencia's voice broke Sena's concentration.

"Hey, yourself. How you feeling?" Sena got up and walked over to the bed to give Vee a kiss and a half hug.

"I'm all right, I guess, considering." Vee still wasn't able to look Sena in the eyes.

"Well, that's good. Look, I want to say I am so sorry for not being there for you when you called me." That still pricked at her conscience. She vowed to never make that mistake again.

"It's no problem, but I did tell you to start answering your phone even when you don't know the number. I could be on the side of the road dying, and you wouldn't know 'cause you avoiding a bill collector." She half-laughed, not wanting anything to move her body.

"I know. I know. I'm glad Moochie was able to come help you. Why didn't you call Kidd?"

"I was scared of the way he would react to my call. I didn't have time to explain why I disappeared. I just needed help. You didn't answer, but Moochie did. That's it."

"So what happened to you?"

"I don't remember." Valencia wasn't ready to talk about it yet. She'd been living with this dark secret her whole life and wasn't ready to let anyone in on her horrid double life just yet.

"You got some kind of amnesia?" Sena said, frowning her face up.

"I don't know. I just don't remember. I wish I could. I really want to know why somebody would do me like this. I've never done anything to anyone my entire life. Hell! I've never even had a fight before."

"Well, you had something yesterday."

"Hey! Is that Johnna B's new book?"

"Yeah, man, where she comes up with this shit, I do not know. She got to be sick in the head."

"Why? It isn't good or something?" Sena looked at her like she was crazy.

"You know my girl come hard every time. Shit! She just be on some crazy time type stuff."

"You stupid as hell. Was Kidd up here yesterday?"

"Yes, he was, and he was very upset. We were up here for hours; then you come talking about you don't want to see anyone for the rest of the day. We almost broke in here to kick your ass again."

"What did he say? I really don't want him to see me like this."

"Nothing really. He was real quiet. I think I caught him crying a couple of times. Me and Moochie were in our own little world," she said smiling big time.

"You and Moochie? Give me the juice, bitch. Right now, and don't you leave out not one, single, solitary detail."

"It was nothing really. He stayed with me all day and night," she squealed.

"You got the D, you funky whore! Ooh! Was it good?"

"It was wonderful." Sena fell onto the bed with Vee.

"*Ssss* shit, Sena!" Pain struck Vee so fierce she almost lost her breath.

"I'm so sorry, honey." Sena was looking worried as she jumped off the bed.

"Girl, please! Don't worry about that. You finally cleared those coochie cobwebs out, huh? And with Moochie! I'm happy for you. So what does this mean?"

"I don't know. I mean, I like him . . . The sex was wonderful, but I ain't gonna sweat him like that. I really like him, but I don't want to run him away."

"I feel you, but you also want him to know you *are* interested in him, *right?*"

"Yeah, he knows. I left it in his hands when I walked out of my house this morning, and he was still in his boxers." She smiled big time at the thought of him in his boxers.

"You left him at your house? You got to really like him to be leaving him at your house."

"I know you aren't talking. Kidd got a key to your shit."

"I never said I didn't like him."

"True enough, but anyway." Sena had been trying to find a way to change the subject to the Houdini act she pulled. "Where did you go?"

"What do you mean?" She was trying to play stupid.

"You know what I mean, trick. Don't get cute."

"I didn't go anywhere. I just needed time alone to get myself together. I was dealing with the demons of my past and didn't need any interruption, that's all."

"Yes, the hell you did go somewhere! I was at your house every day for three weeks straight! I even slept there for a week, and you never showed up!"

"Really?" Valencia honestly didn't know Sena had been to her house that many times. Raven never went back after she left.

"You could have called to tell me you were all right or something. I was worried sick, and Kidd called me every day looking for you."

"I know. He called me like every day too. I just couldn't pick up the phone."

"I gotta pee. I'll be right back." Sena got up to go to the bathroom.

"Ain't that cute? She came to take care of her BFF." Raven barged in without any warning.

"Oh! Shut up, bitch! Would you just go the fuck away?" Valencia was done playing her games.

"Now you all tough and shit, bitch. You ain't tough. You still need to recognize I'm me, bitch, and don't forget it. I can come and take your life in a heartbeat."

"Not this time! We both will die before that happens, you better believe that. And I mean that. You almost got me killed, and it won't happen again!"

"Whatever. I'll give you enough time to heal. I don't want to be walking around hurting and shit. I'll let you take in some of the pain this time, but I *will* be back, so don't get *too* comfortable. Peace out, bitch!"

"Yeah, whatever. I'll be waiting and ready." Vee was determined not to let Raven take over again. By any means necessary, she would fight to the end.

"Ready for what?" Sena asked as she walked back into the room.

"Shit. I'm ready to eat, but I can't. They're feeding me through an IV. I hope I don't get skinny and sick looking."

"As long as you're still here, it doesn't matter."

"Yes, it does. You're still looking beautiful with no worries about being ugly and alone. I do."

"And neither do you."

"No one will ever want to be with me after what I did." Vee could feel tears coming into her eyes.

"Do you really think getting skinny is going to make that man stop loving you?"

"I wasn't even talking about him."

"Well, who the hell you talking about 'cause you sho' ain't got nobody else?" Sena couldn't help but laugh at her.

"She bet not have nobody else." They looked toward the door to see Kidd and Moochie walking in with about thirty "Get Well" balloons and teddy bears and flowers, looking and smelling wonderful.

The sight of Kidd walking with those flowers took her back to when Kidd had first stolen her heart. She looked him up and down, and he'd never been more beautiful to her. Her heart skipped what seemed like ten beats before it returned to its normal rhythm.

"I thought you two weren't coming till later on this evening." Sena looked to the duo.

"Yeah, well, peanut head over here wanted to get out here ASAP." Moochie pointed to Kidd.

"How you doin, ma?" Moochie kissed Sena on the forehead first, then Valencia.

"I'm good. How 'bout yourself?" She was staring at Kidd, admiring him. The man was beautiful inside and out. He was her reason for living. He looked like he was trying to look at anything in the room but her. Sena took notice of the expression she was giving Kidd.

"Hey, Moochie, come buy me some lunch. I'm starving." She stood up and grabbed his arm.

"We just got here." He looked at her like she was crazy.

"Well, you just leaving, now, come on." She gave him a look that said *come the hell on.*

"A'ight, man. Y'all want anything?"

"Yeah, bring me a T-bone with a baked potato and side order of sweet potato pie," Valencia blurted out.

"Girl, please. What you eat will be pumping in you through that water hose you got coming out of your arm!" Sena yelled over her shoulder as she pulled Moochie out the door.

Kidd was just standing there, staring at her, not really knowing what to say. She had bandages everywhere. She looked so fragile. It angered him to see her this way. The beautiful, strong woman he had come to love looked so broken. The spirit that was once bright and vibrant was gone. He didn't know if his heart could take it if she was to be taken from him again. He didn't even know where to start, and he had so many questions. But he didn't come to argue with her. First, he wanted to wrap his arms around her and let her know that he still loved her, but he had to, at least, try to play hard. No matter how badly he wanted to be mad at her, he couldn't stay that way because his heart wouldn't allow it. She had a death grip on his heart and wasn't letting go.

"Well, are you going stand over there the whole visit?"

"My bad. I didn't know if you wanted me here or not." He walked up to her bed.

"Why wouldn't I want you here? I've missed you like crazy." She patted a spot on the bed next to her. They just sat there, staring at each other. Not knowing what to say, there was a long and deafening pause in the air. The room's walls closed them into a small box that only they could fit into together. Tunnel vision kicked in, and they only saw each other. Their heartbeats reverberated off the walls and said what their mouths couldn't. Tears filled Valencia's eyes, and she willed them not to fall. But it was inevitable they betray her.

"I'm sorry." She looked down at the covers.

"So, what happened to you? I mean, where did you go all that time you was gone?" Kidd said, finally breaking his silence as he sat down on the bed next to her.

"I had get away to clear my head from the things that were happening so fast around me. I felt as though I were falling with no ground in sight." Half-truths seemed be the thing these days.

"So you up and left me without so much as a good-bye or nothing? I thought we were better than that." His eyes were full of hurt.

"We are so much better than that, but I told you in so many words that this would happen." She tried to explain without giving too much information away. If she could take Raven to her grave, she would.

"When? You never told me you were just gon' up and disappear on me. I would have never put myself or my heart out there like that." He stood up livid and breathing hard, not believing what she was saying. At this point, he didn't give a shit about her being in a hospital. She was on some straight bullshit.

"I told you she would come back. I prayed and prayed she wouldn't come, but she did to claim what she called hers."

"Who is *she?* What are you talking about?" He sat down, looking at her. Finally, he would get some answers.

"I don't know how to explain it to you. I am indebted to her because she saved my life, and I had to go away for a while to repay that debt. All I can remember is a month later, I woke up in the hotel room not knowing where I was or how I got there." She was in tears all over again. "I didn't think I had any more tears left."

He softened up a bit and tried to wipe her tears away, but new ones immediately replaced the old ones.

"I know me disappearing was wrong, but there was nothing I could do. I would never do anything to deliberately hurt you. I knew from the first time I looked into your eyes I would love you some day. Hell, it may have been love at first sight. I didn't know what I was feeling, but I knew I was feeling something, and being away from you for so long made me realize what I was feeling was love."

All he could do was sit there, looking at her. He didn't know what to say as he was still at a loss for words. He wanted to curse, yell, and scream. But looking at her, all he really wanted to do was hold and protect her. He didn't know if he should continue with the relationship or not because she had a lot going on, and he still didn't have the whole story. He didn't want to press the issue, but something just wasn't sitting right with him. But he knew one thing for sure, and that was, he loved her and didn't want to be away from her again. So he decided to chalk it up and help her through it.

Taking a deep breath, he said, "I love you too."

"Why? How could you love me after this? You deserve someone that can make you happy for the rest of your life, and I don't know if I'm that woman." Like a river flowing into the ocean, her tears broke loose.

"Well, you let me be the judge of that, and anyway, I have known for a while that you were the one I wanted to be with, so let's not sweat the small stuff and just roll with the punches. Can you do that for me?" He pushed her chin up with his finger, so she was looking at him.

"Yeah," she whispered, looking unsure. Once again, she found herself praying to a God that seemed to never be on her side. She prayed that Raven was gone for good for her true, uninterrupted happiness. She prayed for peace in her heart. And she prayed that she could keep Kidd in her life.

Chapter 21

A New Love

"All I need in this life of sin is me and my girlfriend, down to ride till the bloody end." The phone sang as it vibrated across the dresser.

"What's good?" Moochie asked, already knowing who it was. She had set that ring tone for herself and told him he better not change it and she better not hear it ring for anybody else.

"Hey, sexy. Are you busy? I got this itch I can't seem to scratch." He smiled at the sexy melody of Sena's voice coming through his phone.

"I think I can assist you with that little problem." He hadn't seen her in a few days and was ready to get his fix. Since getting with Sena, he hadn't even thought about another woman. She consumed his mind and was quickly taking over his heart.

"You think? Naw, I need you to *know* that you can help me. Otherwise, what do I need you for? I have a thinker at home. And he thinks he's doing it right, but that's what I got you for." The sex appeal in her voice made him play along with her game.

"Oh yeah? No doubt I got you, ma." He unconsciously grabbed his crotch.

"Good. Meet me in the bar at the Radisson Hotel in thirty minutes." She hung up, smiling from ear to ear. She had never done anything like this before, but she felt she had to step her game up if she was trying to keep him in her life. She had a very sex- and fun-filled night planned for him.

Sena sat at the bar, sipping her third Midori Sour, tapping her fingers as she was waiting patiently for Moochie to come through the doors. She still couldn't believe she had put this little shindig together. Her feelings for Moochie were overwhelming. She knew she loved him. She just wasn't ready to admit it, at least, not just yet. She had fallen for him, which wasn't part of the game plan. She knew he didn't want to be in anything serious. Their relationship was going just fine without adding emotions into the equation. But she always wondered if it was going to go any further.

Her thoughts were cut short when she saw Moochie walk through the door. She had to cross her legs to stop her woman parts from jumping. At the sight alone of him, it made her juices flow. She watched as he sat down at the bar as she twirled her room key in her fingers. Then she got up and sauntered over to him. He hadn't noticed her yet because she was undercover.

"Hey, you," she whispered into his ear. He tried to turn around, but she stopped him. "No, don't turn around." She slid her hand down his chest, dropping the room key in his lap. "Give me five minutes, then come up to Room 629."

With that being said, she walked away. He turned to see her hitting the corner. If it hadn't been for her coat, he would have never known it was her. She sported a bleached blond wig that went down to her ass. The red leather pea coat stopped just short of her ass itself, the red fishnet stockings made her legs look thick and juicy, while the red leather pumps made them look long and flexible.

"Aye, let me get a shot of Patrón," he yelled to the bartender.

He looked back toward where Sena had gone and decided he needed a little more. "Make that two double shots." He downed the shots and headed for what he knew was going to be a fun night. As he approached the room, he could hear music coming from the door. He opened the door to see Sena lying in the middle of the bed, her legs cocked open with one hand massaging her clit and the other working on her nipple. She moved her body to the music as she watched him enter the room. She had candles all over the room, and the candlelights flickered and danced off her skin, freshly covered in a sweet-smelling oil, the scent, of which, rivaled the aroma coming from the candles.

"Have a seat," she whispered as she pointed to the chair directly in front of her.

Moochie did as he was told and walked over to the seat and watched her bring on an orgasm he wished he had participated in. His dick was so hard he thought it would implode. He had to squeeze the tip the relieve some of the pressure.

"Come taste me," she moaned as she pulled her fingers out of her soaking wet pussy and placed them in his mouth. He licked all trace of her juices off her fingers. Then he moved from her fingers to her nipples on down to her secret passage to heaven. She moaned in delight at the sensation of his tongue circling around her sensitive area. He finally let go of her clit and moved up to her mouth and planted a sensual kiss on her lips that made her damn near rip his shirt off his body.

"I want you inside of me right now!" Sena panted as she pulled and tugged at his clothes. Roughly she pushed him down on the bed and climbed on top of him. Positioning herself over his dick, she slid down on it with no hands.

"*Sssss*," Moochie hissed as he felt her walls constricting around his pole.

She dug her nails into his chest as she sat all the way down and felt him hit the back of her hot box. Once she got used to the feeling she moved her hips to the rhythm of the song that was playing in the back. Ironically, R. Kelly was in the background telling her to slow wind for him. And that's exactly what she was doing. She rubbed her hands up and down his chest as she grinded her vagina all over his rock-hard phallus. Then she firmly wrapped her right hand around his throat and whispered in his ear.

"Fuck me like you hate me."

"Say no more." He obliged her request as he stroked her long and hard all night long. When he awoke the following morning, she was gone and had left a note on the nightstand with $200 sitting on top of it. He picked up the note along with the money and laughed.

Hey, you!
Thank you for a wonderful night. You were all that I hoped you would be and more.
I couldn't have dreamed last night would be so perfect. Until next time, keep me on your mind, and, if I'm not already there, find a small place for me in your heart.
Smooches, Kiss Kiss,
The Lady in Red

He smiled because he knew she already had his heart. He read the letter three more times before he put it down. He looked at the money and started to laugh again. *Is this how women feel when the sex is over and all they get is a funky-ass $200? Shit! I know my shit was fire and deserved, at least, a guap.* He laughed again.

***

Kidd was there every step of the way helping nurse Vee back to good health. Every day and night, he was at her house. Anything that needed to be done, he was doing it. If it wasn't him doing it, Sena was there. They were fussing over her day and night. She couldn't lift a finger without one of them yelling at her and telling her they would do it. Valencia thought surely she would go crazy, loving and hating the attention at the same time.

Valencia was finally back to good health. She didn't lose as much weight as she originally thought she would. In fact, she lost it in all the right places. To celebrate, they were all going out to party.

Bzzzz Bzzzz Bzzzzzz. Valencia heard her phone vibrating across the table.

"Get that for me, Sena," she yelled from upstairs.

"What's the business?" Sena answered the phone trying to sound hood, but it wasn't working. Kidd only laughed at her.

"Yeah, man, you been around my brother way too long with yo' half-hood ass," he said while still laughing.

"Whatever, punk. What do you want?" She studied all the eyeshadow Valencia had on her dresser while he talked.

"My woman. Where she at?"

"Upstairs in the shower."

"Tell her don't get dressed."

"Eeeewww, gross. I don't need to hear that shit from you." She scrunched her face up.

"Get ya mind outta the gutter. I got her something to wear tonight. I'll be there in a minute, man."

"Oh, okay. I'll be sure to give her the message." She hung up and started putting different colors up to her face. She was happy for her girl. Vee was finally happily in love. She and Moochie had been getting their Bonnie and Clyde thing on. They had sex everywhere . . . in the car while driving, in the backseat, all over the house, even at Vee's. He would have to hold her mouth to keep her from screaming out loud and waking Vee and Kidd up. She got chills just thinking about the time he gave her some mean head while she drove with one leg on the gas and the other on his shoulder. She was in love and in love with the thought of being in love. But she couldn't help but think, was *she* the only one in love?

"Hey, Kidd said don't get dressed yet. He got something for you to put on tonight," Sena told Vee while she wiped the fog from the bathroom mirror so she could start putting her face on. Not that she needed much makeup, she just wanted to get her eyes looking good and put on a little lip gloss.

"Why you ain't using the bedroom mirror? It covers damn near the whole wall?" Vee questioned as she stepped out of the shower.

"The lighting is so much better in here," Sena waved her off. "And I got to get my bedroom eyes right."

"I wonder what the hell he got me to wear. He looks like he got a li'l taste about himself but dressing me? I hope he ain't setting me up to hurt his feelings," Valencia said as she got out of the shower and put on her sea-blue silk bathrobe.

"I know, right? If he comes in here with some bunk shit, we gon' clown him together." They gave each other high fives.

"How he gonna, at the last minute, tell me not to get dressed? I got to put my face on according to what I'm wearing, and what about shoes? I already got something hot to wear."

"Ah, trick, quit whining. I wish somebody would call me and tell me not to put something on 'cause they bringing me something to wear. I would lie across my bed ass naked, waiting on them to walk through the door."

"I don't see how you didn't have sex for so long before my brother started tearing your back out," Kidd said as he walked in and dropped three Gucci bags on the bed. "'Cause you sure do have a lot of freaky tendencies."

"Don't hate, nigga. Ya brotha loves it." She got up, shaking her butt and dropping it down low. "Hate on *that,* punk," she pushed him as she walked out the door.

"That girl is a mess. What do we have here?" She peeked into the bag.

"This is your bag, so you go get dressed with Sena, and I'll get dressed in here. I know how she might need you to wipe her ass, or you'll need her to snap your bra or some shit."

"You being real cute right now, jerk." She picked up the bag.

"Oh, I'm a jerk now?" He walked up to her.

"Yeah, and what you gonna do about it, *jerk?*"

"I got you." Turning around to walk away, he turned back around real quick and grabbed her, then threw her on the bed and started tickling her.

"Okay, stop, please stop." Tears were now running down her face. "You are messing up my makeup!"

"I'm a jerk?" He tickled her even more,

"No, I'm sorry. No, no, you not a jerk."

"I thought so." He leaned down and kissed her softly on her lips. She wrapped her legs around him, pulling him closer to her. Their hands explored each other until they couldn't take it anymore. Kidd pulled the string on her bathrobe and let it fall open. It had been awhile since they were last intimate, but they were ready. Vee's whole body was on fire. The temp in the room had gone up a hundred degrees. Kidd's hands roamed her body, touching and caressing. He couldn't wait any longer. He flipped her over on her stomach and pulled her on her knees. He knew this had to be a quickie because they had company arriving in less than thirty minutes. He tongue kissed the back of neck as he slid in from the back.

"Ummm . . ." She moaned as she grabbed at the sheet. The girth of him was overwhelming. He filled her up and took her breath away in one stroke. She buried her face into the pillow so Sena wouldn't hear her screams as he went in for the kill. He stroked and hit every inch of her walls. She had begun to run away, but he grabbed her by the waist and held her down so she couldn't get away.

"Uh-uh, don't go nowhere," he gritted. He could feel the nut that was ready to explode all the way from his toes. He loved to watch the waves flowing on her cheeks each time he stroked her.

"Oh shit! Yes, right *there*. Keep it right *arrgggggg!*" Vee screamed into the pillow as her body shook violently.

He gritted his teeth as he felt her walls gripping his love stick, especially when she was coming. It was like he could feel her heart beating around his dick. His nuts were tingling something fierce.

"*Grrrrrrrrrrr,*" he growled as he came hard and collapsed on top of her.

"Shit! I don't even want to go nowhere now," Vee laughed.

"Right!" he said as he rolled off her. She slowly got up to go get into the shower. He admired her ass as she walked to the bathroom. "Girl, that jiggle of yours . . ." he said as he got up to follow her into the shower. After they washed each other up, they went to get ready for the festivities.

"Oh, and you a punk," she said as she grabbed the bag and jetted out the door before he could catch her.

"Yeah, a'ight. This ain't over. You better believe it," he yelled down the hall.

"Yeah, whatever, jerk. I mean, punk," she yelled back.

"Girl, what the hell is wrong with you? Shit! You scared the hell out of me, busting in the damn door like that," Sena said, trying to get her heart rate back to a normal beat.

"Running from his stupid ass." She was all extra giddy and happy, and Sena noticed.

"Look at you all super in love, and I'm so happy for you. I can't describe how it warms my heart to see you smiling all the time." Sena grabbed her hands. "I ain't trying to get all emotional or nothing, but you deserve this."

"Thank you. I'm the happiest I've ever been in my life. I just don't believe in fairy-tale endings and happily ever after, though. You know what I mean?" Vee was trying to hold back the tears that were starting to fall. She was scared that Raven would come back and mess everything up. She knew she needed to tell Kidd about Raven, but she just didn't know how.

"Yeah, I feel you, but it looks like you will get one after all. And all you gotta do is hold on to it with a death grip and don't let go. You give me hope that I too will find my dream man."

"What about Moochie?"

"What about him? We cool. I mean, I really like him. No, scratch that. I am sooooo in love. I just ain't ever been into making a man love me. It should just happen." Sena flopped down on the bed.

"You right, but if you saw what I saw you wouldn't be sitting there talking like that. Put that pride aside, honey. That boy loves you. You'll see." Valencia winked at her as she finished getting dressed.

Kidd was getting ready, preparing himself mentally for tonight's events. It would surely change his life forever. With no doubt in his mind, Valencia was the woman he wanted to spend the rest of his life with. He wanted to grow with her, have plenty of kids, and live out his dreams with her. He couldn't wait to hear her say yes. In such a short time, he couldn't imagine his life without her. She was his smile, laughter, and joy. No woman had ever made him feel that way. When she would call, he would get the biggest smile on his face, so anybody around him knew it was her calling. She gave him butterflies. He *had* to keep her in his life.

He was putting on his boxers when he heard a scream and what seemed like a million footsteps getting closer. He smiled real big because he knew he did well. Valencia burst through the door and jumped into his arms as they fell back on the bed. She placed kisses all over his face.

"Thank you, thank you, thank you, oh, thank you," she continued with the kisses. "I love it. I love it, I love it!" She kissed him one more time, then got up and ran back to Sena's room.

"You're welcome!" he yelled as the door shut.

When Valencia opened the bags, she couldn't believe it. First, she pulled out a Gucci camel-colored and gold Jersey dress. But what shut shit down was the camel-colored thigh-high Gucci boots. They were spectacular with the gold toe tips and "Gucci" going down the side real big in gold letters. Once she put those on, "Bad bitch" wouldn't even be able to describe her. She was getting ready to put the bags down when she saw something else in them. A long black box. While she was getting the box out, she heard Sena say "yes." Sena was in a whole other world.

"What the hell you yes'ing for?" She looked over to see Sena posing in the wall-length mirror with her boots on. She just started laughing.

"Girl, shit, I can fit these muthafuckas, so best believe I'm gon' let you get your wears in, but I'll be back."

Opening the box, tears came to her eyes instantly. There was a necklace and bracelet set covered in ocean-blue diamonds. The necklace had a charm with the letter *W* on it covered in the most beautiful, clearest VVS diamonds she had ever seen in her life. She had money and a lot of it, but he had M-O-N-E-Y.

The girls heard a big commotion going on in the living room. Everybody was apparently meeting at Valencia's house. She was damn near having a heart attack at the thought of all those shoes being on her carpet. And Sena could see it all over her face.

"Look at you. You about burst out into tears over that damn carpet. I can see it all in your face. Hopefully, Moochie or Kidd made sure they saw the no shoes sign. Come on. Let's go give them a piece of our minds, damned jabronies." Sena was teasing Vee, and she knew it.

"To hell with you, skank. I'm trying to stay focused, but shit, it's killing me." She was adamant about not having shoes on her carpet. She had never worn any on the fluffy white carpet and hoped like hell she wasn't about to have to wreak havoc tonight. They finished their makeup preparing to make their grand entrance.

The girls walked in the room striking a Charlie's Angels pose. Tony started singing as he walked up to them. *"I love your girl, wife beater with the denims. I love your girl, she keep them heels on high. I love your girl,"* he sang as he put his arms around both their shoulders. The girls were shuttin' shit down for sure. Both of them had their hair blown out and flat ironed bone straight. Sena had Chinese bangs while Vee's was parted down the middle.

"We gonna need the guns tonight, ain't we?" Kidd said as he eyed the duo.

"Yes, sir." Moochie walked up to Sena and gave her a wet one on the lips, then took Li'l Tony's arm from around her. "Get cha own, nigga."

"Why? I just told you I loved your girl."

Sena was also killin' 'em with her high waist True Religion jeans and come fuck me boots. Her tight-fitted button-up and her push-up bra had her breasts spilling out of her shirt.

Vee was staring at Kidd in the male version of her outfit. Looking good enough to eat, she wanted to jump on him right there on the spot and get round two started. In his tan Gucci slacks and white button-up Gucci shirt, and to complete the outfit, he wore a tan fitted Gucci hat with the matching boots that had a big gold G on the side of them.

Sena broke her concentration.

"Girl, look at you. You about to burst open, ain't you?" Sena rubbed Shay-D's big watermelon-shaped stomach.

"I know. I can't wait till this is over with any day now. I'm handing over the baby to Kaylin; then I'm skipping town," Shay said rubbing her stomach in frustration.

"Don't believe that shit," Skillet rubbed her stomach too.

"And don't you be rubbing on any bellies. That shit is contagious." Vee looked to Sena.

"Let's get going, man." Moochie was trying to get as far away from that conversation as possible. He was happy and loving life, but he wasn't ready for daddy-hood just yet.

"All my single ladies, all my single ladies" came blasting through the speakers at Bar Louie in Central West End. Every woman in the bar jumped up and started dancing, doing some part of that video. It was karaoke night, so it was jam-packed. The girls were picking out a song to sing. Vee loved doing karaoke, so, whenever she

could suggest it, she would throw it out there, knowing that was what they would be doing for the night.

"This is my shit!" Sena yelled while dropping it low and sweeping the floor. The girl thought she was Beyoncé for real.

"Sena, what you want to sing?" Shay-D yelled over the music.

"You know damn well she gonna pick some Beyoncé or Destiny's Child," Vee laughed.

"Right! That's my biiitch!" Sena sang while she swept the floor with her ass.

"Okay, I got it," Shay said with a smirk on her face.

"What did you pick out?" Vee peeked at the sheet. "Oh yeah. I'm Beyoncé in this one." Vee waved Sena over.

"Girl, I already know it must be 'Cater to You.'"

Sena knew 'cause she always did Kelly's part. Kelly's part was a little freakier, and Sena always went with the nasty.

"So I guess I'm Michele," Shay-D said with a pout.

"That's okay, babe. You show them how Michele is really supposed to do it," Skillet said, trying to encourage her. Sena snatched the paper and ran it up to the DJ.

"The DJ said we got one person ahead of us," Sena said as she pulled Vee up so they could finish dancing. The guys were digging into the food on the table. It was covered with hot wings, fries, nachos with spinach dip, and mozzarella cheese sticks. It looked as though they had bought the whole menu of appetizers.

While Vee and Sena were dropping it like it was hot. Kidd noticed trouble walking up and thought for sure he was going to throw up. He kicked Moochie in the shin. When Moochie looked up, Kidd nodded to his left, and Moochie smirked, knowing it was about go down. Sena's elevator had stopped going to the top floor and Vee seemed to have a bit of a chemical imbalance herself, so this was to be very interesting, to say the least. Kidd didn't feel like any drama tonight, but he knew for sure he was going to get it.

"Hey, babe. How you been? I haven't seen you in a while. What's up with that?" His ex cuddy buddy Janelle asked. He hadn't seen her in months, and they weren't even that serious, but she had it in her head that he was her man. She was a top-notch chick. He just wasn't feeling her at the time, but he could feel her getting too attached. He wasn't into playing with a woman's feelings, and he didn't believe in wasting time. He wanted to either be with you or he didn't and vice versa. There wasn't room for a gray area. But when he met Valencia, he had it set in his head that he was gonna make her love him. He never bought Janelle anything, and the only place they went was to a bed, and never his. But somehow, she had come to the conclusion that there was something between them other than sheets. He had stopped talking to her a little bit before he met Vee, and hadn't talked to her in months. But he knew her. She didn't like the fact that he just up and stopped calling her, then when she finally sees him again, he's with another chick.

"Hey, fellas. How y'all doin?"

Moochie put up the middle finger while everyone else either frowned or turned their head. Moochie never liked her because she was drama with a capital D. She put her arms around Kidd's neck and kissed him on the cheek. Meanwhile, Vee danced watching the whole thing, but she kept her cool. Sena, on the other hand, had already started taking off jewelry and started counting to see how many girls Janelle had with her. Not that she was scared, she just liked to know how many possible victims there were.

"I'm good, and yourself?" Kidd said as took her arms from around his neck. He cut his eyes toward Vee. She seemed calm, but, if he knew her like he thought he did, any minute some shit was about to pop off. She wasn't crazy like Sena, but he could see the fire in her eyes. Janelle saw him looking at Vee, and she could see his face tighten up. She knew he really wasn't for the drama. But her girls were there, so she had to save face.

"I see you sure are looking good." She pulled out Vee's seat and attempted to sit down, but Vee wasn't standing for too much more disrespect.

"Excuse me. This is my seat." She could feel her anger surfacing.

Janelle smirked. "I didn't know this seat was taken, but how 'bout I sit over here?" Vee saw her head go to the side. Vee thought she meant the other seat but, in fact, she was talking about Kidd's lap.

"See? Now you trying to be funny. I'm not into playing with other people's kids. Now if you would excuse yourself, we were having a night out. You can call him in the morning when he leaves my house."

Janelle's face got real tight, and you could see she was thinking about doing something stupid.

"Please do it, please do it," Sena said, noticing the look in Janelle's eyes.

"Did you hear this bitch?" Janelle looked to her friends and started laughing. Everybody at the table could see Sena picking up the ketchup bottle. Shay-D was wishing like hell she wasn't pregnant but found herself taking off her heels anyway.

"You sit yo' hardheaded ass right here and don't you fucking move." Skillet could read her mind, and it wasn't going down. He understood she wanted to help her friends, but it wasn't happening tonight. He would have to kill any nigga or bitch that put they hands on her.

"Man, Janelle, would you just leave. We ain't here for all that shit tonight." You could see the muscles in Kidd's jaw twitching.

"Look, baby girl, I see you trying to prove a point. He *used* to be yours. I get it. If I'm ever done with him, I'll give you call so you can come get him." Vee's eyes turned dark. She snatched the girl out of the seat and pulled her close, so they were eye to eye. Janelle didn't even have time to react it happened so quickly. "Now beat it, bitch, 'cause it's about to get real ugly around here real quick." Everybody looked at Vee. They were shocked because no one expected that kind of reaction. She was normally the one to step back and let Sena take over. Janelle tried to react but, once again, Sena, who was so used to taking care of her friend, came over Vee's shoulder with that bottle so hard and quick that if you blinked you would have missed the whole thing.

"Bitch, you need to check out the situation before you step into a bad motherfucking decision 'cause, where I'm from, we beat bitches first, and *then* ask questions." Sena, then, turned to Janelle's friends. "She ain't worth it. You hoes don't want these types of problems on your hands 'cause I cause big headaches." Sena was just as calm as a person could be. You would have thought she was just having an everyday normal conversation with them. She didn't believe in using unnecessary energy. All that rah-rah shit wasn't for her. The girls didn't know whether to help their friend or walk away quickly.

"Yo, man! You crazy as a muthafucka, man. Get yo' gal, Mooch."

Moochie just sat there laughing. He'd found the yin to his yang. He was so ready to throw Sena on the table and fuck her right there. Sena had pushed Vee in back of her, but Vee was ready to get her shit off too. But she couldn't get anything in because security was now rushing over.

"What's the problem, Kidd?"

"We cool, man. Just get this bitch away from me." Kidd looked like he smelled something really stank.

"Damn, Kidd! I thought you were something like a pimp. I thought you had your hoes in check." Skillet was laughing hysterically. This was too funny to him. "You know I never liked that bitch anyway. Good going, Ms. Zena," he joked.

"Yeah, yeah, we know." He turned to Vee. "You a'ight, ma?" No answer. "Vee?" Everybody was looking at her now, and no one was laughing anymore. "Vee?" he grabbed her hand. She looked down at it, and then looked back up.

"Huh? You say something to me? My mind had gone somewhere else." She laughed it off.

"We see, you good?" Sena looked at her concerned.

"Yeah, I'm good, bitch. Is you good? You came back down from that adrenaline high, Bonquisha?"

"Well, you know me. I'm good. I just wish I had more time to get that bitch, who came over here trying to carry somebody. Like we ain't us. I ain't no killa, but push me." She scrunched her face and made a face like she was appalled.

"Man, you two chicks is crazy, and three bellies over here done took her shoes and shit off like she finna to do something, knowing damn well if nahn one of them hoes had put their hands on her, they would have gotten they muthafuckin' noodles knocked." Skillet was now rubbing her stomach again.

"Nigga, please, don't count me out. It was about four of them hoes. It was not going down like that, homeboy. Shit! Push this stomach to the side and slap a bitch real good with a six-inch stiletto." Everybody was laughing 'cause she was dead-ass serious, when she couldn't even pull all the way up to the table her stomach was so big.

"Okay. Can we get back to our night?" Kidd was ready to get this night over with while he still had the nerve.

"Aww! You mad at me for knocking your girlfriend down? Go get her. I'll apologize." Sena was being funny.

"Whatever, man. Weren't y'all dancing or some shit?" He couldn't help but laugh at her too.

"And next we have 'Pretty in Pink'!" the DJ announced.

"Who the hell is that?" everybody looked around to see who had chosen the name.

"That's us," Sena told everybody.

"That is *not* the name I chose," Shay-D stated.

"I know. I told him to change it. I like this better. This way, if we embarrass ourselves, nobody will know our real names."

"Speak for yourself. I can sang, honey," Vee said while walking up to the microphone. You couldn't tell them they were not Destiny's Child. The music started, and the girls started rolling and moving to the beat.

"Get 'em, baby!" Kidd cheered from the audience because he knew Valencia could sing since she often sang to him. Everyone had stopped what they were doing to watch the beautiful trio. Sena and Vee had a routine already, but they had Shay, so they had to improvise. They rolled and slow winded so hard all they needed was a stripper pole and a thong. Even Shay got down. People could clearly tell how she had gotten pregnant. When they were done, the crowd was on their feet. The men were whistling, and the ladies were in awe. By the end of the song, they were in their men's laps and sweating like pigs.

After catching their breaths, Sena got up to request a song.

"Ah, ma, I'm sorry about that little situation," Kidd tried to explain to Vee.

"No need to explain. I know you have a past. I'm good as long as the past stays in the past." She kissed his lips and joined Sena at the DJ booth. On their way back, Jaheim's song "In My Hands" came blasting through the speakers. As they got closer, Kidd stood up and pulled Vee in front of him. Then he went down on one knee.

She looked around at everyone smiling at her. Her mind went blank as the realization sank in of what was happening. She started shaking, and tears instantly stung her eyes. She thought she would faint for sure.

Sena was crying. She knew all along. That was why she went to the DJ booth to request the song. Shay-D was clapping and jumping up and down.

"Valencia Ball, I knew from the first time I saw you that you would be my wife, no matter how much you tried to fight it." Everybody chuckled. "I love you with all my heart and soul. I never thought I would love this way." The music got lower. "I want to grow old with you and have a house full of kids. Live out my dreams with you, and turn my dreams into our dreams. You are my smile, my joy, my laughter. When I'm not with you, life doesn't seem right. You will bring so much joy to my heart if you will be my wife."

If the people around him didn't know any better, they would have thought he was on the verge of tears also. The room was so quiet that you could hear an ant sneeze. Damn near every woman in the room was in tears. A million reasons why she should say no ran through her head, but a million and one reasons also flashed on why she should say yes. The tears were really running down now. It was a good thing she had on waterproof mascara.

"Yes . . ." she whispered, nodding her head. Everybody jumped and cheered. Kidd picked her up, spinning her in the process.

"Congratulations!" everyone yelled in unison.

"I told you, you would be my sister-in-law." Moochie gave her a big hug and kiss on the cheek.

"Uh, I hate to ruin this most sentimental moment."

Everybody looked down at the disturbed face of Shay-D.

"This being my first child and all, I don't think I'm supposed be in a restaurant when a big gush of water burst out of me."

Everybody looked down.

"Her water broke!" Sena yelled, and everybody went into a frenzy.

Everybody was throwing purses and money. Skillet dropped five big face hundred dollar bills. He was super-excited and couldn't wait. He didn't know what the baby was. They wanted to be surprised.

Everybody stayed at the hospital till the baby was born. After baby Kayla came into the world, everyone went their separate ways.

Chapter 22

Till Death Do Us Part

"You got any Lyfe on this iPod of yours?" Vee asked while she searched through it.

"What you know about Lyfe Jennings? Not nothing, young grasshopper."

"What? Are you crazy? That's my nigga. He's the most slept on singer out there. I know every song he's ever made and featured in."

"Yeah, a'ight. Whatever. What's his best song?" He turned his mouth up to the right, waiting for her response.

She found Lyfe on the iPod and pressed play when she got to her favorite song. "I Can't" came blasting through the speakers.

"What? That's my shit too!" He was too excited. "I knew I loved you for a reason, and I'm going to spend the rest of my life showing you just how much." He grabbed her hand and kissed it. He was convinced he had found his soul mate. He always thought his soul would burn in hell for the sins he had committed, but Vee gave him hope. She would never know how much that meant to him.

"You already have. If you couldn't do anything else for me for the rest of our lives, what you have done so far would be enough."

"That was the most beautiful thing ever. You should have seen it," Sena gushed.

Sena still had stars in her eyes from watching the baby being born. She, Skillet, and Vee were in the delivery room. They hadn't known Shay-D for that long, but they felt like family. Shay asked them to come in with her. She was scared to death and didn't know what was in store for her. Skillet was driving her crazy and, if she had to listen to him the whole time, surely she would have jumped off the roof.

"Nah, I'll pass on that any day, I heard it was gross, but I'm glad you enjoyed yourself, though." He laughed at her.

"Yeah, well, you'll change your mind once you see your own little bundle of joy being born one day."

"Well, until then, I'm steering clear of the delivery room." She was just looking at him kind of strangely.

"You want something to drink?" she asked, getting up off the couch to go to the kitchen. They were at Kidd's house. It was practically Moochie's house because Kidd was always at Vee's house.

"Yeah, get me some Kool-Aid!" he yelled out.

"You act like you so high class but keep a cup of ghetto-ass Kool-Aid in your hand." She laughed at him.

"I will not even dignify that with an answer."

"You know, if I didn't know Kidd so well and look at him as family, I would have thought he was a li'l metrosexual or something." She looked around the house. It was immaculately well kept and had too many womanly features for her taste.

"Why the fuck would you say some shit like that?" Moochie asked as he rushed into the kitchen not even trying to hide his anger. Sena just laughed at him.

"Look at you. Running in here with your chest all swollen and shit. Get some of that air out cha chest. What, you ready to fight or something?" She patted him on the chest. He had to laugh too. He had a tendency to overreact when it came to Kidd. "Calm down! I'm just saying it looks a li'l suspect round these parts, that's all."

"Didn't you come in here to get something to drink?" He folded his arms across his chest.

"What? I'm on a time schedule on how long I can stay in a certain room or something?" She looked him up and down.

"Don't start any dumb shit." He slapped her on the ass and walked back into the living room.

"What if I told you I was pregnant?" Sena asked as she sat back down next to him on the couch.

Moochie damn near dropped his cup. He got that feeling in the pit of his stomach like when the police pull up behind you.

"Are you?" He prayed she wasn't. He knew he wasn't ready to be a daddy. That was Kidd's dream, not his.

"You can't answer a question with a question." She was looking at him, trying to get a read on him, but he wouldn't look her in the face.

"Are you, man?" You could clearly hear the frustration in his voice.

"What would you say?" She had been trying to find a way to tell him for about a month now. She was almost two-and-a-half-months pregnant. And now she just wished she could crawl under a rock and die. He had this sour look on his face. For the last two months, she had been floating on cloud nine above the heavens. But now she was back to the reality of things that she might be the only one happy about it.

"Are you pregnant or not?" Sena could see the veins popping out of his neck.

"You still haven't answered my question, but you want me to answer yours?"

"I would ask who the father was. You know what they say—Momma's baby, daddy's maybe." He could tell that stung a little, but she kept her game face.

"Do you ever plan on having kids?"

"Yeah, in the future. Not now, but, if it happened, it is what it is." He hunched his shoulders. "Now are you pregnant or not?" He finally looked at her and could tell something was wrong with her. Her eyes looked a little glossy.

"No, you can breathe now. I was just feeling you out." She looked to the ceiling and was fighting so hard not to cry. She wanted him to be happy like she was. She wanted him to smile with joy at the possibility . . . but he didn't. "Uh, I gotta get going. I just remembered I got something to do early in the morning."

"Yo! You gotta be shittin' me, right? You just all of a sudden got something to do?" He looked at her like, *"are you for real?"*

"Yeah, I'll call you." She stood up and started getting her things together.

"Man, you on some bullshit," he said as watched her putting her shoes back on.

"How am I on some bullshit because I got something to do?" She was really yelling now and fighting back those tears. "You know what? Don't answer that. I'll see you around."

"What you mean you'll see me around? What the fuck is wrong with you? I ain't even did nothing. Now it sounds like you ready to stop fuckin' with a nigga. What's really good?" He could feel his heart about to stop. She couldn't be serious. No, she couldn't leave him. For what? What had he done in the last ten minutes to make that happen? He tried to replay their conversation again in his head so he could see where he may have gone wrong.

"Ain't nothing wrong with me. I'm good. I just got something to do."

"Are you fuckin' pregnant, man?" If she was, he would gladly take on the daddy role, even though he knew he wasn't ready.

Sena had already made up her mind that she was getting an abortion. She didn't want to bring a child into the world without two loving parents. No, she wouldn't put a child through a childhood like her own. She never had a father. She was never daddy's girl or little princess, and she wanted that for her unborn child.

"I told you no. It was just a question." She stopped moving and looked at him.

"What you got to do that's so important that'll make you get up and leave in the middle of the night? What, you got a nigga at home waiting on you?" He knew she didn't because she was loyal to the bone. He just couldn't find anything else to say.

"Why? It wouldn't matter to you. I'm not your woman so you couldn't give two shits about me. I'm just a fuck buddy, ain't I?" It hurt her to her core to even think he felt that way about her.

"If that's what you think, then you are as dumb as you sound right now." He couldn't believe what she was saying. He thought he had shown her every damn day how much he loved her. He did everything for her, no questions asked. He would give her his last if that's what she requested. Only thing was, he had never flat-out told her that he loved her.

"Well, how do you feel about me? What are we? I mean, let me know." She had gone all the way into left field and didn't know why. She was just fine with their relationship, or, at least, that was what she thought. The baby really had her emotions in an uproar.

"What? Because yo' girl got proposed to, you want me to propose to you too?" He regretted those words the moment they left his lips. He knew what she was saying.

She just looked at him like he had a bag of dog shit sitting on his face as the tears began to fall. Then, she chuckled a little bit. She had to laugh to keep the floodgates from opening up. Her heart was being shattered with every word he spoke.

"You still haven't told me shit!" She held up her hand to take a deep breath. "You know what? I don't want you to do a muthafuckin' thing but stand there and shut the fuck up while I walk out this door." She walked to the door. "Like I said, I got something to do in the morning." But, before she walked out the door, she turned back around. "If, and when, my man proposes to me, it won't be because I suggested it. It will be because he wants to spend the rest of his life with me. I'm not into keeping up with the Joneses. I asked a question and never got an answer. But you know what? I *did* get an answer." And, with that, she slammed the door. But Moochie wasn't letting it go down like that. He still didn't know what the hell had happened to make her go off the deep end. He rushed out the door. He had to stop her from walking out of his life.

"What's wrong?" he yelled as he ran after her. Confusion couldn't even begin to describe how he was feeling. What happened? was all he could think.

"Don't worry about it. Just go back to your life." She was crying and running to her car.

"Wait a minute! Don't leave like this! Please tell me what happened. What did I do?" He grabbed hold of her arm, turning her to make her face him and saw that she was crying.

"You didn't do anything. It's me. I'm going through something right now, and I don't need any extra luggage. Just go on back to your life." She tried to walk away.

"So I'm extra luggage?" He was totally outdone by that remark. "You say you going through something, so, instead of going through it with me, you'd rather go through it alone? How the fuck is we supposed to be together and you won't let me in? This shit is new to me, and even I know that don't sound right." He threw his hands up in the air.

"Why are you doing this to me? I understand you're young and want to live your life. I'm not trying to tie you down." She didn't know what she was doing. She just knew she had to get away.

"Tie me down with what? Why would you say that? If I didn't want you in my life, you wouldn't be here." It broke his heart to even think of her leaving. Now here she was standing in tears, and he didn't even know why. "Tell me what happened. I don't even know what I did."

"I told you. It's me, so just leave me alone! I'll call you when my head is clear. Maybe then I can explain to you." She could finally see the love he had in his eyes for her. He really wanted her to stay. But she couldn't. She didn't want to be the one who ruined his life.

"I was doin' just fine till you came along. You got a nigga all in love and shit. Now you want to pull a 180 on me? I don't put my heart out there like that. Now you 'bout to just walk away with it? What type of shit is you on? What the fuck happened in the last hour? Nah, better yet, scratch that. What if I *wanted* to be tied down?" He pulled her chin up so they were looking eye to eye. "What if I said that you are the only woman for me and that I wanted to be with you and only you? What if I said that I love you and really don't want you to leave?" He was looking into her eyes and tried to wipe away some of her tears, but she moved her face out of reach.

"I would say please go on with your life and let me go on with mine. Trust me, this is for the best." She turned and ran to her car. The waterfalls started. She could barely see to get the key in her door. She was so distraught that she clearly forgot she had a remote to open the doors. She got into the car and drove off as Moochie watched her from the middle of the yard, but he couldn't move.

He wanted so bad to go after her and tell her how much he really loved her. But he could tell she had her mind already made up.

She was everything he ever wanted in a woman. Her smile was like fresh air, and it melted his heart every time she did it. The way she would make sure she was touching some part of him in her sleep to make sure he was still there. He loved the way he got lost in her moans while they made love. But, in reality, he wasn't ready for this yet or just didn't want to be ready. Whatever the case, he watched his perfect match drive away, crying, and, in the process, shattering his heart.

"Well, this has been an eventful night, I—" Valencia's sentence was cut short as Kidd stepped into her personal space.

"You think so? That's funny, because the main event hasn't even started yet." He kissed her lips hungrily.

"Oh really?" Vee had to bite her bottom lip to keep her excitement down a little.

"Really." He picked her up and started toward the bedroom.

Kidd laid her down on the bed and began to crawl on top of her. In the process, he pulled his shirt over his head. Vee found herself rubbing all over him. She couldn't keep her hands off of him. He licked and kissed her from her face all the way down to her toes, not yet getting to her sweet spot. He left her toes and began going up her legs with long strokes of his tongue. He made it to her throbbing clit and sucked it right into his mouth, making her scream out in ecstasy. He was happy she wore no panties. The fewer obstacles the better. His tongue was driving her into a frenzy.

"Damn! She wasn't lying. Sheesh! You do have a vicious head game," Raven laughed.

He stopped moving and looked up at Valencia. "What'd you just say?" he asked, trying to make sure he heard correctly.

"I said, 'She wasn't lying when she told me you were Grade A. Don't stop. Keep going.'" she smirked.

"Yo, what the hell is going on, Vee?"

Laughter filled the room and seemed to suck the very air they were breathing right out.

"Oh my God, Kidd, just leave, right now, please!" Valencia was mortified and scared to death. This isn't the way she wanted him to find out about Raven, and especially not at that moment. He'd just proposed to her, and they couldn't even enjoy the moment.

"What the fuck you mean just leave. Not this shit again, Vee." He sat up in frustration.

"Just trust me, please. I'll explain later."

"No, I let you do that shit before. Explain now!"

"Get the fuck outta here. She ain't gotta explain shit to your ass."

"Why you talking in the third person and shit?" Kidd studied Valencia's face and could see a mischievous look spread across it.

"Ummm, let me think . . . because this is the way I talk, nigga."

"Stop talking like that!"

"Wanya, can you please just leave! Please listen to me!"

"Man, wat the fuck is going on, Vee?"

"You's about a dumb muthafucka, I swear."

"Stop talking like that. Vee, why you talkin' like that, baby?"

"Because there is no more Valencia, sir. Ding dong the bitch is dead!" Raven sang.

"Huh?"

"Did you miss me?" She smiled at him.

"Raven?" Confusion flushed his face.

"I was wondering when your dumb ass was gonna figure it out." She laughed a little louder.

"What the fuck is going on, Vee? Why you sound like Raven?" He was now up and almost out of the door.

"Because, dumb ass, I *am* Raven." She stood up to put her clothes back on. "I am she, she is me, we are one!" she said in a little kid's voice as she held up her index finger.

As he looked at her, everything started to add up. He couldn't believe he hadn't put two and two together. Was he really that blinded by love that he couldn't see what was right in front of him? Why couldn't he tell that the woman he loved the most was living a double life right in front of his eyes?

"Wait! Please don't leave! Let me explain. Please don't leave like this." He heard Vee plead with him. He stopped walking.

"Vee?" He stopped and turned to look at her.

"Yes. Please listen to me before she comes back!"

He could see the tears rolling down her face. "What the fuck you mean before she comes back? Here we go with this shit again." He threw his hands in the air.

"Please wait. Raven, she's the she I was talking about," she tried to explain as quickly as possible.

"So what? You got two different personalities or some shit?" He frowned up and stepped away from her.

"Duh, dickhead! How the fuck could you *not* know the woman you in love with is a nut job? And how could you not know that we were the same fuckin' person? Y'all really are some dumb muthafuckas." Raven gave him a look that said dumb ass.

"I'm getting the fuck out of here. You two muthafuckas have a nice life together." Kidd ran down the stairs into the living room.

"Why would you do that, you dumb bitch? I love him, and you will not keep me away from him." Vee ran down the stairs. "Kidd, please wait a minute! Don't just leave. Let me explain, and, if you still want to leave, I'll understand." She had tears running down her face. He hated to see her crying, so he stopped to listen.

"When I was younger, I went through a lot with the people around me. I guess I couldn't handle my life anymore because somewhere along the line, Raven came in and took over. And I let her. She lived through all the pain and suffering I went through as a child. Nobody loved me. Sometimes, I didn't even know where my next meal was coming from. I never had a problem that she didn't handle. We came up with a plan that she could have the nights and I would live the days. And I never had a problem with it until—"

"Until she met your punk ass and wanted to renege on our arrangement!" Raven interrupted.

"Would you shut up for one fuckin' minute!" Valencia yelled. "When you came along, I wanted to live my life. I wanted to be with you. I wanted to be loved and to fall in love, which I did, and she didn't like that. Now, she is doing everything in her power to keep us apart."

"So, she's the one you was talking about when you said you owed someone a debt. So, when you disappeared, you didn't really go anywhere. She just took over?" He looked real confused, but he was trying to understand.

"Yes," Vee answered, exhausted.

"So what about Sena? Does she know all this?"

"She doesn't know either. I've lived this way for more than half my life without fail."

"Oh, okay, enough of this bullshit, bitch. Let his ass go. All this emotional shit is for the fuckin' birds."

"Would you shut the fuck up and let me talk!"

Kidd was just standing there watching her talk to herself. If he wasn't standing there watching, no one would have been able to convince him that this shit was happening. He felt like he had just taken a leap into the Twilight Zone.

"Ah, look at this shit. This nigga's a pussy. He getting all misty eyed and shit. I see why you two muthafuckas are together. Ole sensitive ass. Fuck is you cryin' for? It's just pussy," Raven taunted.

"Yo, bitch, you got one more time to disrespect me." He was losing his cool. He was trying to understand, but this bitch Raven was working his nerves.

"Please ignore her. Before you leave, I want you know that I love you with all my heart." She started walking toward him, but he backed away. "I know you will never be with me, and I can accept that. I just want you to know that you are my heart. You are the reason I smile. You have my heart, and I don't want it back." She stepped forward, and, this time, he didn't move. He wanted her to touch him to make sure this was really happening.

"Ah, nigga, fuck you, pussy." Instead of the loving touch he longed for, Raven slapped him in the face. "Love don't live here anymore," Raven spat as she turned and walked away from him.

"I am so sorry," Valencia cried. She watched in horror as his facial expression changed to disgust. She knew he would never look at her the same—ever again. The love she once saw in his eyes was now replaced with repulsion.

Vee had to take a deep breath because Raven wouldn't let her finish her sentence. And Kidd looking at her like she had the plague wasn't making things any better.

"I'm so sorry for this. I can't control her. She's always been around. She comes and goes as she pleases. I just don't know what to do anymore." She could see the look of uncertainty written all over his face.

"You muthafuckin' right, bitch! It's you and me for life, till death do us the fuck part." Vee looked defeated.

"So what do you want from me? I ain't with this schitzo shit." It didn't matter how she explained it. He knew they could never be together again. The more she talked, the more his happily ever after slipped further and further away.

"I don't want anything from you. I just wanted you to know that I appreciate everything you did for me. I now know what it feels like to be loved. And that's all I ever wanted in my life. As you can see, I can't seem to stop her." She was crying even harder now as she walked over to the bookshelf and pulled out the Bible. "I will always love you."

Chapter 23

Revelations

Moochie was up, on his way to Valencia's house. He needed to talk to someone about what had happened. As he drove down the streets, he couldn't help but think about his situation, not knowing what to do about Sena. He couldn't wait for his brother to come home to help him out. No, he needed him at that very moment to school him and drop some knowledge about this thing called love. Was he supposed to chase after her or let her breathe? He didn't know what to do. But what he did know was he wouldn't be any good if she didn't come back soon. He hadn't expected her to invade his heart that way. She snuck in through the back and caught him by surprise. Unfortunately, for him, it was already too late when he realized it.

When he got to the door no one was answering as he knocked. But he could clearly hear yelling and crying. So he went around to the back to see what was going on. The back half of Valencia's home was glass so he knew he would see whatever was going on. When he got to the window, he thought his eyes were playing tricks on him. Kidd was standing in the middle of Vee's living room with her on the other side with a gun pointed at him. He checked his hip to make sure he had his gun on him.

Vee was waving the gun real crazylike. She kept pointing the gun back and forth between her and Kidd. It looked like she could barely see. Her eyes were so black from the black makeup she wore around her eyes. She pointed the gun back at Kidd, and Moochie was fed up with that shit for real.

He picked up a huge vase that Valencia had in her back-yard filled with flowers and threw it through the window. The glass shattered everywhere, but Moochie took no time to assess the damage. He rushed right in. He came in gun drawn, ready to shoot now and ask questions later.

"Ah, now, ain't this shit too cute. You came to save yo' big brother, so you don't just save hoes. You save niggas too, huh?" Raven laughed at him.

Moochie looked at Kidd, but he just hunched his shoulders and nodded back toward Raven. He wouldn't know how to explain this situation if his life depended on it.

"What the fuck is wrong with you, Vee? I can't just let you shoot my brother. Bitch, I will shoot the shit out of you with no second thoughts about it." He kept his gun aimed, never breaking eye contact.

"You see this shit, Vee? Don't you call him your brother. You see the people you trying to leave me for?"

Now Moochie was really looking confused and looked at his brother again, and Kidd just raised his eyebrow and nodded toward Raven again.

"Moochie, I'm so sorry," was all she could muster up to say. She was at a loss for words as she watched her world come crashing down around her.

"What's going on, sis? Why you waving guns and shit?" Moochie asked softly now that he assessed the situation a little closer. She was crying hysterically, and Kidd didn't seem too worried.

"I'm not about to explain myself to this nigga. Bitch, is you fuckin' him too? Jeez, Louise!"

"I am not waving guns at anyone."

"Well, what the fuck *is* you doin'?"

"I don't know anymore."

"So since, technically, I'm not Valencia, can I test the goods? Sena just raves about how good you are! And I'm tryin'a see what that be like." Raven laughed at Moochie's facial expression.

"See, now you doing too much." Kidd gritted. Raven was about to see what he was really about. He'd never hit a woman before, but he would make an exception for her.

"Moochie, shoot her!" he heard Vee's voice say.

"Shoot who?" He was looking around the room. He still hadn't caught on yet.

"Her! Me!" she pointed to herself.

"What kind of dumb bitch are you to ask somebody to shoot you? Uh-uh, you see how crazy she is?" Raven said sarcastically while twirling both her pointer fingers in circles around her ears. "I mean, if you really loved her, could you really shoot her? I mean, if I loved somebody, I don't think I could shoot 'em." Raven walked around the room with the gun down by her side.

"Yo, Kidd! What the fuck is going on?" Moochie walked closer to his brother.

"She *is* Raven."

"What?" He stood up straight and let the gun fall to his side. "Come again?" He needed to hear that shit again.

"I know. You ain't even got to say nothing," Kidd said, reading his brother's mind.

"I'm so sorry. I didn't know how to tell you. I just wanted to be loved and know what it felt like to love someone. Just remember, I did love you like a real brother, and I would never do anything to hurt you or Kidd. This gun isn't for him. It's for me," she cried. She didn't want to be in the world any longer if she could never be around them again. She knew neither Kidd nor Moochie would ever be with her or around her now that they knew about her horrid secret.

"The hell it is, bitch. What you think you going to do with this gun? Shoot me? How you gonna shoot me without shooting yourself?" Raven smirked, figuring she hadn't fully thought her little plan through.

"Wait a minute! You don't have to do that. You can get some help." Kidd finally found his voice. He knew he couldn't be with her, but he would never wish death on her. The world without her spirit just wouldn't be right.

"No, she will never leave me alone, and I know she will never let me be with you. I can't even fathom my life without you. It would be like making me breathe in a plastic bag. Just can't do it. Eventually, you die. You, Kidd, taught me how to love. Please remember you were my first and only love. And I thank you for loving me."

"Please don't do this, Vee. You don't have to do this!" Now Kidd was getting hysterical. "What about Sena? You would put her through this again?" He knew she loved Sena, so he threw her in there, so she would know that it was not just him and Moochie that would be missing her.

"Fuck that bitch! She ain't never did shit for me! I couldn't even call on her when I needed her the most, so she could go suck on a sandpaper dick!" Raven was spitting real venom now.

Moochie felt his trigger finger itching. Raven had hit a soft spot with him.

"Vee, you don't believe that. She almost had a nervous breakdown last time you got hurt. Don't do it again," Kidd pleaded.

"Fuck her and this damn Brady Bunch shit y'all tried to create."

"Vee, you are stronger than her."

"Noooo, she's noooottttt," Raven sang sadistically.

"Yes, you are, baby, you can do it. Fight it."

Moochie was still in shock. He hadn't said a word since the revelation.

"See what I mean? I can't control her. Plus, I promised myself that I would never let her play with my life again. First, she took you away from me. Then, she almost got me killed. Now she's back to take what she believes is hers. But it's not hers; it's mine, and, if I can't have it all to myself, I don't want it at all."

"Nooooooo!" Kidd tried to tackle her, but he got to her too late.

Chapter 24

Shattered Hearts

Valencia finally woke up to the sounds of the machines constantly beeping. She looked around the gloomy hospital room, and it felt like déjà vu. Only, this time, she was all alone. She didn't have anybody to call. She was too scared to call anybody. She knew Kidd and Moochie didn't want to see or hear from her, and Sena . . . She wasn't sure if they had told her what happened. She wondered if the bitch Raven was lurking around waiting to appear. She felt around her body because she couldn't believe she was still alive. But, in reality, she had only grazed her head. With her shaking hands and the sight of Kidd running toward her, she had missed her mark.

Where is Kidd? How come I'm not in jail? Why aren't I dead? She had so many questions.

She turned her head, looking for the call button, not realizing she had one right by her face, and it was sensitive to the touch.

"Yes, how can I help you?" a young patient care technician asked as she walked into the room.

"I didn't know I called." Valencia turned her head toward the young lady. "I was actually looking for the call button." She looked around the bed.

"Oh, here it is," she smiled at Vee.

"I wanted to see if I could talk to the doctor."

"I'll tell the nurse." The young girl smiled and walked back out of the room.

Valencia took a deep breath as she picked up the phone. She knew she needed to call Sena no matter if Kidd and Moochie had already told her the story. She needed to tell her own side of the story.

"Hello."

"Well, I can't believe you answered," Valencia exclaimed in excitement.

"Hey, chic-a-dee! What you doing?" Sena really wasn't in a talkative mood, but she needed to speak to her friend.

"I've been better. Have you spoken to Moochie?" she asked, trying to see what Sena had heard.

"Naw, we broke up last night." Sena got choked up, and her voice cracked a little.

"Why? What happened?" She was surprised by this revelation.

"It's a long story. I'll tell you when we're face-to-face. Where you at?"

"At the hospital," Vee answered, not knowing how else to answer.

"Hospital? For what?" Sena went from zero to Code Blue in one second.

"I'm okay. Like you said, it's a long story. You can come and get me. I'm ready to get out of here." Valencia was glad that Moochie hadn't gotten to Sena before she could explain her own story. She got out of bed, almost forgetting that quickly that she was hooked up to the IV machine until she felt a pull in her arm. "*Ssssss*" she hissed at the pain. She made a quick assessment of her surroundings and noticed she only had to unplug it to get the bathroom, which she did, and pulled it along with her to the bathroom as she walked there. Passing the mirror, she saw the bandage that stretched along-side her face, and her knees went weak. She grabbed ahold of the sink to get her balance. Once she was stable, she began pulling the bandage off and was instantly sickened by the sight of the wound that stretched from her cheek to her temple. It looked to be about a thousand stitches. But in reality, it was only sixteen.

"Look at this. What did I do?" she cried. Images of hurt and fear in Kidd's eyes flashed in her mind. It hurt her even more to know she had caused him more pain. But it wasn't her fault. It was Raven's. It was all Raven's fault. Why wouldn't she just leave well enough alone and let her live her life?

She couldn't believe her life had come to a full halt. Why had she sunk so low? So low she tried to end her own life . . . Was it really that bad? She ran her finger along the stitches and sighed. "Life must go on." She examined the wound one more time before walking out of the bathroom. Though she was trying to go on with her life, she knew her life would never be the same. She didn't think she would be able to even go back to the way things were before Kidd came into her life.

Knock Knock Knock!

Valencia heard someone at her door, and she jumped at the thought of it being Kidd. But the sight of the nurse walking in quickly dashed her moment of hope.

"Yes? You wanted to see me?" the nurse smiled.

"Yes, I wanted to know what happened to me." She unconsciously rubbed her wound.

"Well, according the guy that came in with you, he was teaching you how to use your new gun. You dropped it, and it went off. When his little brother found you two, the young man broke down the window in the back to get to you, and they called the police." Valencia thought about the story for a minute. It was somewhat believable. She would go with it since Kidd had already put it out there.

"OK, thank you."

Twenty minutes later, Sena came walking in.

"What the hell did you do?" Sena asked as she walked up to Valencia's bed.

"Have a seat." She scooted over and patted a spot on the bed for Sena to sit on.

"So you know how you joke and say, 'Girl, what the hell is wrong with you? You got double personality or something?'" Valencia laughed at herself at how she sounded while mocking Sena.

"Um, yeah." Sena gave her a strong side eye.

"Well, you weren't wrong in your observations."

"What hell you talking about, girl?"

"Remember when that girl in the mall got me mixed up with a woman named Raven?"

"Yeah . . ." Sena answered slowly.

"Well, she was correct."

"What hell are you talking about? Stop talking in riddles and give it to me raw, dammit!" Sena was becoming impatient.

Valencia looked at her with tears in her eyes, fearful of losing her only friend in the world. She looked at her with questioning eyes. Will she believe her? Will she run for the hills? Will she stay around?

"Listen, honey, I'm here with you. You can trust me. I will not judge you. You will always be my sister," Sena reassured her after noticing the uncertainty in Valencia's eyes.

"Well, when I was younger, I went through a lot, as you know. So I won't go into all those details. But somewhere along the line, I developed another personality to help me get through everything I was going through. She took in all the pain I was supposed to be going through. Raven came at a time in my life when I was at my most vulnerable."

"Wait a minute, so you're serious?"

"Let me finish while I have the gall, please, ma'am." Valencia chuckled a little at Sena's anxiousness.

Sena threw her hands up in surrender. "Carry on."

"I won't make this too long."

"We ain't got nothing but time, chile," Sena interrupted again.

"OK, so me and Raven came up with a game plan that she would come out at night or when I needed her, which means when I was angry or hurt, she would come in to protect me. And I would live throughout the days."

"You mean like a night shift and day shift type of deal?"

"Yeah, something like that. Any who, we never coexisted. So I didn't know of the things she did when I slept. Until recently. Then I found out she's a lesbian who likes to beat and torture women."

"Wait—what!" Sena yelled.

"Yeah, I didn't find that out until she came back and tried to take over for good."

"Wait—what? So she was out here killing women?" Sena sat back a little, then a lightbulb went off in her head. "So that's her on the news they been talking about?"

"Yes, that's her. She's sick and twisted, and I don't know where it came from, because I never had problems with women."

"And when you disappeared?"

"She took over and tried to take my life from me. But I guess one of the girls she had left for dead survived and came back with revenge on her mind."

"I'll be damned. This is too damn much." Sena took in a deep breath, not knowing how to process all of this information. "OK, so let me get this straight. You have multiple personality disorder, she took over your life when you disappeared, and she's a fuckin' nutcase lesbian serial killer?"

"Yes."

"I can't believe it. So, all this time, you've been living with that your whole life?" Sena asked in disbelief. How had she not noticed this? But, then again, she would always ask Vee if she was bipolar because, some days, she seemed different.

"Yeah, I didn't know how to tell you. What was I supposed to say? Hey, my name is Valencia, but, sometimes, it's Raven." She put the pillow to her face to block the scream that so desperately wanted to come out.

"OK, so what happened last night?" Sena needed all the details before she made her assessment. See would never leave her friend high and dry, but she would definitely encourage her to get some help.

"Me and Kidd were about to have sex; then she showed up and showed out in a major way. She was still upset that I chose him over her. And, of course, he flipped out, and then, Moochie showed up. I couldn't take the way they were looking at me. I knew those looks meant they would never want to be around me again. And I couldn't fathom the thought. So I decided if I couldn't live my life, no one would."

"So you would leave me like that?"

"I'm sorry, Sena, but in that moment, I just didn't want to live anymore."

"But you would leave me when I need you most?" Sena thought about the unborn child growing in her stomach and started to cry.

"I'm sorry." Valencia joined Sena in the shedding of tears.

"So where are they?"

"Probably somewhere never wanting to see me again."

"I'm sure Kidd didn't say that. You have to give him a chance to adjust. Shit, it's a lot to take in." Sena reached out and grabbed Valencia's hand. "Shit, I'm still over here at a loss for words. I have so many questions, but they won't come out."

"I just want to give up, friend. I'm tired. I'm so tired of fighting her."

"You can't give up, babe."

"I can't fight her any longer, Sena. She's draining me. Look at me." Valencia pointed to the wound on her face.

"Look, we'll come up with something. I can't lose you again."

"OK, can we come back to that later? I just want to talk about something else for minute. This has been consuming my life for so long. Enough about me. Now, why did you and Moochie break up? What did you do?"

"Why do you just assume it was me?"

"Because I know you. What did you do, woman?"

"I'm pregnant," Sena whispered.

"Come again."

"I'm pregnant." Sena finally looked back up at Valencia.

"Bitch!" Valencia yelled. "OMG, I'm gonna be an aunt!" Valencia's smiled faded. "Wait, did that nigga leave you when he found out you were pregnant?"

"No, I never told him."

"What do you mean? Well, what happened?" Valencia was confused now.

"I started to tell him. But I panicked when I looked into his eyes. He had this look of horror in them that said he wanted no part of having any children. I didn't want to be the one who ruined his life."

"You didn't even give him a chance, babe." Though Valencia was going through her own crisis, she was trying to be there for her friend, but Sena wasn't making any sense.

"I can't tell him." Sena shook her head. All she kept seeing was his eyes when she mentioned the possibility of him being a father.

"Why not? How will he find out if you're not talking to him and I'm not talking to him?"

"I will not give him the chance to reject my child. All I need is you and my baby." Sena looked out the window at the sky and breathed heavily.

"I understand that, but the man has really done nothing wrong for you to keep him away. He may not be ready to be a daddy, but I believe he would make a great father.

If not, you know Kidd would gladly help. And besides, I don't know how long I'm gonna be around to help out. It would ease my heart to know you're being taken care of." Vee could feel tears starting to form in her eyes. What would she do now? She needed to come up with a plan to keep Raven away. She wanted her life more than ever now. She wanted to be the best aunt ever, and she wouldn't let Raven take that away from her. Raven had already taken the love of her life away. She wouldn't be taking anything else if she could help it. She was tired of crying, so she shook the tears off.

"What do you mean? Isn't she gone?"

"You never know. I hope so, but, just in case, please tell him."

"Well, what we gon' do?" Sena was willing to help her in any way she could.

"I don't know. I never thought about actually getting rid of her. She's always been around. Though right now, I want her gone. But in the beginning, I don't think I could have survived without her."

"Yes, you could have. You just didn't know, but you are much stronger than her."

"I don't know about that. But, we'll see."

"I'm gonna tell Moochie when I'm ready. I just have to build up the courage."

"OK, if you say so." Valencia didn't understand at all what Sena was talking about. How could she just give up on the love she and Moochie shared because she was afraid? She would never have given up on Kidd like that, and for that, she felt a little jealousy.

"You ready to get out of here?" Sena asked, breaking Valencia's train of thought.

"Yes."

Chapter 25

Want that Old Thing Back

The past four months had been hell for Sena going through the pregnancy alone. Valencia tried to be there for her, but it wasn't the same. She couldn't hold her at night or make love to her. She missed Moochie very much. She just didn't know how to approach the situation with him. How would he react to seeing her after all this time? Then, to top it off, she was now six-and-a-half-months pregnant, so there was no hiding it. She had found out last week that it was a girl. She had returned to work, but Valencia never went back. She didn't have a fat savings account to live off of like Valencia. The bills had to get paid, and she wasn't into asking people for handouts.

Her stubborn pride was standing in front of her happiness because she knew Moochie would have taken care of her, especially if he knew the situation.

"Johnson and Associates, please hold." Sena was back to her old routine and hating every bit of it. She looked up from her desk . . . and Kidd was standing right there. She almost pissed her pants.

"Uhh . . . Kidd . . . How you been?" she stuttered as she scooted up closer to try to hide her protruding baby bump.

"Lemme holla at you for a minute." He studied her face and body and noticed some discrepancies.

"Uhhh . . . yeah. Give me a minute. Go into the conference room on the left." She watched him walk away and wanted to run for the nearest exit, but she knew she would have to face him eventually.

She walked into the room, and his face turned into a ball of anger. "So why we didn't we know nothing about *this?*" He pointed to her stomach.

"Because it's none of your business, that's why."

"Don't fuckin' play with me right now, Sena!" Kidd was pissed beyond measure. His little brother was about to a father, and he didn't even know about it.

"How do you even know it's his?" She put her hands on her hips.

"It better be, and, if my calculations add up right, you're about six months by the looks of things. And if it ain't, if I know my brother, you gonna have a fatherless child." Kidd was dead serious. He knew Moochie would flip the fuck out if he knew Sena was pregnant by another man.

She took a deep breath and slid down into a chair. "I'm so sorry. I didn't know how to tell him," she pleaded.

"You sound like your friend now," he countered sarcastically.

"Whoa, pa'tna! Leave her out of this." No matter what, Valencia was still her girl, and nobody would be disrespecting her in any way, shape, or form. "She's the one who told me to tell him. I just didn't want him to hate me." She started crying.

"Why would he hate you?" He looked away for a minute. He hated seeing women cry. It always reminded him of his mother.

"'Cause this ain't the life he wanted, and I didn't want to force him into anything." She wiped the tears away. "When I met him, he made it pretty clear what he was about. Sex and money, and I was fine with that. Then, we started getting closer, and I was getting more attached than he was. Then, I found out about the baby. And I just panicked. I had to get away." She kept looking at the floor.

"So are you gonna tell him?" He couldn't help but think, *Damn, this is supposed to be Vee and me.* He felt a slight pain in his heart.

"Yeah. I mean, I really have no choice now that you know. Please let me tell him. I don't want him to find out that way." She sat up and leaned forward.

"Okay. I'll let you tell him, but if you take too long, I'll have to tell him." He felt his brother had a right to know about his seed. He had heard the story on what went down and thought it was totally stupid of her to just leave for no reason. If Valencia didn't have issues, there was no way in the world he would have let her leave his life.

"I know. I know. Well, welcome to uncle-hood." She smiled and rubbed her stomach.

"Damn right! I'm gonna be an uncle. Damn! Moochie 'bout to be a daddy," he said excitedly. "So what is it?"

"A girl. She's gonna be a little minime."

"Naw, homie. She ain't gonna be no li'l freak monster." He laughed at her.

"Shut up, punk. You know what I mean. Anyway, how's he been doing?" She didn't know if she wanted to hear the answer, but she wanted him to be miserable like her.

"He been all right. I guess you know Moochie gon' always be Moochie. How you been? You been all right going through all this alone?"

"Yeah. Well, I haven't really been alone. Vee has been a really big help. Catering to my cravings, rubbing my feet, dealing with the gas. Hell, I think she's more excited than me. She has more stuff for the baby at her house than I do. She lives on the Internet and has all these baby magazines and ordering all this high-priced stuff." She laughed a little. "She was telling me about the Bentley of strollers, and I told her my baby is a Chevy type." They both laughed.

"How's she doing?" She still held his heart. No matter what he did, she was still there in his memories to remind him of yesterday. He wanted to see her but didn't know how to go about it. He was scared of the possibilities of Raven being there too.

"She's taking it day by day. She quit working here and is really staying to herself. Vee doesn't really go anywhere for fear that Raven may come back. As of yet, we haven't heard from her." She hunched her shoulders.

"Why isn't she on any medicine for that?"

"She said she doesn't want to become addicted to anything."

"So she's just gon' live her life like that?" He was trying to get some understanding about the situation.

"To tell you the truth, she has really given up. She's just waiting for Raven to come back, and she's not going to fight it." Sena felt sad all over again.

"Why would she just give up like that?"

"She said if she can't live the life she dreamed of with you, she doesn't want it at all. I don't know what I'm gonna do without my best friend. But I know she doesn't want to live like this. When you left, you took the best of my friend with you. Now, I'm not blaming you for nothing. I'm just letting you know."

"What was I supposed to do, Sena? I had never in my life seen no shit like that." He tried to explain.

"You were supposed to love her through it. Let her know she wasn't alone!" Sena raise her voice.

"You not gonna blame all this on me, Sena."

"I'm not blaming you, but you just left and never looked back."

"You think I never looked back? I think of her every day. I dial her number a hundred times a day but am too afraid to press 'call.' I'll always love her, and she will always have my heart. But I don't know if I'm the guy for this kind of job."

"Bruh . . ." She reached out and grabbed his hands. "You are the *only* guy." There was long pause.

"Well, we'll be at Happy Hour Bar and Grill this Friday playing a little pool if you want to come and talk to my brother." He had a lot of thinking to do. He wanted to go see about Valencia, see her smile and hear her laugh. But he knew it wouldn't be the same. No matter how much he loved her, he couldn't deal with the craziness. He felt his phone vibrating as he walked out of the office. He gave Sena a nod and answered his phone.

"What's the business?"

"Not shit. At Goody Goody, 'bout to attack these cheese grits and chicken," Moochie said while chewing in his ear.

"Order me two waffles and two chicken breasts. I'll be there in ten."

"Shit. I'll be done by the time you get here. I guess I could get a couple of waffles for myself."

"Get off my phone, fat ass." He hung up, laughing at his brother. The boy could eat a whole horse if you let him.

Kidd walked into the restaurant and bent the corner. He knew they always ate in the back. It was just a habit to always be able to see the door. He looked at the table and shook his head at all the food on it.

"What's good, my dude?" Moochie reached out for dap.

"I saw Sena today," Kidd said as he sat down. Moochie looked up, and Kidd could see the concern that stretched across his face.

"Where at? How's she doing?" Moochie still wanted to be with her even after everything. They were good together. After she left, he went back to his old ways and put a deadbolt lock on his heart.

"You'll see Friday. I told her to come hang out with us at Happy Hour."

"You do know them chicks coming, right?"

"So what that mean? Like you care? I sure as hell don't." He stuffed some chicken in his mouth.

"So because you don't care about ruining your chances for some ass, you wanna cock block mines."

"Li'l thot gon' fuck regardless."

"That's why you don't care, nigga," Moochie laughed.

"That could be the case, but you and I both know you couldn't give two shits about them chicks. Besides, when you see her, I bet you'll put ole girl in a cab." He looked at his brother with a knowing look.

"How's she lookin'? Is she fat and bald headed?" He wanted her to be suffering for what she had done to him.

"No and no. No, she is actually more beautiful than I remember." Kidd was referring to the expecting glow she had.

"Anyway, so how she say Vee doing?" He missed her and thought his brother should have handled the situation a lot differently.

"She said she doing all right. I just don't understand why she won't get on any medicine or get help." He hunched his shoulders.

"You don't understand why she won't take any medicine? You of all people should understand that, if you don't understand anything else. You should be able to see why she won't take no medicine." He looked up from his plate and stared Kidd in the eyes.

"I know you don't start getting sick until they start healing you, but this is different." He tried to justify his actions.

"A sickness is a sickness. Don't matter what kind." Before Kidd could respond, his phone started to vibrate.

"Hello?" Moochie could tell it was something serious by the way his brother's facial expression changed. Kidd flipped his phone shut.

"Yo! Who was that?"

"Mr. Jackson. Says he needs to see me. He needs a favor."

Chapter 26

Mending Hearts

Kidd could have fallen the fuck out when Mr. Jackson threw some pictures of who was supposed to be his next victim. They were pictures of Valencia and a white girl who looked to be in her late teens. His heart felt like it was gonna beat through his chest cavity. His poker face was slowly fading the more Mr. Jackson talked.

"Are you listening to me?" Mr. Jackson asked.

"Yeah," Kidd answered with a faraway look in his eyes. The thought of Vee being dead was a thought unthinkable. There was no way in the world he could do it. What had she done to get on his shit list?

"Now, I want her tortured and killed. This is very important. She is the last person to see my precious daughter Kennedy alive." He paused to look at the picture of his twin daughters on their fifth birthday.

"Did she kill your daughter?" Kidd couldn't believe what he was hearing. No, not his precious Vee.

"I'm not certain of what happened, but I do know that my daughter left with her alive and returned dead. That is *not* acceptable."

"I'm sorry for your loss, but you know I don't kill women." Kidd couldn't take his eyes off the pictures in front of him. His heart felt like it was going into cardiac arrest.

"Well, I need you to overlook that little rule of yours. If this wasn't important, I wouldn't ask because I understand that you are out. But I want this done efficiently, and I know you can do it." Kidd sat there, just staring at the picture. "You will be greatly rewarded," Mr. Jackson stated in a matter-of-fact tone. Kidd knew he couldn't say no. Mr. Jackson wasn't asking him to do this. It was an order.

Kidd left Mr. Jackson's house in a daze. He drove around aimlessly. He couldn't imagine killing Vee. No matter what they went through, she didn't deserve to die. Did she really have something to with his daughter's death? What kind of person was Raven? It had to have been her because it was a club party picture, and Vee didn't go to clubs. Vee was so kindhearted and tender. The thought alone of her killing someone was ridiculous, but Raven . . . she was a whole different story. Kidd knew in the end he had just signed his own death certificate because, if he couldn't commit to killing Vee, both he and Vee would die. He had to figure out something quick because he knew the timeline was short.

"So I saw Kidd today." Sena finally found the right time to tell Valencia. They were at Sena's house putting the baby crib together. Tears instantly came to Valencia's eyes. She missed him so much she didn't know what to do with herself. He was somewhere in the world living his life with her heart in his hands. He had taken any happiness she ever felt with him and didn't look back. She put her hands to her face and started crying tears she thought were long gone. Sena pulled her into her arms.

"I'm sorry. I just thought you should know," Sena said while trying to wipe away her own tears.

"I miss him so much, Sena. Why did this have to happen? I feel like I'm in quicksand. Every step I take to get over him, I fall deeper, and now, I feel like I'm drowning. It hurts. I feel like I can't breathe."

"I know, honey. Get it out." Sena knew exactly how she felt because she felt the same way when she walked away from Moochie. Valencia sat up and looked at Sena.

"You know I never told you how stupid you were for walking away from Moochie." Sena frowned, but she let her finish. "I'm not trying to hurt your feelings. You told me to hold on to my love with a death grip, and you just let yours go without a fight. If I could go back in time, I would change so much in my life. I'm only telling you this because I love you." Sena looked surprised. She had never said that before. Vee could read her mind. "I know, right? Anyway, I now know what love is, but I have no choice in the matter. I will never feel love like that again. And to tell you the truth, I have come to grips with that. But I don't want that life for you. You have a lot of love to give, and I know Moochie would gladly accept and return it," Vee said sincerely.

Now, Sena was in a fit of tears, and her friend was right. How could she have let something beautiful go for no reason at all? At first, she thought she had her reasons, but now those reasons seemed so asinine.

"What did I do, Vee? He's never gonna forgive me for this." She looked down.

"Yes, he will. What happened to the Sena who thought everything was possible?" They shared a laugh.

"She died that night." Sena looked up into her friend's eyes and could see the pain behind them. She didn't want to live with that kind of pain anymore.

"No, she didn't. I still see that sparkle in your eyes. Don't let it go 'cause it's not time. Your baby is gonna need to see that when she looks into your eyes."

"I'm supposed to meet them at Happy Hour Bar and Grill this Friday, and I don't know what to do."

"You gonna get your man back. What the hell you talking about?"

"What you gon' do about Kidd?"

"What can I do? *I* wouldn't even want to be with me." She looked to the ceiling to keep the tears from falling again.

"He still loves you. When he asked about you, I could see it all in his eyes."

"I wouldn't want to put him through that again," she said, shaking her head. "Let's work on getting your man back. These damn sweat suits ain't gonna get it."

"I am not about to go shopping with this big-ass watermelon sticking out the front of me."

"You act like you gained a hundred pounds, girl. Come on." Actually, she had only gained about fifteen pounds. "Your cheeks gained all the weight, and we ain't dressing your face." She pinched Sena's cheeks since they had gotten so full. "We going to get fried, dyed, and laid to the side. Then, it's off to do some serious shopping, and my wardrobe needs some serious updating."

The girls were having a good time. It felt good for them to get out and hang out again. They got facials, massages, manis, and pedis.

"All right. I'll see you in a little bit." Vee waved to Sena as she went to the other side of the beauty shop.

"Why you being so secretive about your hairdo?" Sena knew Vee wasn't going to do nothing different. She loved her hair like she loved herself.

"You'll see, honey." She walked away.

When Vee walked from around the back, Sena just knew she wasn't seeing what she thought she was seeing.

"Ahhhh, what the hell did you do?"

"You like?" Vee had cut her hair all the way down. She took it back to Halle Berry in the James Bond movie 007.

"Yes, I love it. Oh my God! I would have never guessed. I thought you were going to come out with some blond highlights or something to that effect, but never this." Sena looked at her friend in awe because she would never have the courage to cut her hair off.

"Well, I'm starting anew. I felt the need for a change." She rubbed her hands through her hair. "I donated it all to Locks of Love."

"Damn, girl. I wish I was that brave." Sena admired her haircut. She really loved it.

"Okay, now. Let's go wreak havoc on the mall."

They were in Motherhood maternity store, having a fashion show. Sena really didn't have to shop there since she really didn't gain too much weight. She was all stomach.

"Hello, ladies. My name is Reagan, and I'll be right over there if you need anything. So, do we know what we are going with over here?" The young saleslady had been try-ing to get closer to the pair for about thirty minutes. She knew Valencia from somewhere but didn't know from where. There was something about the woman standing in front of her that sent chills up her spine.

"Everything! I have a few more months to be pregnant, so I may as well look good," Sena said, rubbing her stomach.

"How far along are you?" She asked Sena the question but couldn't keep her eyes of Valencia.

"Six and a half months."

"Excuse me. I'm sorry, but do I know you from some-where?" she asked Vee. She was really trying to figure it out.

"I don't think so." She knew it was a mix-up with her and Raven again. Sena could see the fear in her eyes.

"They say we all have a twin somewhere in the world," Sena said, trying to help Vee out.

"I had a twin. Her name was Kennedy, but she was murdered a few years ago." They could see the pain in her eyes, but that had nothing to do with them. "We were named after our parents' favorite presidents."

"I'm sorry to hear that," Vee told her; then she carried the clothing to the counter.

"Why is this girl telling us her life story?" Sena asked.

"I don't know. Maybe mentioning twins brought some-thing out. Stop being mean."

Reagan stared at Valencia the whole time she checked them out. Valencia wondered where Raven knew this girl from. Obviously, it wasn't a good encounter. Sena went into her purse.

"I got it, girl. Don't say I never did anything for you." Valencia handed the girl her credit card. She read the name but nothing popped into her head. The name wasn't familiar, but her face was etched in her mind for some reason.

"Oh, well, thank you, girl. Shoot, I should have gotten more if knew I was on a free shopping spree," she laughed.

"Whatever. Let's go."

When Sena and Valencia finally left the store, Reagan ran to the back of the store to look at the surveillance tape. She knew it was something big because it kept eating at her like somebody was trying to tell her something. She watched as they laughed and joked. That smile gave her goose bumps as she fast-forwarded a little, then stopped when she saw Vee doing a little two step before she helped Sena put her shoes back on. She remembered it like it was yesterday. Raven was the last person to see her sister alive.

But this girl on tape said her name was Valencia Ball. Could it be a coincidence? she asked herself.

"She acted like she didn't know who I was, but my sister and I were identical. No, that's her. It's got to be her. That's the bitch that killed my sister." The tears started falling down her face. "She was right here in front of me, living and laughing like nothing ever happened. But I'll change all of that . . ." She continued to watch the tape and imagined shooting Valencia in the head. Soon, she picked up the phone to make a call.

Chapter 27

One More Try

Valencia sat in the living room playing *Madden*, thinking of her time with Kidd. She could still see him sitting next to her, pouting because she was beating him. She missed the energy he brought around. The love could be felt throughout the room. His scent was intoxicating. She needed his touch so badly that her imagination would play tricks on her, because, at times, she thought she could actually feel him touching her.

"So what you gonna do?" Raven asked her.

"About what?" She really didn't want to have any kind of conversation with Raven. She missed the times when they had their own times of the day and they never had to interact with each other. Now, it seemed like Raven came and went as she pleased with no warning, and the headaches had gone away too.

"Kidd. You know what I'm talking about." For some reason, Raven felt bad about the way Vee was feeling.

"There ain't too much I can do about it. He never wants to see me again. And I don't blame him. Why do you even care? Isn't this what you wanted?"

"Yes, well, not all of this. We used to be happy and out in the world, laughing and having fun. What happened?"

"First of all, *you* were the one having all the fun. I was just existing, and, second, I'm not stopping you from having fun. I've never stopped you before." She could feel the tears starting to fall.

"Whether or not you believe it, I am sorry. I never wanted it to come to this. I won't interfere with your life anymore. I was here because you needed me, and now you don't need me anymore. I get it. I never thought it was that serious until you tried to kill both of us. Well, like you told Miss Sena, go get your man." Raven had finally come to grips that this wasn't her life to live anymore. Vee no longer needed her. No matter what, she did love Vee. They had been together for over fifteen years. Now, it was time for her to move on.

"Yeah, right. You expect me to believe that?"

"Like I said, I'm sorry."

"Are you serious?" She got no answer. "Raven, answer me! Are you serious?" Still no answer. Was she really gone? She started yelling. "Why would you do this? I don't want this life. Now that you've fucked it up, you want to leave? Don't do this. Take it! I don't want this, please. My life is already over. You can have it."

She fell to her knees, not understanding what was going on. She should be happy, but she was not happy at all. There was no way she could just go on like nothing ever happened. The damage was already done. What was making her leave now—after she had caused so much pain and heartache? Vee had kind of gotten used to her life and the life she began to put back together after Kidd left. Raven's words ran rampant through her mind, but the one thing that stood out the most was, *Go get your man.*

Kidd sat at his mother's grave site, crying his heart out and talking to his mother.

"Momma, I don't know what to do. I chose this life, and I know it was the wrong choice. You wouldn't be proud of me, and the worst part is, I brought Moochie into this shit. Is this the payback for all my sins?" He looked at the pictures of Vee scattered around him. How could he kill the love of his life, the woman who was supposed to bear his kids?

"I need you here, Ma. If you were here, I wouldn't be going through any of this. I know you would help me through anything." His life had gone from to sugar to shit in a matter of one conversation. He hadn't even told Moochie yet, because he didn't know what to do. He did know that he couldn't kill Valencia. He heard someone walking up on him and pulled his hammer as he turned his upper part of his body. He let it fall when he saw Moochie walking toward him.

"What's up, man?" Moochie questioned with a worried look in his eyes.

He could see his brother had been crying. He had been trying to reach Kidd since nine that morning, and it was now going on three o'clock in the afternoon. It was very unlike Kidd to not answer his phone. Day or night, he kept his phone close. So he hit the locator on his phone to find out where he was and came to see about him. Moochie looked at all the pictures lying around and picked one up. "What's this about?"

Kidd looked up, and tears started falling all over again. "He wants me to kill her." He looked back down at the ground.

"Who? Mr. Jackson?" Moochie asked, shocked.

"Yeah, he says she was the last person to see his daughter alive. What the fuck am I supposed to do?"

Moochie couldn't answer that question. He himself didn't even know what he would do had he been faced with the same predicament.

"Did she do it?" Moochie asked. Moochie really didn't care if she did or didn't. He didn't want to see her dead either.

"I don't think so. It looks like Raven." He handed Moochie the picture. He could see how his brother couldn't tell the difference. Raven's eyes were cold and sinister. She put you in the mind of the cat that ate the canary, while Vee's innocence shined brightly through her eyes. Her aura was loving and caring. Plus, he couldn't even get Valencia to go to a club, and this was definitely a club picture.

"I don't know, man. Did you tell him you knew her?" Kidd shook his head no. "You know I got ya back on whatever you come up with. Just make sure you can deal with the consequences."

"I can't. That's the fucking problem! So it's gonna come down to either kill her or they kill us both." Kidd was speaking just above a whisper, but Moochie had heard enough.

"Well, I know for a fact the second one won't be happening. I'd burn down the whole fuckin' city of St. Louis. Shut this muthafucka down. So you better come up with something quick 'cause you know I choose you over her any day."

"So you could kill her?"

Moochie got quiet.

"I didn't think so."

"If it came down to you or her, I would share her brains with the world, plain and simple. Come on, man, I don't like to see you like this. Let's go have a few drinks and ponder this situation over. We'll come up with something, even if we have to leave the fucking country and take her crazy ass with us." He chuckled a little, and Kidd followed.

Sena walked into Happy Hour with her stomach doing a million flips. She didn't know if it was the baby kicking or her nerves getting the best of her. She was clad in some maternity skinny jeans and a loose cowl neck sweater and flat rider boots. She looked to the left and could see Kidd and Moochie with some girls playing pool. Her heart sank to her feet when she saw Moochie with his arms around the girl's waist. She walked to the right and sat at the bar facing them. They hadn't seen her come in. She watched how Moochie interacted with the girl. She looked to the makeshift stage they had set up. There was a guy who was messing up Marvin Gaye's "Let's Get It On." She couldn't help but laugh because he sounded horrible. It was karaoke night, so she knew it was going to be entertaining. She immediately thought about Vee and how she would have loved to be there. If there was singing going on, Vee was always in the building. She looked back at Moochie and his date. She wondered if she was his new girlfriend. Did he love her? Did he touch her the way he used to touch her? Did she make him laugh? Why had Kidd invited her if he knew Moochie would have a date?

That was enough wondering. Her stomach had finally stopped flipping, and her nerves had calmed down a little. She got up and slowly approached them. Moochie looked up and saw her standing there and couldn't believe his eyes. It was as if the room went black around her, and there was a bright light shining on her. Kidd noticed his brother's sudden change in demeanor and looked in the direction he was looking and saw Sena standing there. He walked over to her and gave her a hug as Moochie just stood in the same spot still unable to move. He couldn't help but to stare at her stomach. The mere sight almost made him want to throw up. The thought of her being with another man fucked with his mental. She stood in her spot too, not moving and watching him watch her. She wanted to know what he was thinking, like, did he hate her? Was he just as happy to see her as she was to see him? She smiled at him, and his body loosened up.

"I didn't think you were going to come." Kidd broke her out of her trance. "You took so long."

"I wasn't, but you know Vee. She was very persistent. You didn't tell me you all had dates," she whispered in his ear.

"Who? Them? Don't go being no punk now, not Miss I'll Shut Any Bitch Down." They laughed, and Moochie just watched her. He missed that laugh and her smile. He walked up to her. But that didn't shield the hurt and rage flowing through his heart.

"What's up? How you been?" Moochie looked down at her stomach wondering how far along she was and who the father could possibly be. Jealousy had him wanting to make the man disappear. He reached out to get a hug. This was supposed to be his life. *She left me to go get pregnant by some other nigga,* he thought. He put his arms around her and didn't want to let go. It felt good to have her in his arms again. This was right. There was no other way. They released each other.

"I've been all right, trying to make it through this craziness." She laughed and pointed to her stomach.

"I see. Congratulations. How far along are you? You don't look that far along." She saw something flash through his eyes when he said that. A closer look and she would have seen fury flow through his eyes. He was hurting, angry, and just clearly pissed off.

"Umm, six and a half months." She waited for his reaction as he added up the time.

"Six?" he asked to make sure he heard her right.

"Yes."

"Six as in the number between five and seven?" He looked over at Kidd, who just smiled and held up his beer.

"Congratulations, li'l brother!" Kidd yelled. Moochie turned back to Sena.

"So, this my seed?" A wave of relief washed over him. Because, for one, he didn't want to have to kill anybody, and, two, it was his. He was going to be a father. He placed both of his hands on her stomach gently and rubbed.

"Yes, yes . . ." was all she could say. She couldn't seem to come up with another word.

"Maaaaaaan." He was totally amazed. That was his baby growing inside of her. He pulled her into his chest and squeezed her tight. No words needed to be said. Everything had already been said. He missed her like crazy and needed her back in his life. He was still mad over the bullshit she had put him through, but he'd get over it.

"So are we celebrating or what?" Kidd walked up to them and put his arms around both their shoulders.

"Damn right!" Moochie was so excited, he had totally forgotten about his date.

"Aye, baby girl, I'm sorry, but you gotta bounce," he told his date as Sena smiled on the inside and out.

"What the fuck you mean bounce? Nigga, you got me fucked up." The girl was irate. "I'm leaving this mutha-fucka the same way I got here—in your car." She poked him the chest. Sena felt herself getting upset, and she didn't like the fact that the girl had put her hands on him. It didn't matter if he was wrong as two left feet.

"Don't make a scene. It ain't that serious. I'll just pay for a cab." He tried to calm her down. He knew it was wrong as hell, but he didn't really give a fuck. She had to go.

"You's about a dirty motherfucker, but it's all good. I hope you and ya li'l family have a nice life." She walked away. Sena was surprised because she herself would have been swinging some bottles by now.

"Now, can we get this party started?" Moochie turned toward Kidd and Sena.

Kidd watched them fall back in love in a matter of minutes. He couldn't believe that his happiness would never be. In his heart of hearts, he knew his boss would never allow them to leave the country. He was too well connected. Why did this have to be his situation? He was sitting there with his date wishing it was Vee. It wasn't the same without Vee. This was a pretty girl, but she was no match for his one and only love. But she'd do, and it damn sure beat being alone.

Valencia watched them at the table having fun debating on whether to approach them. Kidd had a girl sitting next to him, and she wanted to snatch her bald so bad. He still looked good. She wanted to reach out and touch him. He looked like a tall glass of rich chocolate milk. Every time he laughed, she could see his one dimple in his cheek. She just wanted to kiss it. The girl sitting next to him kept laughing and touching him, and it was driving her crazy. She looked to the stage and laughed at the group of girls singing Salt-N-Pepa's, "Push It." Then she got an idea.

"Hey, excuse me," she called to the bartender.

"Yes, what can I get you?" the waitress asked.

"A Midori sour. And could you do me a favor? Well, not really a favor because I'll pay you for it." She could see she had the bartender's attention.

"I simply need you to take this to the DJ and give it to him. Let him know I want to go up next." She handed her two hundred-dollar bills, one for her and one for the DJ. She continued to watch them at the table and down her drink. She had never sung in public by herself. She usually would have Sena to back her up.

"Okay. We got 'That Girl' coming up next!" the DJ announced.

"Here goes nothing," Valencia whispered to herself. She stood up and made her way to the stage. They hadn't looked her way yet, and they hadn't even been paying attention to the show all night long. The music started.

"I know you're here with somebody, but I just want you to know how I'm feeling," she said getting her intended target's attention. Everyone at the table turned to the stage at the sound Valencia's voice.

Sena was too happy. "Woo! Get 'em, girl!" she yelled across the room.

I remember when you used to be mine, way back when; I was too naive to love you right."

Everyone in the room could see the tears running down her face. Kidd was looking on, holding back his own emotions. She looked so beautiful up there just the way he remembered her except her hair was different. He really liked the haircut. It fit her face perfectly. He never imagined she would have cut it all off.

Sena was in tears too, happy her friend had come to her senses.

" *. . . I keep on praying for another chance just to have you back.*"

The crowd was up and on their feet cheering. It was like Mariah Carey had coached her through the song herself. Sena could barely contain herself, almost jumping over the table to get to the stage. Kidd's date looked over at him and could clearly see the gorgeous lady singing to him. He had a look of love and admiration in his eyes. He was also misty eyed. She couldn't blame him, though. She too was a little misty eyed as well. But she couldn't help but think, *What the fuck? Is this a love reunion night or some shit?* She got up and left. Kidd didn't even look her way.

"*Maybe we can bring it back,*" Vee sang before she walked off the stage to the crowd cheering and whistling. Sena rushed her.

"Girl! That was the bomb. When you hit that note, I thought I'd die!" Sena was elated.

"Thank you, babe." The duo hugged, and she looked at Kidd, staring at her. She let go of Sena and headed toward the exit.

"Wait! Where are you going? Don't leave like this. At least, go talk to him," Sena pleaded with her.

"No, I have to go. I just want to let him know that I still loved him. Now I have to go." Kidd watched her going toward the exit practically running to the door.

"Man, go get her and don't let her leave like that. She just poured her heart out to you. Least you could do is talk to her." Moochie tried to get Kidd to move, but he didn't.

"I don't know what to say to her." He looked at his little brother. Knowing what he had to do, he didn't want to look at her, let alone talk to her. Why didn't Moochie understand that?

"I don't care what you say. Hell, don't say nothing. Act like the white people in the movies and run up to her and kiss her." They laughed, but Kidd's laugh faded when he saw Valencia driving past.

"She's already gone," he said as she drove by.

"So, you not gon' go after her?" Sena said as she came over to them and rested her arms on her stomach.

"Already, huh? You acting Sena'ish," Kidd laughed at her.

"You damn right. Ain't nothing change but the times. Now, are you going after her or what?" Moochie just watched her, amazed at how much he had missed her craziness. But he could see his brother's hesitation, knowing he was thinking how could he run to her and pour his heart out, knowing the circumstances.

***

Valencia paced back and forth in her living room questioning herself. She didn't know why she had left like that. She wanted to go over to him, wrap her arms around him, and confess her love one more time. She knew she had said it all with the song she had chosen. She had gone back and forth between Mariah Carey's, "Mine Again" and Toni Braxton's, "Unbreak My Heart." She felt they represented how she felt at the time, but MC hit the nail on the head because she wanted what they had before she wanted that kind of love in her life again. She did believe they were made for each other's arms. Something brought them together, whether it was fate or destiny, but she knew they were made for each other. She went to her bed and just lay down and cried. She cried her heart out. She wanted to get all the pain out, and this one last cry was going to be the start of a new beginning. She wept for love she would never feel again. She wept for her aching heart. And she wept for her dying soul. Exhaustion consumed her as she lay there and closed her eyes.

Kidd looked at the keys he held in his hand, knowing once he used the keys, there was no turning back. There behind the door, he was pacing in front of was his future. He had no doubts of that. He already made up his mind. He would help her deal with everything. If she needed him to go with her to get help, he would do whatever it took to get them back on track. They were going to leave the country together. Wherever she wanted to go, they would go. He would follow her to the end of the earth if that's where her footprints led him.

He took a deep breath and put the key in the lock and took the first step to making things right in his life. He walked into Valencia's home and took the route to her room that he had taken so many times before. Vision of the night everything went down flashed before his eyes, but he didn't let that deter him.

When he got to her room, he saw her curled up in the fetal position in the middle of the bed with her clothes still on. He sat in a chair he had sat in so many times before. He could remember sitting in the chair watching her get ready for something or just watching her sleep like he was doing now. She looked so peaceful, as if she had no worries. She didn't look like she had the weight of the world on her shoulders. He didn't know whether he should wake her up. He liked this moment. Everything was at peace. No yelling, no crying. It was him, her, and the quiet. He rested his head against the wall.

Valencia woke up and was surprised to see a sleeping Kidd sitting across the room. She pinched herself to make sure she wasn't dreaming. She watched him sleep for a minute, but she couldn't stand being that close to him without touching him. She got up and slid out of her clothes. She stood in front of him with only her bra and panties on. He was leaning back with his arms crossed over his chest. His head was resting on the wall. She watched him a little longer and picked up the remote on her nightstand to press "play." Alicia Keys's voice melted out of the speakers. She closed her eyes and took in a deep breath before straddling his lap and caressing his face. He opened his eyes to see her looking at him.

"Hey, you," Kidd said as he put his arms around her waist.

"Hey." She broke eye contact.

"I'm—" He opened his mouth to say something, but she stopped him with a passionate kiss. This was not the time for talking. They had already missed out on so much time together. His hands began to roam all over her body, missing the feel of her skin. She melted into his arms as goose bumps formed all over her body at the touch of his hands.

"Every time you hold me, hold me like this is the last time" Alicia whispered in their ears.

He stood up with her arms and legs wrapped around him and walked over to the bed. He gently laid her down on the bed and watched as she hurriedly pulled at her bra and panties to get them off. He followed suit and pulled his shirt over his head, then got back on top of her.

"I missed you," he whispered into her lips as they kissed.

"I love you," she moaned. His hands felt so wonderful rubbing all over her body.

"Say it again." He looked into her eyes. He wanted to see her say it.

"I love you with all of my heart." She looked him in the eyes.

"This doesn't feel real. I never thought this would happen again." She caressed the sides of his face.

"Well, it's happening, and I ain't going nowhere."

"Promise me you'll never leave me again." Tears rolled down the sides of her face.

"I promise," he whispered.

"Can I keep you?" she asked, using the question he had asked her in the beginning.

"I'm yours."

They made love numerous times that night, catching up on lost times . . . with an audience watching the whole thing through the bedroom window.

Chapter 28

Vengeance Will Be Had

Reagan had been following Valencia ever since she'd seen her at the mall. She'd gotten her address with her credit card information. She was going to kill her, but when she saw Kidd walking up to the door, she figured she'd wait. He was innocent, and she only wanted Raven to suffer. Whether or not Valencia admitted it, Reagan knew she was Raven. And she was going to deal her the same fate she'd dealt her sister. She felt no one in the world could understand what it felt like to lose a twin. Raven thought she got away with everything she did, but Karma's a bitch.

"Ahhhh!" Sena was awakened out of her sleep with a pain so fierce she thought somebody shot her in the stomach, causing Moochie to jump up.

"What's wrong?" He pulled the covers back and could see clear slimy stuff mixed with blood flowing between her legs. "Aww, man." He hoped she wasn't losing the baby.

"I don't know. Aaaahhhhhh! I need to get to the hospital." She was in so much pain she couldn't move. He put on some basketball shorts and a tank top, grabbed his phone, then picked her up and carried her to the car.

"Please, don't let me lose my baby. God, please," she prayed.

"Fuuuuuck!" he looked over at her and could see she was in agonizing pain. He picked up the phone to call his brother.

"Hello." Kidd sounded asleep.

"I'm on my way to the hospital. I think Sena's in labor, man."

"What!" Kidd jumped out of bed and started looking for his clothes.

"What happened, babe?" Vee looked at the clock. It was six in the morning. She was now up, looking for something to slip into.

"Sena's in labor."

"Wait. It's way too early." Now it was her turn to go into a Code Blue.

"I know. Come on. Let's go. What hospital y'all going to?"

"St. John's," Moochie and Valencia said in unison. He looked over at her.

"It's the only hospital we go to." She could tell what he was thinking.

"We're on our way." He hung up.

When they stepped off the elevator, they could hear Sena yelling down the hall. Not because of the pain but because the doctors didn't know if the baby would survive once it was born. They had a heart monitor on the baby, and she was still alive. Valencia ran to the room and literally jumped on the bed with her. Moochie was pacing back and forth not sure what to do. Kidd walked up to him and hugged him. It hurt him to see his little brother in this kind of pain.

"Man, I don't know what I'ma do if my baby doesn't make it," he cried into Kidd's chest.

"Shhh. She gon' make it, so don't talk like that. She gon' make it." Kidd was trying to convince him of something he wasn't so certain of.

"My baby, Vee. Why they trying to take my baby?" Sena looked to her with pleading eyes. "Please don't let them take my baby. That's all I want. I'll give up everything, just don't let them take my baby, Vee, please, please. Ahhh!" She was having contractions and couldn't have an epidural since it was too late for that. Moochie ran back over to her. "They trying to take our baby!" Moochie was lost. He didn't know what to say. Sena placed his hand into her stomach. "Don't let them take her."

The doctor came back into the room. "Okay, it's time to check her again. I need you all to step out for a moment."

"No, I want them in here. Please don't leave me."

Kidd stepped over to a place where her va-jay-jay wasn't in view, and Vee sat right where she was at. It was gonna take the whole police force to get them to leave, and the doctor could see that.

"No problem." The obstetrician placed a glove on and pulled the cover up from her feet. He saw the baby's head coming out. "Are you ready to see your baby 'cause we are ready to deliver?" He went to the door and called out for help. The nurses and doctors weren't far away because they knew it was going to happen soon. And they needed all hands on deck to help the baby survive.

"Is the baby still alive?" Valencia asked.

"Yes, ma'am. There is still a heartbeat." He pointed to the heart monitor that was still on. "OK, I need you to push."

Sena looked around at all the people waiting on her baby to come and seeing the incubator waiting for her baby. She gave one big push and felt the baby being pulled out. Everybody watched as the baby came out with Moochie and Vee in tears. Kidd was holding on to Vee as they all prayed the baby would make it. After a few seconds of no crying, it wasn't looking so good. They could hear the doctors over there working on her. "Come on, baby. Cry for me," the doctor kept saying as she rubbed her finger up and down the bottom of her tiny feet.

"Please, baby girl, don't die on me," Sena pleaded another second or so, and then, everybody in the room heard the most beautiful sound ever . . . a faint yet resilient cry. "Thank you. Thank you. Oh my God, thank you," Sena cried. After a few more minutes, they brought the baby over to them.

"Here is your beautiful baby girl." A nurse put the baby in Sena's arms. She was so small and looked so fragile.

"She is so beautiful, babe." Moochie had never seen something so wonderful in all his life. He was a father, and there was no greater feeling in the world.

"Look at my goddaughter. Ain't she precious," Vee gushed.

"She takes after our side, of course," Kidd joked.

"Whatever, hater. You know I'm hot to def."

"Not right now, you ain't. You are in dire need of some Carmex." Kidd pointed to her white lips.

"Okay, ma'am, we have to take her to the nursery and make sure everything is okay. Someone will bring her back later, or you may have to come visit her in the nursery."

"Okay, thank you so much," Sena said before the nurse left.

"Well, you're not done yet. We have to get the afterbirth out," the doctor told her.

"Okay, I don't think I have to see that. Congratulations, honey. I love you. And you be thinking of a name that rhymes with Valencia." She and Kidd stepped out of the room.

"Let's go to the gift shop. I want to buy her some more stuff." Valencia was excited. He laughed at her.

"Okay." He felt around, realizing he had left his wallet at home. "I don't have my wallet."

"That's okay, I brought my purse. Shit, it's in the car. Let me go get it."

"Naw, I'll go get it."

"Oh, whatever! Just go and pick out some stuff. I'll be right back. The car is right outside the door. What, you scared some sexy man will come and sweep me off my feet?"

"Do I have to worry about that?" Kidd walked up to her and pulled her into his arms. They shared a kiss that made them want to go get a quickie.

"Umm, never." Vee blew him a kiss as she walked up the ramp to the doors.

"Aye," he called out to her.

"Yes, babe." She turned to look at him.

"The song is 'You Bring Me Joy' R. Kelly." He turned and walked toward the gift shop. *Yeah, we gon' be okay,* he thought. They were leaving for Egypt in a couple of days and would travel the world for a while till they decided where they wanted to live.

Valencia had just gotten to her car when an odd-shaped minivan covered in flowers pulled up beside her, and someone snatched her inside the van.

Kidd had noticed she was gone a little too long, so he decided to look for her. Only thing he saw was a minivan with flowers all over it leaving the parking lot and another one sitting next to Vee's car. He noticed someone was sitting in it and went to see if the man had seen what happened to Vee.

Just as he got ready to knock on the window, the side door flew open, and three men jumped out with machine guns aimed at him. Right then, he knew what had happened to her. She had gotten snatched by Mr. Jackson's people. Next thing, everything went black.

***

When Kidd came to, he couldn't see anything, and his mouth was duct-taped. But he could clearly hear Vee crying real close to him. Valencia saw his head moving from side to side. She had watched them drag him down into the basement three hours ago and had been waiting for him to wake up. Her arms and legs were tied to the chair she was in. He was sitting no more than maybe a foot from her. She could see him, but he couldn't see her. And it was a good thing. He probably would have had a heart attack at the damage they had put on her body. Her body was numb to the pain. All she wanted to do was make sure Kidd survived the whole ordeal.

"Hey! Are you awake?" She barely got the words out. She could hear him mumbling something, but he wasn't coherent. "Do you know what they want?" He nodded his head. He knew they wanted her dead, and he was the reason they were both down there. "Did you do something?" He shook his head. "What did I do?"

"I'll tell you what you did. You fucked with the wrong family," Mr. Jackson said as he walked back into the room.

Kidd's head swung up trying to hear where his voice was coming from. Mr. Jackson snatched the bag from over Kidd's face. Kidd was horrified at what he saw before him. They had beaten Valencia something terrible. There was blood running down her face and neck and a big gash in the middle of her forehead. He struggled against his restraints, trying to get to her. It broke him down to see her this way. He had promised he wouldn't let anything happen to her . . . but he had failed.

"I don't know what you're talking about," she said as more blood spilled from her mouth where a tooth had just fallen out.

"Oh, so now you don't know anything." He picked up the bat they had already been beating her with and swung it at her shoulder. You could hear her bones crack all through the house. Kidd's screams could be heard, even under the tape. He bucked and struggled to get free. This was way more horrible than what he had expected. They weren't just going to kill her. They were going to torture her, and he was going to have to be there.

"Please tell me what I did! What did I do?" she screamed.

"Now, you, Kidd, you really disappointed me. I had such high hopes for you. But you let the likes of this bitch take you down." He looked at Kidd in the eyes and could see all the hate and rage Kidd had in them. It sent chills down his spine. He knew if Kidd walked out of that basement alive, there would be hell to pay. That was why he was there. He couldn't leave such a job to amateurs.

"I asked you to do me a favor, and this is what I get—you sleeping with the enemy." He got close to Kidd's face. "I told you she killed my daughter, and you fuck her and think you're going to run off into the sunset together. I tell you what, either you or she will die tonight, or both of you. You choose." He snatched the tape off Kidd's mouth.

"No, no, it's me. Just do it. I did it!" Valencia pleaded. When she heard that she had something to do with his daughter being killed she knew it was Raven's doing. She refused to let Kidd die over something Raven had done.

"No!" Kidd yelled.

"I can't let you die over something she's done."

"Valencia, no," Kidd pleaded.

"I can't let him hurt you, baby. I love you too much. And she has done so much."

"Vee, just calm down and let me talk."

"No, Wanya. I can't let you die tonight because of me. I can't." She took a deep breath and turned to Mr. Jackson. "It was me; just get it over with."

***

Moochie had been calling his brother's phone for a few hours. At first, he wasn't alarmed. He thought maybe Kidd and Vee were somewhere freaking off. But hours later and still no response, he was way past worried. Just as he was about to activate the locator button on his phone, it made an alarm sound. That meant Kidd was in trouble. He kissed a sleeping Sena on the cheek and ran out of the hospital like the ground was made of hot coal.

When they first started out, he and Kidd had these chips placed under their armpits. So if there was ever an emergency, all they had to do was press it and their phone would lead them to wherever the other was. They couldn't always trust the locators in their phones because kidnappers broke phones and disposed of them. Wherever his brother was, he prayed he would get there in time. And that all the culprits were still there, so he could kill every last one of them.

"So, Mr. Brown, who's it going to be?"

Kidd sat there stone faced. He wouldn't give him the satisfaction of pleading for his life. He knew Mr. Jackson would never let him walk out of there alive. He just prayed Moochie would get there in time to save them both. The gunman released his hands under Mr. Jackson's orders. He still wanted Kidd to kill her. Mr. Jackson wanted her to die at Kidd's hand. He tried to hand Kidd the gun.

"Don't hand me that. It wouldn't be good for any of us." He was dead serious. He was willing to go out in a hail of smoke. But if there was any way Vee could walk out of there alive, he would try to make sure that happened. The gunman never took the gun off of him. They had one to the back of his head and one on each side of his neck.

"Just take the gun, baby. Do it," Vee pleaded with Kidd. He just sat there staring at her trying to remember her voice and pictured her before all this mess came about. Everybody turned their head to the click clacking of a pair of high heels walking into the dingy basement. Vee started to feel a horrible headache worse than the one she already had. She knew what was about to happen. Raven was coming to her rescue once again. Even though it was Raven's fault she was even in the predicament, she was thankful she came to take on her responsibility.

"I guess I can introduce you all to my precious daughter Reagan. The twin of the girl you killed."

"That bitch is a fucking slut bucket just like her sister was," Raven spat. Raven was no punk, and, if she was going down, she was going to speak her mind. "I could have fucked them both." Kidd laughed because he knew it was Raven. Valencia would have never said anything like that. Reagan snatched her nine millimeter out of her waistband and brought it down hard on Vee's head.

Raven was a little dazed, but it didn't deter her. "Fuck you, bitch, and your freak-ass sister. I have to admit her pussy was fire. Do you taste anything like her?"

"You shut up! Don't speak on my sister like you knew her!" Reagan yelled.

"I knew her good enough for her to munch on my dick like a starving child in the back huts of South Africa." Raven knew it was her time to die. She was remorseful for how things would end for Valencia because all she wanted was to protect her by any means necessary, and, instead, she ended up putting her on a death sentence. But there was no need in crying over spilled milk. If she was going out, she was going out like only she could.

"*Arrggg,*" Reagan screamed. She was furious. She began to rain blow after blow down on Raven, causing blood to fly everywhere. The gunmen held Kidd down on the ground. He fought hard trying to get up to help Vee. *Where the fuck is Moochie?* he thought. If Moochie didn't get there soon, they would surely kill Valencia.

Moochie was creeping down the basement stairs. He had just laid out seven guards with his silenced pistol. His stomach was doing flips. He hadn't been so scared in all his life. He didn't know what was to come when he stepped around the corner. But he did know he would go down blazing for his brother. He peeked his head around real quick and came up with a total count of five people. Three men were holding Kidd down on the ground, and some girl had a gun to Vee's head with Mr. Jackson standing there watching everything. He had to wait till those men had their guns pointed away from Kidd's head. He leaned back up against the wall.

"Bitch, you could never kill me because I been dead," Raven spoke venomously as blood ran out of her mouth. "I made my peace, bitch, so get it over with." Raven was in so much pain, but she would never let them see her cry. She looked over at Kidd on the ground. They locked eyes. "I'm sorry" were the words he heard. By the look in her eyes, he could see she really meant it. She had no more teeth in the front of her mouth, and one of her eyes was damn near hanging out of the socket. But you could still see her smirk.

"We'll see about that." Reagan put the gun to her head and pulled the trigger.

"Nooo!" Kidd screamed watching the side of Vee's head being blown out. His heart imploded at the sight before him. Never in all his life had he imagined this would be his fate. How had he ended up on this end of the shit stick? Why would God do this to him?

Moochie ran in like he was doing target practice.

He took aim and knocked off the three gunmen in a matter of seconds. Before anybody could figure out what was going on, Moochie already had Reagan in a choke hold with his gun pointed at her head. Mr. Jackson could have kicked himself for forgetting about Kidd's watchdog of a brother. Kidd shook the men off him and rushed to Valencia's side, but she was long gone. His heart had shattered into a million pieces as he held her dead, flaccid body in his arms. Moochie's anger rose to a whole different level seeing how bad Vee looked. He cocked his hammer and returned the favor to Reagan.

"Noooo!" Now it was Mr. Jackson's turn to mourn. He had told her not to come down, but she had to get revenge for her sister. He held his dead daughter in his arms and rocked her back and forth.

Kidd was in daze. He couldn't believe Valencia was really gone. There was no coming back this time. He couldn't wrap his mind around the fact that she was gone.

Moochie noticed that Mr. Jackson was still alive, and he couldn't have that. He filled him up with lead, tearing his face off in the process. Neither he nor his daughter was going to have an open casket.

"We got to get out of here." Moochie touched his brother's shoulder. But Kidd wouldn't budge. He couldn't. His mind wouldn't let him leave her side. Moochie tried to pick up Valencia, but Kidd wouldn't let her go. "Come on, man. We have to go!" He shook his brother. Kidd finally looked up at his brother. It broke Moochie's heart to see him like that. Kidd got up with Valencia still in his arms. He just imagined she was sleeping, and technically, she was; she just was never going to wake up again.

***

Sena sat at Valencia's grave site, and it still felt weird to her. It had been almost a year, and the memory of that day was still fresh in her mind. She couldn't believe the happiest day in her life had turned into the most horrible day. They hadn't told her all the details of what happened, but they did tell her it was because of something that Raven had done. Her sister was gone, but at least Vee got to meet baby Deonna before she passed. She was cleaning the leaves around the area and had asked the boys to wait a little longer to come up because she wanted some alone time. But she could see them walking up now. She really felt bad for Kidd. He had been through so much with Vee, only for her to be taken away again, only this time, in front of his eyes. He had lost her before, but there was no coming back this time.

"Hey, you all right?" Moochie asked as he and Kidd walked up. Kidd was holding the baby.

"Yeah, I guess so." She wiped the tears from her face.

"Hey, sis," Moochie said as he placed the yellow lilies on Valencia's headstone. He helped Sena up off the ground.

"We'll let you talk to her," Sena said as she patted Kidd on the shoulder.

He stood there, reading her headstone for what felt like the thousandth time. *Valencia Renée Brown, Born July 13, 1982, Deceased April 2, 2016. Beloved Wife, Sister, and Friend.* He kneeled down to finish what Sena had started and placed her favorite flower, birds-of-paradise, down in front of the grave. He stared at her name. It had cost him a pretty penny to get them to change her last name. They weren't married by law, but they were in their hearts.

"Hey, you know I ask myself every day why I didn't go outside with you that day. I feel so guilty for what happened to you. I miss you so much. At first, I didn't think I would make it. I see why you kept Sena around for so many years. She a little crazy, but you couldn't have picked a better person to be your sister. She helped me through everything. I was supposed to be there for her, yet, she was comforting me. It was like I finally got you back; then you were snatched away again. Man, nobody will ever know what that did to my heart. I am so sorry I wasn't there for you. I will have to live with that for the rest of my life. I love you and know that no one will ever replace you. You are still my heart, my smile, and my happiness. I will love you for life, Mrs. Brown."

He cleared a couple more leaves away and got up. Then he kissed his index and middle fingers and placed them on her name. He walked away knowing she heard everything he said and was smiling up in heaven looking down on him.

BIO

Johnna B is a St. Louis, Missouri, native and still resides there. She ascertained a passion for reading and writing at an early age. She currently has six novels published: *Beautiful Nightmare, Vengeance: A Never Ending Nightmare (Part 2), Wydow Maker, Sins of Destruction,* and *Sex On The Rox,* which is a short story.

Her sixth title is signed under Write2Eat publishing, *Wicked Deceptions.* She is also featured in Anna J's, *Erotic Snapshots, Volume 6.*

Johnna decided to give the world a glimpse into her own imaginative thoughts and become a part of the literary world. She is hard at work on her next novel. In the meantime, make sure you are caught up on all of her titles: *Wicked Deceptions, Sins of Destruction, Wydow Maker, Vengeance: A Never Ending Nightmare (Part 2), Sex On The Rox,* and *Snapshots: Peeping Tom.*